hopeless

GEORGE K. JORDAN

urban
soul

URBAN BOOKS

http://www.urbanbooks.net

URBAN SOUL is published by

Urban Books
10 Brennan Place
Deer Park, NY 11729

ISBN-13: 978-1-59983-023-0
ISBN-10: 1-59983-023-X

First Printing: December 2007

10 9 8 7 6 5 4 3 2

Printed in the United States of America

hopeless

Chapter 1

"Oh my God, Josie, it will be the best weekend ever," Jeanne Archer was screaming on the phone. "We will have so much fun." Fun was a very subjective term in my mind. To Jeanne, it made sense. I mean, she had just invited me to Atlanta to be one of her brides-maids in her uber bougie wedding to an investment banker or lawyer or something. I blanked out. All I could think about was another bland dress to wear so the bride could shine, another barrage of ugly, mean, spiteful men, all trying to holler at me at the reception while their girlfriends stepped on the dance floor. But worst of all was being the only single girl in the bridal party. I had been through this torture several times before and was praying for a way to get out of it.

"My schedule is real busy here at the clinic, Jeanne," I said. "Can't I just buy you a very expensive gift?"

"You have to come," Jeanne whined. "You're like my best friend." *Liar.* Actually, we were pretty good friends in college, but like most school relationships, distance could strain even the best of them. Once she opted for graduate school in Atlanta, and I chose to stay in Chicago, we became more like e-mail buddies. But in a wedding situation, a bride to be could call the friend marker and you almost had to attend. Even though your bond might not have been more than sharing a dorm for a semester or crushing over the same boy junior year. A college friendship almost guaranteed your attendance at their wedding. And, if you were single, like I was, you were immediately inducted into the bridal servitude camp.

I had been drafted more than a few times within the last several months, and it always ended up the same: spend tons of money getting to the wedding, get ridiculed for being single and barren and alone, and then erase your so-called friend's number on the plane ride home. I just didn't think I had one more wedding in me.

"Josie, you have to come," Jeanne pleaded. "It won't be the same without you." I didn't know about that, but I did know her mother was friends with my mother, Pamela. And if I refused, I would never hear the end of it. Besides, my schedule at the clinic had been nonstop. Being the only doctor was usually a manageable obstacle. But as more women came to my clinic, it got busier. I was almost burnt out every six or seven months. Maybe a break would do me some good. At the very least, I could hit the mall, do some damage to the old credit card. It had been a long time since I'd walked through a mall and been able to try on clothes and shoes.

"Okay, I'll come. But I am not going to be matron of honor," I said. "I am just going to support you and eat cake." We both laughed.

"That's fine, sweetie," she exclaimed. "I am so excited. I can't wait to see you."

"Me, either," I fake screamed, too. "Just e-mail me the dates and information."

"Will do. Ciao," she said. The second I hung up the phone with her, I knew I needed reinforcements if I was to endure this wedding. I punched in Jason's number.

"Yeah," an agitated voice answered.

"Hey, Jason," I said as I smiled through the phone. "Guess who's coming to ATL to visit you?"

"Nope. Sorry," he said. "I'm busy that weekend."

"Jason," I yelled. "I didn't even tell you what weekend it was."

"Pick one," he said. "I'll be busy."

"Jason," I whined. He busted out laughing.

"You know I am kidding," he said. "I finally get you to come visit me down here." Jason was one of the few school buddies I did keep in contact with. His maligning, judgmental humor seemed to match my own. Plus, he was gay, and we had great fun clockin' which of the straight boys we met would call me and which ones would call him after they called me.

"I am coming to attend Jeanne's wedding."

"Tall, ugly Jeanne or cute, bitchy Jeanne?" he questioned.

"Cute and bitchy," I said.

"Wow, some man is willing to deal with her drama," he said. "God bless 'em."

"Yeah. Who would have thought?"

"Not me," he said. "So how long will I have you for?"

"I think my mental stamina will only be able to

withstand four days," I said. "And I will have to be drunk the entire time."

"You know I have a bar in the house," Jason said. It was good to know I had a friend who was sympathetic to my issues. "So are you the OSB again?"

"The what?" I asked.

"The OSB, the only single bridesmaid."

"Probably, knowing my luck," I said.

"Then I better double up on the liquor," he said.

"No doubt," I said. "Well, let me break the news to my mother that yet another woman has passed me in the race to having children."

"Why do you even call her with stuff like that?"

"Better she hear it from me than from Jeanne's mother, who will rub it in even more."

"I say just announce you're a lesbian and get it over with," Jason teased.

"She'd probably still be mad I haven't found a partner who could teach her golf. And she would be all over me about when I was going to adopt our Cambodian baby."

"Jesus," Jason said. "There is no pleasing that woman."

"Naw, not really." I laughed.

"Well, just tell me when you're coming, and I will make sure we have some fun," Jason said. "All right. I actually have real work to do here at the office, so . . ."

"Are you playing the Xbox again?

"Yep, the new Spiderman came out, and I am beating my assistant by way more digits than he will ever see on his paycheck."

"You are retarded."

"Just call me. Gotta go! Bye!" Jason hung up, and I sat looking at the phone. Was I once again going to another wedding? How did I always get caught up in these situations? I decided to spare myself the phone call to my mother until tomorrow. No sense getting Pamela all riled up for nothing. And the last thing I wanted to do was have to defend why I was the hopeless single girl.

Chapter 2

"Explain to me why everyone else seems to have no problem getting married," said Pamela, starting in over the phone. "But my only daughter just doesn't seem to want to be happy."

"I am happy now," I argued.

"No one is happy alone, dear," she corrected me. "I am just trying to make sure I see some grandchildren before I die."

"You're only sixty, Pamela," I said. "And in perfect health, I might add. I check you every year myself."

"Yes," Pamela sighed. "I can still say my Josie is a very successful gynecologist, but you know that only goes so far."

"How far do you want it to go?" I joked.

"This is serious," she said. "Being married is one of the most beautiful experiences you ever can have in your life."

"You divorced Dad," I said.

"And I would divorce him again in a minute," she blurted out. "But don't use one bad example to tarnish the institution of marriage."

"Jason said I needed to admit to you that I was a lesbian." I just knew that would get a rise out of her.

"Oh, that won't work," she said matter-of-factly. "You're too bossy to be a lipstick lesbian and too pretty to be the dominant one."

"Lipstick lesbian," I said. "Have you been watching the *Tyra Banks Show* again?"

"I keep up on things, my dear," she said. "But the most important thing I am keeping tabs on is my daughter's dating life."

"Nothing to report," I said quickly.

"That is because you don't put yourself out there and date more."

"You mean be a slut?"

"No." I could hear my mother breathing hard. She was getting frustrated with each passing minute. "I mean, see what your options are. Have you joined a church, like I told you to?"

"I am not joining a church just to find a man, Pamela," I said.

"It's not just to find a man." She laughed. "But it wouldn't kill you to find a man that has at least seen the inside of a church, instead of all those heathen men you normally date."

"I just called to tell you that Jeanne is getting married, and that I am going to yet another wedding," I said. "I was not calling to be ridiculed."

"You and your father always took everything I said as ridicule," she said. "It was just constructive criticism. I just always wanted the best for you both."

"Well, sometimes being silently supportive is a good thing," I added.

"I'll keep that in mind," she said. "Well, I must

attend to my chicken before it gets dry as a coyote's mouth in the oven."

"Well, I will keep you posted if I elope within the next three days."

"You know, if you spent more time finding a man than coming up with smart-aleck jokes, I would be on my way to my second grandchild by now," Pamela blew through the phone. It was so much fun pissing her off.

"But what would be the fun in that?"

"Good-bye, child." Pamela clicked off the phone, and I went to bed, satisfied with my mission for that evening.

Jeanne had told me the wedding wasn't for another seven months. But most things I dreaded had a habit of sneaking up on me, and before I knew it, I was on a plane to Atlanta. When I arrived at Hartsfield Airport and grabbed my luggage, I was mortified to see Jason holding a sign that read: SINGLE BLACK WOMAN.

"Could you please put that sign away?" I pressed down on it with my hand.

"Are you kidding?" he said. "I got six numbers already."

"Too bad you're gay," I said.

"That's all good," he cheesed. "I am sure I can auction off these numbers to the highest bidder at my gym." He put down his sign, and we hugged long and hard.

"I missed you so much," I said.

"Me, too," Jason said. "God, it's been almost a year, right?"

"Something like that," I said. "I think you came to see me in Chicago last October."

"Yeah," he said. "Coldest winter ever."

"That was the fall," I corrected him.

"To Atlanta people, Chicago weather in the fall is winter weather. So when do you have to see Jeanne?"

"Not until tomorrow," I said and breathed a sigh of relief.

"Then you are caught in the wedding party from hell."

"It may not be that bad," I said. "Jeanne has been so cool on the phone."

"Don't fall for it," Jason said. "Once you let down your guard, she will pounce on you."

"I am telling you she has been cool," I said as Jason picked up my bags and guided me to the parking deck where he kept his car.

"Okay, I could be wrong." I caught Jason rolling his eyes. "Tomorrow I will drop you off at the hotel. But don't say I didn't warn you."

As we rode down the freeway, laughing and reminiscing about our college days, I felt so happy in my decision to come down for the wedding. Maybe it was me. Maybe I was being so jaded and not enjoying these opportunities to hang with my friends.

I knew how some weddings went and how I was treated. But this time it just felt completely different. There was no sense of dread as the day approached. No yearning for an escape route. I think Jeanne and I had both matured enough for me to enjoy her wedding and for her to relish her special day. Boy, was I wrong.

* * *

The next morning, after a night of laughs, drinks, and a great dinner, Jason dropped me off at the Intercontinental Hotel, the official hotel for Jeanne's wedding. I had barely stepped into the lobby before I heard "Josie!"

Jeanne ran up to me and held me tight. "I am so glad you could make it. We are going to have so much fun."

Fun consisted of a three-page to-do list and a reservation for a rental car (I had to pay for it, mind you) in order to get everything on the list. Though Jeanne wanted to spend lots on the wedding, the one thing she had refused to do was seek the services of a wedding planner.

"Why would I need to do that when I have you guys?" she said in her hotel room. But I noticed her eyes were fixed on me. "There are just a few items to pick up, Josie."

A few items included her mother from the airport; the diamond earrings from Tiffany's that she wanted to wear at the ceremony; the Prada pumps and flats for before and after the wedding, respectively; and the gift bags for all the bridesmaids and groomsmen.

Of course, the gift bags weren't assembled, and it took me four hours to stuff them with disposable cameras, T-shirts, gift certificates, and other useless paraphernalia, which would only serve to get the recipient of such a gift stopped at the airport. But I did it all with a grin. That was until I saw the dress.

Chapter 3

"Oh my God, you all look beautiful," Jeanne gushed. She placed her hand over her mouth and jumped up and down. "Those dresses look amazing on you."

Liar. We looked like a cluster of Grape-Nuts left at the bottom of the cereal box. The brown color of the dresses was supposedly called cocoa but looked like shit. The dresses had no waistline and were supposed to plume at the sides. But with my small frame, I was swallowed inside the massive amounts of fabric. The other girls didn't fair too well, either. Most were so big, they stretched the sides to their limit, making the dresses look like a weird second skin on their plump bodies. This was why I didn't like weddings.

"My husband is going to freak when he sees how this dress is hugging my ass," the girl with the cute bob hairstyle and chubby face said. "He be getting jealous when other men be staring at me."

"I know my Vic told me, he doesn't go out with me, 'cause he is tired of all these guys hitting on me," another girl, with stylish glasses and small diamond earrings, added.

"Omar isn't jealous like that," Jeanne interjected. "He knows he is the only one for me, and I am the only one for him."

"Clearly," said the third girl, with the ponytail weave that cascaded down her back. "I mean, he is spending all this money on ya'll wedding. He must know you're the one."

"I know one hundred fifty thousand dollars is a lot," said Jeanne as she rolled her eyes and put her hands on either side of her head. "But like Omar said, if you are going to do something, do it right."

I stood there looking at Jeanne, trying to force my hands not to slap her. For $150,000, she could buy a home, pay off her student loans, and pay me back the thousands of dollars she'd borrowed from me over the years. We went to college together and were basically inseparable until she moved to Atlanta for grad school while I stayed in Chicago. She wanted to be a psychologist, and I wanted to be a physician. We talked about opening a dual clinic together. But right as we both turned thirty and finished our schooling, something happened to Jeanne. She started complaining about how she would never be married and didn't want to die alone. I felt her concern but just never thought I would be alone. I was busy in school, and once I figured out a career, I was sure a man would follow. Jeanne couldn't wait that long, and every four months for the next three years, she proclaimed she'd found Mr. Right.

As I went about setting up my practice, picking a location and a staff, Jeanne went about finding a husband. Our dream of a dual clinic died a slow death when she met Omar, an African investment banker, who talked about money almost as much as he spent it. When he proposed to her, he gave her a ring so big, she could use it as a compact mirror. That was that. I was summoned to Atlanta to be bridesmaid and doormat for four days with a bunch of overweight married women.

"You lucked out, girl," the girl with the bob said. "An investment banker from New York. I know he is paid."

"It's not about the money," said Jeanne as she turned to the mirror behind her and did a last-minute check on her make-up. "Omar just completes me. I know it sounds so cliché. But he finishes my sentences and protects me and gives me all the things I pretended I didn't want or need when I was single."

"Oh, I know single girls are always lying to themselves," said weave girl, placing her hands on her hips to accent her point. "I don't know about ya'll, but I hated being single. Coming home all alone to my apartment, dating all them trifling men, and all them STDs and AIDS and stuff. Too much."

I looked around for a place to hide, because I knew where this conversation was going.

"I know, and if they don't have a disease, the men are gay or married or in jail," said the girl with the glasses. She was adjusting Jeanne's veil as they talked.

"We can't just blame the men, girls," Jeanne interrupted. "We do it to ourselves. We go out there, get these great jobs, and then emasculate men for not having what we have. If they do one thing we don't like, we dump them and then complain that there are no available men."

"I didn't think there were," said the chunky-faced

bob girl as she patted her hair. "Until I met my husband, I thought it was hopeless."

Then, as if on cue, Jeanne and I locked eyes, and she turned around. She tilted her head and smiled. "Ladies, I think we are scaring Josie."

She got up and walked toward me and put her arms around me. "Girl, it is not hopeless. Your man is out there. And one day you will be as happy as we are."

"I am happy," I interjected.

"Oh, I'm sure you're happy," said Jeanne, nodding in the most condescending way. "I am sure you're happy, but we mean the kind of happiness that only comes when two souls are joined together."

"You mean when one person gives up her identity so her man can run the show," was what I wanted to say. But I kept most of my comments to myself.

"Don't get me wrong," eyeglasses said. "I thought when I was single, I was happy, too. I mean, I had a great job as a civil engineer, lots of friends, but when I met my husband, it was just different, ya know."

Did these women think I didn't want to be married? Like I was carrying a sign on my chest that said, DON'T MARRY ME! Of course, I wanted to find a husband, a man who understood and supported me. But for some people, it takes a little longer to find that right connection.

"Ya'll don't understand," said Jeanne. She smiled. "Dr. Josie Green over here is too busy saving the world to find a man."

"You're a doctor?" weave girl asked.

"Yeah, I'm a gynecologist," I said.

"She owns her own clinic on the South Side of Chicago," Jeanne said.

"Well, no wonder you're scaring the men away," eyeglasses said.

"Excuse me?" I said.

"You have this powerful job, and you work in the medical field," said weave girl as she shook her head. "You have already alienated most black men."

"Yeah, it would be different if you were a nurse or something," eyeglasses concurred. I stood there trying not to be stunned by my sisterhood. Were they indirectly telling me I should not be a doctor? Were they saying that to get a man, I couldn't do anything that threatened them?

"Well, I thought whoever my husband was would accept me for me, and not be threatened by what I do or how much money I make," I replied. I watched the ladies' faces after I said this. There was a pregnant pause before they buckled over in laughter.

"Josie, that is a fairy tale," Jeanne said. "Do you think my Omar would be okay if I was traipsing off, trying to have a career, leaving him alone?"

"Well, I would assume we would both share things, be a partnership," I countered.

"Men don't want a partnership," weave girl said. I was so glad I couldn't remember their names. Because if I could, I would have put a hit out on their lives. "They want a silent dictatorship, where you do what they say, cater to their needs, and don't complain."

"That doesn't sound like much of a marriage," I protested.

"Oh, they will take care of you, too," eyeglasses said. "Men are just like children, though. Spoiled, selfish, and they want to be number one."

"And you're cool with that?" I asked. I was fascinated

by the latest colored version of the Stepford Wives nest, which I had somehow discovered.

"Do I get tired of always having to clean up after my husband, baby him, feed him, sex him up, and then do it all again the next day?" chunky face said. "Of course, sometimes, but I know in the end he is worth it." The ladies all sighed and agreed, and I began looking for the off button on the back of their necks. Surely, this could not be a modern woman's future. I wished I could say this conversation surprised me, but it didn't. This was the sixth wedding in fourteen months, and the conversations were all the same: a bunch of married women praising Jesus for their men and feeling pity for the one single girl stupid enough to be a bridesmaid at the wedding. It was almost as if they had to make sure I knew how sad I was for not having a man, as if I never felt lonely myself. It was like the married woman's form of a singles' intervention.

Get with it, you single cow. Do you want to be going home alone forever?

The truth was, I did want to be married, or at least in a long-term relationship with a man. And I had done my share of dating. But once you're past thirty, you begin to realize that no matter what happens, you have to carve a life for yourself. If I sat at home and worried whether or not I would ever be able to wake up with someone who made me laugh or held me during scary movies, I would never get anything done in my life. And my life was good. I was a doctor with my own practice. I had a mother and father who loved me, even though they got on my nerves sometimes. I had friends who I hung out with all the time. If I were a man, I would be a lucky bastard. But because I was a woman, I was inferior to the segment of the sisterhood who managed to lock down their man.

"Omar has so many single friends, girl. Don't worry. We'll get you married yet," said Jeanne as she hugged me again. If I had had a sharp object, I would have stabbed her right there. I would have punctured her fifteen-thousand-dollar dress and watched her have a heartache when she felt the blood seeping on the fabric. Better yet, I wouldn't have had to stab her; I could have just cut the wedding dress into tiny shreds of cloth and watched as she fell to the ground, shocked to death by a ruined wedding.

"Josie, you are smart and pretty," eyeglasses said. "I am sure you will find a man in no time." We had now entered the reassuring portion of the single-girl intervention. After belittling and berating the woman, all the married ladies rally around the lost single soul, console her, and convince her that all is not lost. Marriage was right around the corner, and I would be as happy as they appeared to be. I was more upset, I had spent all this money to have my so-called friend insult me.

The only way I would be able to save myself would be to remind them of the real reason we were all there. "Hey, I think it's about time for someone to walk down the aisle." I let my voice rise, and I smiled, hoping Jeanne would take the bait.

"Jesus, you are right," said Jeanne. Got her. "I am so nervous, girls."

"There is nothing to it, girl," weave girl said. "You just take a few steps, say a few words, and walk into your new life."

Jeanne dabbed at her eyes with a handkerchief she pulled from under her sleeve. "Josie, you always want to carry something to catch the tears so your make-up won't run," Jeanne offered. I smiled and looked at my friend. Despite everything, I still did love her and wished her the best.

"You really do look beautiful," I said, and we hugged one last time.

"Thank you," said Jeanne. She pushed some stray hairs back on my face, then turned her head to the rest of the circle. "Let's go, girls."

She let the others walk ahead of her and stopped me as I headed for the door.

"You are my best friend, Josie," Jeanne said. "And I thank you for being here."

"Thank you," I said. "I am so happy for you."

"Oh, and don't worry," she said. "I know you will not be single forever. You will find that special man. I know it. It's not hopeless."

I looked at her and managed to feign a smile. But all I could think about was, *Where is a knife when you need one?*

Being the only single bridesmaid at a wedding is like living in a small village that just discovered the cure for the plague. But instead of thanking Jesus they are cured, they go around tormenting the poor souls who couldn't afford the vaccination shot. Such was Jeanne's wedding.

After being asked at least seven hundred times when I planned on getting married, and if I was gay or abused or just a hater, I decided after the reception toast to politely leave the main table and sit at the table I knew no one would go near—the one holding all the empty plates.

Someone said, "Yo, Ma, give one good reason I

shouldn't be helping you out of that dress right now."
I rolled my eyes, ready to cut somebody, but burst into a fit of giggles when I realized where the deep voice originated.

"I know this is Atlanta and all, but I don't go for DL boys," I said as I punched Jason on his arm. He flinched like it hurt.

"For the record, I am not a down-low thug," Jason protested. "I am a semi-closeted homosexual who just happens to like beautiful and angry-looking black women who like to sit alone next to half-eaten chicken bones."

"It was the only place I could truly hide," I said. "Do you have a cigarette?"

"Dr. Green"—Jason shook his head—"you quit, remember?"

"I did?" I questioned. I knew it had been several months since I'd puffed on a cancer stick. Perhaps it was during the last wedding I attended. "Well, they're all out of cake. What do you expect me to do?"

"Make a quick dash for the car with me," Jason said. "The straights are boring, with their golf and matching baby strollers. What this place needs is a strobe light and a few Ecstasy pills."

"That has got to be the gayest thing I have ever heard come out of your mouth." I fell on my friend, comfortable in the fact I had at least one man in my life I could count on to make me laugh.

"See, there is a smile on your face." Jason rose to his feet. "I've done my job, and you've done yours, babe. Let's go."

"I can't. They have more pictures to take."

Jason rolled his eyes. "I thought they did that night after the ceremony."

"They did." I played with the small glass of vodka I'd brought over from the wedding table. "But they want natural reaction shots of the reception."

"Here's my reaction . . . lame," Jason said.

"I know it's lame, babe, but that is why you need to be a bride, so that nothing is lame. Everything is about your special day."

"Don't they say stuff like that to slow children. 'This is your special day.'"

"Don't kill the bridesmaid," I said. "I don't want to be here any more than you do."

"Then let's dip," Jason prodded.

"I have a responsibility," I said.

"Honestly, Josie, I sort of have to go."

I turned to him. "If you say you have a date, I am going to throw this drink in your face." I thought about that statement and downed the last of the alcohol. "I'm going to throw this ice in your face."

"Look . . ." Jason smiled. I knew our time had ended. "You came down for the wedding; we hung out. I even went to this little starter-kit, bougie wedding. By the by, she got fat, and it will never work."

"I love you."

"And I love ass." Jason threw a high five in the air, which I didn't slap back. "And I am about to get some peace."

"So you are just going to leave me stranded?"

"You know everyone here."

"I hate them."

"You're pretty," he said.

"They hate me."

"I'll tell my friend to pick me up."

"No, no." I threw my hands up. "The hotel is down

the street. I am sure someone can drop me, or I can catch a cab."

"I feel bad now." Jason poked his lips out.

"No, you don't." I pushed him in the direction of the door.

"No, I don't, but I love you," Jason said, walking to the exit. "Brunch tomorrow before you leave?"

"If I feel like it." I blew a kiss at Jason and watched him practically run to his car. I was stuck alone and decided to head back to the main table for the final humiliating beat down before I went home and cried myself to sleep . . . because I forgot my vibrator.

"Josie." A voice as distinct as it was sexy called my name from behind. I turned around, hoping, praying, it was who I thought it was.

"Craig," I gushed and felt immediately guilty for doing so.

"Oh my God, what are you doing here?" he asked.

"I was in the wedding," I said. "Didn't you see me during the ceremony?" Dammit. Now he was going to think I wanted him to notice me. And I hadn't even known the man was here.

"I came late," Craig said, his pearly whites still lighting up a room. "The groom is frat."

"Some friend you are." I laughed. "Showing up hours late to your boy's wedding."

"Hey." He put his hand on my bare arm, and I felt the tingling in my body. "I drove from a sales conference in Memphis all the way here."

"All right, you're off the hook."

"I take it you're a friend of the bride?" Craig asked as I ignored the fact his hand was still holding, no, caressing, my arm.

"I thought we were, but she put me in this dress."

We both chuckled a bit, but I could feel the tension between us.

"You look stunning," Craig said.

"Thank you," I said. I tried for a joke, but seriously, at your lowest point in life, who wouldn't want a fine brother complimenting you while in a tacky dress?

"So, um, was that your boyfriend?"

"How long have you been watching me?"

"Long enough to see him walk out."

"We're just friends," I said.

"Oh, he's gay." Craig smiled.

"Now why does he have to be gay?"

"Because he is a good-looking brother, and you are the most beautiful woman in the room," he said. "If he hasn't found the right woman in you, he must be looking for something else."

"I believe *ass* was the term he used." We both laughed.

"I can't be mad at that," Craig said. "So do you need a ride somewhere?"

At least he'd kept his manners. "No thank you. I mean, I have to stay and take more pictures. It's going to be a while."

"I'll wait," he said. And he did, for two more long, inebriated hours. Most everyone in the wedding got drunk, danced, and took pieces of their clothes off to the loud tunes of Earth, Wind & Fire. By the time we left the wedding and headed back to my hotel in Craig's car, it was well after 2:30 a.m. Every so often I glanced over at Craig, and his eyes were locked on me. He wasn't trying to grab a sister on the way to the bathroom or slip his number to the waitress with the banging ass. He waited on me. I had to admit, for a second, I did contemplate giving him some. But again that would be like rewarding a person for not killing someone. You don't get points for doing what's expected of you.

When we reached the front entrance of the hotel, I turned to say good night, and he already had his lips on mine. Not in a nasty, sloppy way, just soft, sensual, and sexy. I was all set to let him up when the memory of this man started seeping back inside my brain.

When I met Craig at a desperate black women's forum, also known as a poetry reading, I wasn't interested in meeting anyone. My girl Deana had dragged me to the event so she could read some of her erotic poetry. The idea of watching my friend and a horde of shameless single women writhe around a microphone while reciting a million colloquialisms for genitalia was a nightmare I dreaded. To my surprise, I found a fellow hater in Craig, who was seated next to me.

I had been trying to hold in my laughter as a sister with a flowing weave and a damn near see-through top waxed poetic about how her pussy was a direct descendant of Cleopatra's.

"I guess everyone would be real mad if I asked to check the score of the game on the television," Craig whispered in my ear, and I burst out laughing. I had been trying not to giggle, but the idea of interrupting this woman's ode to clitoris hour with a football game sent me over the edge.

The woman narrowed her eyes at me as if I wasn't deep enough to understand her art. But I got it. She was horny, had got tired of eating chocolate, and wanted to share her frustration with the masses. *Get a vibrator, and be done with it, sister*, I wanted to yell, but

I decided this was the perfect time for a cigarette break.

I had barely got the lighter out of my purse when the man from inside was leaning over me, cigarette held between his soft, ample lips.

"Help a brother out?" he said. I lit his cigarette, then mine, and we stood in silence as we inhaled the smoke. As we blew the smoke back out into the air, I kinda of thought I liked him.

"Wow, that was like watching the ghetto version of *The Vagina Monologues*," he said as he smiled at me with the most perfect set of white teeth I had ever seen. I smiled back, and I knew I really liked him then. "Do you write poetry?"

"Are you crazy?" I said. "I can hardly write prescriptions for patients."

"Oh, so you're a doctor?" *Shit*. I hated revealing that information too soon. Many a brother had been intimidated when they found out I was not a stripper or didn't have some other job where minimum wage and an intercom were involved.

"Yeah," I admitted.

"That's cool," he said. "I am in pharmaceutical sales."

"You're a drug dealer?"

"Baby, you gone have to upgrade your opinion of the brothers. Sometimes pharmaceutical sales means selling pharmaceuticals."

"Sorry. Reflex."

"I will accept your apology if you let me take you to dinner this week."

"Is that the only way?" I smiled, and he leaned in as if he was going to kiss me right there.

"Yep."

"All right, you twisted my arm."

"Whoa, whoa, I am not in to all that kinky stuff."

We both laughed. The man stepped away from me and tossed his cigarette into the street. Under the streetlight, I realized just how fine this man was. Wide shoulders framed a tight, muscular body, and thick calves pressed against the back of his jeans. His chestnut eyes looked as if they were inspecting my body in ways I definitely wanted to explore later.

"Craig Peron," he said. He extended his hand, and I took it.

"Josie Green."

"I gotta say right off the bat, you are one of the most beautiful women I have ever seen," Craig said. "And let me tell you I have only used that line about four times tonight."

"Wow, only four?"

"It would have been five, but one of the ladies turned out to be a drag queen, so I don't think that applies."

"There are a lot of things wrong with that last statement."

"That is why we are having dinner. So I can explain my weird statements."

"I see. So I suppose you want my number."

"Definitely." Craig whipped out his phone and punched in the numbers I gave him. He gave me his number in return. And that's when the Top-of-the-Heap Syndrome, or THS, developed. THS is a common disease in which good men who follow the rules believe they are demigods in the dating world. All they really do is what most people are supposed to do. But because they are black men, whose brethren have serious issues, they believe women should fall down on their knees and suck their dicks in public just because they can balance a checkbook. The thing is, women have been maintaining this juggling act for centuries, and what do we get? We get to bow down and kiss the ring of the one brother in a thousand who has their priorities together.

It crept in slow and quiet at first. We would be talking daily, and then Craig would fall off the face of the earth for days—no call, no text—and then resurface like a Navy Seal, happy and horny.

At first, I just assumed he was dating another woman. That was cool with me, 'cause we had never said we were exclusive, and I was not one of those women who went around claiming men without a ring on my finger.

But as it turned out, Craig didn't have another woman; he just wanted me to do all the work in the relationship. If I called him, he would respond. If I suggested a date, he would comply, but there was no initiation on his part. There was no action. Just reaction. It was a relationship built entirely on my movement and inertia. Every woman, no matter how much she protests, wants a guy who gives her that look of passion when he sets his eyes on her. Not to be confused with lust or infatuation, a look of passion is where the man has to be next to you, touching you, or hugging on you. Women know the difference between a guy who just wants to freak you and a guy who needs you in his life. Craig was always down for freaking, but I never felt like he really wanted me in his life—until I broke up with him.

Once I said I was done, Craig found religion and decided I was the only one in his life. He even cried when I told him it was over. But I don't do do-overs. Once I am done in a relationship, I am done. So we transitioned from boyfriend/girlfriend to stalker/victim. I started getting 2 a.m. crying phone calls, and he would pop up in my parking garage.

I felt really bad for feeling so vulnerable and needy at this moment. I felt shameless for turning to a man I knew I didn't want and who didn't really want me, just because some mean girls talked about me. But right now, I needed someone to hold, to touch.

"Do you want to come up?" I asked.

"Of course."

"Just to sleep," I said. "It's late, and you had a long drive." Craig cracked a smile, just knowing he was going to get some. We got into the room, and I excused myself and went to the bathroom. I heard the television click to life. I took off my freak show of a dress and removed all my make-up. I had no energy to do anything else. I put on the pajamas I'd left in the bathroom and walked back in the room.

And there was Craig, all of him. He was buck naked and waiting for me. He was on hard and holding it in his hand as if to prove it was real or something. I had already rode that pony. No surprises there.

It started as a tickle in my throat and ended up with me bursting out laughing.

"What?" he said.

"Nothing." I shook my head, but I couldn't stop laughing. "I'm sorry."

"What?" I could tell he was getting upset, 'cause he'd stopped stroking himself.

"I guess you just knew you were getting some."

Craig gave a sly smile. "Not exactly," he said. "I was just getting comfortable."

"I can see that," I said. "You allowed all the blood from your head to relax and travel south." I got into the bed and made sure I was under as many covers as possible. I might have been turned off, but I was still human, and the boy was fine. One rub too hard and this might have been a different conversation.

"I mean we used to be together, Jos," he said. "And how we met like this. It seemed like fate." *You mean, it felt like fuck, as in fucking me,* I wanted to say.

"Look, Craig, you have been so sweet tonight, waiting on me and taking me home. I would love to take you to breakfast tomorrow as a thank-you."

"That's cool," he said.

"Well, good night," I said and turned off the lights. It took only a few seconds for him to sidle up next to me. He slipped under all the covers, and I felt him on my butt. I won't lie. I was tempted at first, but Craig had a habit of disappearing when he got what he wanted. And I was in no mood to track him down to whop his butt for being a jerk.

"Good night," I repeated. Craig tried one last time to get the party started. He started kissing the back of my neck, which was my weak spot, but I kept my ground. His hands started massaging my body, rubbing my breasts and thighs. I was getting excited. I wanted to give in, but what would I be getting? A little freaky midnight snack. But the next day I would be alone again. And he would be satisfied. I might have been the bride's slave, but I was not Boofoo the fool.

I leaned away from him a little more and began snoring lightly. Whenever he tried something throughout the night, my snores got louder and louder, until he eventually just moved to the other side of the bed. The only things he got that night were half the covers and blue balls. Not surprisingly, when there was no sex,

Craig became an early riser and left before I had a chance to yawn and have a cup of coffee.

"I got a long drive back, babe," Craig said. "But I will call you."

"Oh, no problem." I smiled under the covers. He slammed the door, and I burst out laughing. That was the last I would see of Craig. Or so I thought.

"I love you, Josie Green," Craig yelled at me through the glass partition as I scrambled to find something to hide behind. Most girls would think their boyfriend standing in the lobby of their job, with flowers, and declaring his love would be the ultimate gesture of affection. Maybe it's because I don't watch Lifetime or read any paperback novels in the checkout line, but I just didn't.

Don't get me wrong. Craig was great on paper: thirty-five, straight, no kids, pharmaceutical sales, the legal kind, churchgoing, good credit, nice-sized penis, funny. But he suffered from the same ailment as most men his age: THS.

"Should I buzz him in?" Gayle, my receptionist, asked. A group of women were in the waiting area, staring at me. They kept moving their eyes between me and Craig.

"No," I said as one woman clicked her tongue at my response. In black woman language that meant, *What the hell is wrong with you? Why aren't you taking that beautiful man's flowers and doing whatever he says to make him happy?*

"I will go out and talk to him," I said and made the long journey from my office to the front lobby. I just knew after our little nixed hookup in Atlanta that we would be officially over. But here he was again. Mind you, after that night he didn't call for three months. He could be dead, and I would only know if they did a special report on brothers who chased unavailable women on CNN.

"Before you start," Craig blurted out before I had a chance to open my mouth, "I have been doing a lot of soul-searching, and I think we should get married."

"What?" I wasn't ready for the marriage proposal.

"I am serious," Craig protested. "I know I have been a little trifling, but I am serious now. You changed my life."

"Craig, I just don't think we're compatible."

"Why?"

"The only reason you are here is because I keep rejecting you."

"That's not true!" I could see a vein throb near Craig's temple.

"When we were dating, I had to push you to do everything: go out, show me attention," I said. "But whenever I pull back, you feel personally challenged."

"I love you, Josie." Craig put his arms around me, and I knew at that moment I was right. He was not holding me like a man who could never let me go. He was holding me like a man who would be upset if I moved on without him.

"But you're not in love with me," I said. "A man that was in love with me would not slip out of a hotel in the morning because he didn't get sex."

"It wasn't like that," Craig yelled. "I mean, yes, that was what happened, but I am different now."

"How many times can you say that before you understand that I don't believe that?" I could hear the toe of my shoe tapping against the ground. "Craig, if you truly have changed and you truly do love me, you will accept that fact that we are not compatible."

There was a kind of silence that only the truth can bring. As much as he wanted to refute my statement, the bottom line was I was not the one for him, and he was not the one for me. Craig slowly dropped his arms and then kissed me on the cheek.

"I do love you," he said.

"I know you do," I said and kissed him back. "But you need to find someone you want to live for, not just live with."

"So what now?" Craig looked so confused. I felt sorry for him, though I didn't really know why. He would mourn me for a few weeks, maybe a month, but then some skinny little twenty-five-year-old girl who had just got her adult braces removed would scoop him up and that would be that. I was the one who would have to deal with the very real possibility of being alone for the rest of my life.

And if I couldn't make it work with a semi-decent, if not misguided, man, how in the hell was I going to make real love work? I offered Craig a hug and then sent him on his way.

Chapter 4

I waved my hand at the brigade of single women. They looked absolutely dumbstruck that I had let a good-looking straight brother walk away. I could almost hear their feet twitching against the linoleum floor, debating if they should chase after the leftovers in hopes of making a brand-new meal for themselves. *Good luck is all I got to say. If you have the energy to track 'em, trap 'em, beat them down, and then make them say I love you, then by all means go for it. I am through.*

I finished my workday, and when I finally arrived home, I was mentally and physically exhausted. I filled up a wineglass with an emergency stash of vodka I kept in my kitchen cupboard. I tried to forget the fact that I had racked up yet another failed relationship. But my brain was my worst enemy. Images of past boyfriends popped up as I downed another glass of alcohol.

There was Gary, the perpetual fraternity boy who spent more time with his boys than with his girl. There was Jay, the gorgeous guy who actually liked guys and later became my best friend. There was

Carlos, the attorney who spent ninety hours a week at the job and the rest of his time looking at Internet porn. Charles was the love of my life, until he tried to shake me. It was a shame I had to stab him in the leg later that night, but I didn't play that abusive shit. Perry ended up having a wife in Jamaica. Terrance had breath that could tranquilize walruses. And then there was Craig. A collection of losers for the biggest loser of them all.

It wasn't until the phone rang, and I fell from the couch to the floor in a sad attempt to answer it, that I realized I had had four drinks. I was drunk and alone. I could not afford to be single and a drunk, too.

"Hello," a voice shouted on the phone, jarring me back to reality.

"Who is this?"

"Is that how you answer the phone?" The correcting tone was unmistakable.

"Hi, Dad." I smiled, thinking that Peter Green was the one consistent man in my life. I was not sure if that was good or bad, but I was grateful to claim anything at this point.

"What's going on, baby?"

"Not much. Just sitting here getting drunk," I said. At this point I had nothing to hide.

"Why are you getting drunk all by yourself?"

"I am feeling sorry for myself."

"Why?"

"Well, in addition to breaking up with Craig and being completely done with all of your kind, I am just frustrated with my life right now."

"Work is going well, right?" My father had a very narrow vision of happy and unhappy. If you were working and paying bills, you should be on top of the moon.

If you were unemployed or, more importantly, borrowing money from him, things needed to change.

"Everything is good at the clinic. I have plenty of patients, all that," I assured my father.

"A man will come, sweetie. You just keep doing what you are doing. He will show up."

"See, that is the problem." I slurred my words together and hoped my father could understand what I was trying to say despite my jumbled sentence structure. "I used to believe that . . . . Now I am just not so sure."

"Please," my father huffed on the phone. "You are a beautiful young woman making your own money. What man wouldn't want you?"

"Plenty, apparently," I argued. "And what is becoming more disturbing is I don't even know if I care anymore."

"What you need is a vacation."

"Why is a vacation suddenly the cure to every black woman's problems? The Bahamas do not cure cancer, and they will not ease my existential crisis here, Dad."

"Well, don't go to a tropical island. Come out here to Denver and spend some time on the farm." My father, who had been a postal carrier in Chicago for twenty-five years, had finally saved enough money to pay off his debt, retire early, and do what he always loved, raising horses. Raising horses had been his only goal in life, but as a Southern-born farmer, with no financial backing and little education, he had had to relocate to the Midwest, hoping for a chance to start fresh.

He married Pamela, and they led a rocky existence until my father revealed his plans to start a working farm in Denver. Pamela opted to move to California, to live near her sisters, and hence both parents left me in Chicago to basically fend for myself, since I was eighteen years old. Praying for some stability of my own, I pursued a career in medicine and attended the University of Chicago and ended up starting my own practice for young women as soon as I finished my residency. And I was happy. But this latest relationship fiasco had me questioning my worth as a woman. And I hated myself for even admitting that. Despite all my accomplishments, being in a meaningful relationship with a man, starting a family, that always seemed to outweigh the other factors in my life. And no matter how much I loved my father, milking cows and picking up horse poop in Denver was not going to make me forget the shitty mess I had right here in Chicago.

"Yeah, I am going to take a pass on that trip, Dad."

"Oh, come on. You'll have fun."

"I just don't think that is going to do it."

"Well, you need to do something. You are getting dangerously close to being bitter, just like . . ."

"Yeah, and of all the things I don't want to hear tonight, the worst is how I am turning out to be just like Mom. No thank you."

"I am just saying—"

"I think you have said plenty for one night, Dad. I will call you later this week."

"We just had a snow this weekend, so it is perfect skiing weather."

"Do you even ski, Dad?"

"This is about you having some fun."

"Well, you hit me up when you start hitting those slopes as well." We both chuckled, and I hung up the phone. I sat in silence, watching the room spin. Wow, I had had too many drinks. I closed my eyes for what seemed like a second, and when I opened them, bright rays of light were in my face. My hair was gathered in my mouth, and I felt like I had to throw up. I dragged myself into the bathroom and prayed a shower would ease the pounding sensation that was gathered around the base of my head. As I lathered up, I couldn't help thinking that maybe a break from Chicago, the job, myself, would not be a bad idea. Since I had entered medical school, I couldn't remember taking more than three days off at a time, and that included my grandmother's funeral.

Maybe a break away from all my responsibilities would give me an opportunity to think and clear my head. But where would I go? Denver was out. The Bahamas were full of desperate single women pretending they were having a good time when they were actually looking for a man who would give them an excuse to escape their female friends. I didn't want to think about men, women, work, or family—nothing. I started to fantasize about all the books I had on my desk in my home office. Books I had been trying to read for months, unable to because of work. *Maybe Palau,* I wondered to myself. *Maybe Honduras.* I would never really be able to escape black men entirely, since many had good jobs and credit just like me, but I refused to pick a stereotypical location. And even if the islands were flooded with them, I just wanted to lie on the beach in a cute little bikini, soak up the sun, and read books until I went blind.

Yes, I was going to take a vacation. I decided I would stop at the little travel agency down the street from my job on my lunch break. Suddenly, being single on a luxurious beach did not seem like such a bad way to spend my spinster years. Sure, being in a relationship would be great, but being served fruity drinks by well-oiled men in a paradise resort . . . I could do worse. I just had to break the news to my staff.

Chapter 5

"Thank you, Jesus," Gayle screamed when I told her about my vacation plans.

"Gee, thanks," I cocked a half smile. Clearly, my staff couldn't wait for me to leave them alone.

"You know we will miss you, Dr. Green," Gayle said as she turned to Marcela and Ruby, my nurse and administrative assistant, for support. They both nodded in unison. "It's just that I don't remember you ever taking a *real* vacation. Ever!"

"What about the trip I took to Boston over the summer?" I replied.

"Wasn't that a medical conference?" Ruby interjected. She pressed her fingers against her glasses as if she were a prosecutor grilling me for answers.

"Yeah, but I took that next Monday off," I said.

"Wasn't your plane delayed?" Marcela chimed in. Damn. They were not giving a sister a break. But they were right. It seemed all my focus had been work related. I wondered how that affected my relationships.

"I get it, ya'll," I said, throwing my hands up in the

air. "I am going to make up for lost time and take a real vacation."

"Where are you going?" asked Gayle.

"I heard Palau is a beautiful island, and not a lot of people have been there. I am trying not to deal with the crowds."

"Wow, like all the hip-hop stars and celebrities go there," Marcela, the youngest one of the bunch, added. She should know. She was constantly reading all those entertainment and rap magazines when she was supposed to be filing patient records.

"Hmm," I said. I could feel my face scrunching up. "Well, I do not want to be dealing with any rappers and their naked groupies following them around everywhere."

"Don't listen to her," Ruby said. "Just go. You will have a fabulous time."

"I was online looking at all these cute bathing suits I wanted to wear," I said.

"That's the spirit," said Gayle. She clapped her hands. She was more excited than me.

"You are sure to meet a man there," said Marcela. She threw her hand in the air, waiting for me to give her a high five. The group just stared at her.

"This is not about meeting a damn man, Marcela," Gayle snapped.

"This is about taking a break and recharging," I gently added, not wanting to sound judgmental of Marcela.

"Yeah," Ruby said. "You know Dr. Green ain't down for no man like that."

"Thanks, I think," I said. I was trying to determine if I was just insulted.

"I mean, you are not sweating being with a man. This is about you," explained Ruby.

"Anyway, we have to talk administration for a second," I said, steering the conversation back to familiar and safe territory. "Dr. Brighton will take care of the exams, and, Ruby, you can deal with everything else. Gayle, reschedule Mrs. Harris's and Ms. Fey's appointments for the following week, when I will be back."

"Will do," said Gayle. She was jotting down notes.

"Marcela, I need all the files updated to the new system by the time I return," I said. Marcela tried not to frown, but the corners of her mouth were already crinkled. "By the time I get back, Marcela."

"I get it," said Marcela as she rolled her eyes.

"So I guess I will leave early on Friday so I can go home and pack and leave on Saturday."

"Wow, nine days," Ruby said and laughed. "My money is you go crazy after three days."

"Hey, I thought ya'll were supposed to be encouraging me?" I replied.

"We are encouraging, Dr. Green," Ruby chuckled. "But this is like giving a person living check to check a hundred thousand dollars and telling them to budget it for a year. It is going to be a very interesting experiment."

"Well, I am going to have fun, and I am not going to break down or crack up or kill anyone," I said.

"I will be watching the news for any reports of a Chicago doctor who stabbed a busboy because she missed her job so much," said Gayle.

"Please. I will be drinking fruity drinks I can't pronounce and making sure my skin gets even more chocolatety," I replied

"You are already a Hershey's bar, baby," Ruby said.

"I am going for deep dark chocolate," I said. The ladies and I busted out laughing.

"I heard that," said Marcela. "At least the island will get to see that gorgeous body you hide under all those clothes."

"I don't hide my body."

"Dr. Green, I love you, but if I had your body, I would be wearing sleeveless, backless tops and mini-skirts every day," said Marcela.

"Thank God, you are not Dr. Green," Ruby said and shook her head. "How is she supposed to care for patients dressed like she is going to the club?"

"They would just have to get over it," Marcela said.

"Lord, help the children," Gayle said.

"Well, believe me, I will be showing more skin on the island," I said.

"Good for you," Marcela cheered.

"All right, everyone. We got a lot of work to get done before Friday, so let's get to it," I said. "Oh, and one more thing—thank you."

The ladies of the Green Clinic enveloped me in their arms as we all hugged. It hit me that over the last few years, this had been not only my staff, but the closet thing to a family I had had since my parents left Chicago. I was going to miss them.

The rest of the week went by so quickly, I could hardly keep track of the time. When I got back to my town house on Friday and saw all my clothes thrown on the bed and couch, I felt overwhelmed. I had started pulling out clothes on Monday in the hopes that I would be all finished packing by Wednesday at the latest. Here it was the night before my trip, and I barely had a pair of shoes in my suitcase.

How did one dress for paradise, anyway? I decided

I didn't want my wardrobe to reflect my personality. I grabbed the twelve best swimsuits I'd purchased over the last week and threw them in a small weekend bag. I tossed in my toiletries and a few mules and sandals. And, just in case, a black, sheer evening gown and shawl, 'cause I believed in miracles, too.

After I finished throwing in my book choices for the trip, I got down on my knees.

"Lord, please do not let me get in the way of me having some fun. I just want an adventure, not to worry about everything, and to take it one day at a time."

I was about to get up but knelt back down. "And just in case . . . there is a special man out there for me, and he happens to be on this island, please let him be genuine and funny and love me for me."

Figuring I had all my bases covered, I climbed into bed and tried to dream of palm trees and fruity drinks.

Chapter 6

"Can't you go any faster?" I yelled at the limo driver as we wove through traffic.

"I am trying my best, ma'am," the man mumbled under his breath with more than just a little agitation. And he was justified. I didn't know if it was the three cocktails I had had before falling asleep, or passing out, which ever way you looked at it, but I woke up an hour before my plane was to take off. When I finally roused myself, both my cell and home phones were flashing their red lights angrily at me. I knew immediately it was the car service, and I was late.

It wasn't until we hit gridlock traffic miles from my gate that I realized how late. Each plane that buzzed above us could have been my escape. And I was getting hotter by the second.

"I am so sorry for not answering my phone earlier and having you deal with all this during rush hour, but is there any other way to get to my plane? I only have twenty minutes."

"At this point you can walk," the man said in such a deadpan voice it scared me. I was one more outburst away from being put out. I decided to keep quiet.

Baggage claim was a blizzard of people scrambling to their destinations. I barely had time to get my tip out of my purse when my door swung open. My bags were thrown on a trolley, and the driver slammed the door as soon as I got out.

"Here you go. Thanks," I said as I tried to offer my tip, but the man was already getting back into the car and revving the engine. The limo skidded off in a huff, and I ran to my flight.

"Ma'am, that plane took off twenty minutes ago," said the woman behind the counter, holding back a smirk. "We ask our customers to arrive at least ninety minutes before departure to ensure that things like this don't happen."

"I know, I know." The customer service people and I were obviously getting along today. "But is there another flight to Palau I can take?" The woman starting clicking the buttons on her terminal furiously as I wondered why airline representatives typed so much just to read aisle or window seat on your ticket.

"The next flight is not until tomorrow morning."

"Really? Are you sure?" The woman offered a half smile that read, *Yes, bitch, I can read and you're late. Get over it.* I meandered over to some empty seats next to the ticket counter, defeated and angry. This was going to ruin all my plans. I would be a day late for everything. And though I had no tours planned, I was very anal and didn't like unexpected hiccups in the plan.

"A woman as fine as you should not have your face all frowned up like that," a man mumbled a little too

close to my ear. I was ready to go off until I looked in
the man's face and something familiar registered.

"Do I know you?" I asked.

"Dallas Sterling." The man smiled back, waiting for
the moment of recognition to sink in. I almost jumped
out of my seat when it did.

"Ohmigosh," I screamed. "Dallas from the Denver
Nuggets?"

"Baby girl, not so loud. I am trying to be incog-
nita." I ignored the fact that he pronounced *incognito*
wrong. He was gorgeous. Not only was he gorgeous,
for some reason, he was talking to me. Now I was
pretty confident with my looks, but usually basketball
players only went for three types: baby momma, Halle
Berry, or groupies. Since I didn't fall into any of those
categories, I was surprised to be garnering Mr. Sterling's attention.

"I think you are great."

"Thank you, baby." Dallas served up a smile that I
was sure would have caused many a groupie to literally fall on their knees in response. I attempted to
pull myself together.

"I am such a fan. It is a pleasure meeting you," I
said as I gathered my little tote and attempted to exit
without embarrassing myself further.

"Why you looking like that? All sad."

"I missed my flight."

"Oh, for real? Sorry about that. Where were you
headed?"

"Palau."

"No shit? I mean for real?" Dallas smiled. "So are
we." He pointed to a small entourage of men who
were standing in a corner. One man was holding
a television camera and was bogged down with

equipment, while another man, who also looked vaguely familiar, was on his cell phone and was jotting notes.

"Were you on this airline, too?"

"Yeah, but we got here late, too."

The man with the familiar face came up to Dallas and me and blurted out, "It's all taken care of. We chartered a private plane." Suddenly, the man's face registered, and I started bouncing around like a schoolgirl.

"Are you Francis Wright from *60 Minutes*?" The man turned and nodded, giving me the classic TV smile I watched every Sunday. Not only was Francis one of the smartest men in broadcasting, he was the cutest, especially on CBS.

"The plane is on the other side of the terminal, so we should get going," Francis said to Dallas and then looked back at me. "It was a pleasure meeting you." Then he was off. It didn't matter that he technically hadn't met me, but rather had politely tolerated my presence.

"What is your name?" Dallas questioned me.

"Dr. Josie Green."

"Doctor? Wow, that is hot." Dallas smiled again. "My little sister wants to be a doctor."

"I am sure she can do it."

"Yo, listen. Since you missed your plane, you should hitch a ride with us."

"What?" My mouth dropped. Catching a plane ride with two of the most famous, rich, and handsome men in the world was very tempting, but I was afraid of the payback.

"Oh, thank you for the offer, but I don't want to impose."

"You ain't imposing," Dallas said. "*Sixty Minutes* is following me around and seeing what I do day-to-day. They have to do what I say, and you were going there, anyway. This way you get to stay on schedule."

"Yeah, but . . ." Dallas looked at me like he already knew exactly where my mind as going.

"Uh, Josie, right?" His smile was intoxicating. "I know you used to a lot of niggas probably gaming you with shit, and you fine, so I know it happens all the time. But I am just offering you a ride. That's it."

"Mmm," I whined. I hated myself for letting the sound come out like that.

"If you don't want to be escorted to an exotic island by the number one point guard in the league, in a private jet, that is on you. But I got a plane to catch."

"What type of in-flight movie will we be watching?"

Dallas chuckled. "I have that new Leonardo movie in my warm-up bag."

"Sold," I said as Dallas shook his head and grabbed my bags.

"You're weird." He laughed.

"So I have been told." I smiled back and gave the woman at the counter a cursory rolling of the eyes for good measure.

As we boarded the plane, I tried to make a mental note of all the people I was going to call from the bathroom of the plane and to brag about what was happening. I was definitely calling the ladies at work. Hell, Marcela would probably faint. Jason would fall out laughing, and even though I wasn't speaking to Jeanne, it would really send her over the edge to know I was flirting with someone richer than her husband. For the first time, it felt like my luck was finally changing. Perhaps this could be a new turning point in the saga known as Josie Green. No longer dating duds and losers, I had upgraded à la Beyoncé to movers and shakers. Wow, and all I did was schedule a vacation. Maybe those other sisters had it right. The key to happiness was only a passport away.

Chapter 7

You haven't lived until you have sipped five-hundred-dollar champagne with an NBA player and TV celebrity on a private jet. It's like being prom queen, head cheerleader, and the first female president all wrapped up in one cashmere-lined ribbon.

"Do you need any more shrimp, baby?" Dallas asked in that boyfriend voice that would have made me giggle if I weren't already thirty-four and bitter. Instead, I offered a coy smile and nodded my head. Hell, yeah, I wanted some more shrimp. Some more wine. I almost forgot the fact that I was supposed to be on a first-class flight on Delta. This was like first class *MTV Cribs* style. Everything was exaggerated. The seats looked more like a small couch, and were covered with Coach leather. A small cart, filled with seafood, vegetables, wine, soda, and fruit, separated me from Dallas, Francis, and the cameraman, who sat quietly in the back, sipping on his bottled water. He seemed to be unaffected by the celebrity wattage that electrified the cabin. He just looked out the window and ignored us all. Lucky him. I didn't have that luxury.

I was admittedly smitten and surprised by the royal treatment and attention. I began to see why some sisters made it their personal credo to seek out ballplayers and celebrities. You might be an object, but you were an object living the good life, if only for a moment.

"So what field of medicine do you practice?" Francis asked, not looking up from his notes.

"I am a gynecologist in the southeast region of Chicago," I said.

"Like Cabrini-Green?" Francis asked. His hazel eyes made contact with mine. I could tell I piqued his journalistic curiosity.

"Yep, around that area," I answered as I debated if I could get away with a few more shrimp without looking like a glutton.

"Wow, that is a pretty dangerous area," he said in almost a questioning tone.

"It can be, but I haven't had any problems," I countered. I hated when people tried to give South Chicago a bad rap. Yeah, it had had some issues in the past, but it was an up-and-coming neighborhood now, with mostly poor but hardworking people. I wanted to open a clinic in the area to offer services that weren't readily available or affordable to people who needed them.

"I didn't mean to offend," said Francis. He must have sensed my agitation. "I was just thinking you would make a great feature story about people giving back to their community."

"Are you serious? Me on *60 Minutes*?" My parents would fall out seeing a profile of me on their favorite television show. There had hardly been a Sunday that went by in my childhood that my mom and dad didn't sit me down in front of the TV, where we munched on dinner, digesting the chicken and the current topic of the day. To think I could be a topic of discussion for some family somewhere almost forced me into hyperventilation.

"That would be great," I tried to say calmly. "Dallas, where is the restroom?"

"Right down the corridor to the left," Dallas managed between chomps of shrimp. I rose and headed to the bathroom. I needed to pull myself together. I closed the door behind me and pinched myself for a reality check. I felt it but did it again to ensure I wasn't hallucinating. *Oww.* That was real. Yes, I was having a great time, but I wasn't going to sleep with either of these men. No. I was going to enjoy this ride and then say good-bye and continue on my vacation as I had planned. This was not about finding a man. But, it wasn't like I had been looking for a man when Dallas appeared. And I certainly hadn't been praying to meet Francis Wright.

Get it together, Josie, I said to myself. Suddenly, the plane dipped, and my stomach sank. I pressed my hands against the bathroom walls to brace myself. *Whew.* I screamed when we looped back up.

"You all right in there?" Dallas asked through the door. I took one last breath and opened the door.

"Yeah, just scared me a little."

"The captain said we need to sit down." Dallas grabbed my hand and guided me back to his seat. He buckled me up, then fastened his own seat belt.

"Tropical islands usually have weird weather patterns," Francis said matter-of-factly, like he had endured hurricanes in search of his stories. Well, in fact, he had covered both Katrina and the tsunami in Asia, so I guess he had a right to be passé about our turbulence.

"Lady and gentlemen, we are going to have to avoid this weather and head in from a slightly different angle," the captain said. "This may delay our arrival by about an hour, but we will get there."

Dallas grabbed my hand and held it in his gigantic palm.

"Uh, I'm not scared," I said.

"Maybe I am," said Dallas. He smiled, but I could tell by his shaking hands that he wasn't kidding.

Then, for one complete second, the shaking stopped. I felt Dallas's grip relax, and I was about to settle back when there as a horrendous clap of thunder and we plummeted hard and fast.

"Hold on, people," the captain yelled through the loudspeaker. I was scared. But when the oxygen masks fell in front of us, I thought we might actually die on this plane. I would die unmarried, with two of the world's most beautiful men on the plane with me. Alanis Morissette's "Ironic" played in my head. I had procrastinated on my dream vacation, and when I finally took it, I ended up dead.

All I knew was if I died, I was going to haunt all my family and friends who had forced me to take this vacation. I didn't know where dead people purchased those scary shackles to make loud noises in the halls, but I planned to stop at the heavenly Home Depot and pick up as many noisemakers as I could. I opened my eyes for a brief second to see the wing of the plane rip off, and then it all went black.

Chapter 8

My nostrils are on fire. That was the first thought that came to my mind. Then I opened my eyes. It was like being in space. Everything was floating in front of me. The delectable shrimp we'd nibbled on; Francis's notepad; several pairs of tennis shoes, which Dallas was supposed to sign while he flew to Palau. Then it hit me. Where was everyone? Double wham! *We are underwater.* I swam to the top of the plane, praying there was an air pocket. My lungs collapsed just as I reached the plane's ceiling. *Thank God. Air!*

I pulled strands of hair away from my eyes and tried to think. *Emergency door!* The plane seemed to be almost level, which meant it had hit the bottom of the ocean, a reef, or it hadn't completely sunk yet. *Okay. Just swim to the other side, open the door, and head for the surface.* I squashed my attempts to hyperventilate and took in as much air as my lungs could hold. Then I dived back in the cold water. I was halfway to the front of the plane when I spotted something shiny under a set of turned-over seats. I squinted to make sure my eyes weren't playing tricks. They weren't. It was a watch. Dallas's watch.

I got to the seats and turned them over. Dallas lay unconscious on the floor. I braced my feet between a seat and the floor and managed to pull him free from his prison. Instantly, he seemed to spring to life, swinging and yelling in the water. I avoided the blows, got behind him, and grabbed him under his arms. He grabbed my arms but must have realized a familiar touch and stopped resisting. We made it to the emergency exit, which was already open. I took a quick peek to see if the captain was in his seat, but he was gone. I pulled Dallas to the surface, which, thankfully, didn't seem that far. But once we hit the cool air, Dallas lost it.

"I can't swim," he screamed as he flailed his humongous arms around in the air. He whacked me right across the forehead, and for a moment, I felt like I would pass out. I maintained my balance.

"Calm down." I tried to sound reassuring to Dallas but really wanted to scream, *Why hasn't your rich ass taken swimming lessons?* I looked around me, praying Palau was nearby. Thankfully, land was not far off.

"Okay, Dallas." I spoke soft and slow. "We are going to swim to the island behind you. If we are calm and take our time, it won't take long at all."

"I just fucking told you I can't swim!" Dallas had managed to hold on to some part of the plane that was floating above the water.

"I get that. But we cannot stay floating out here forever. We will freeze or worse."

"What can be worse than my fucking plane crashing into the goddamn ocean?" Dallas almost spat back, and I wanted to stop treading water and slap him.

"How 'bout you die!" I screamed. "How 'bout I let your ass drown if you swear at me one more time?"

Dallas fell silent. His face flashed a deep purple, as if the nastiest joke had been whispered in his ear by his mother.

"I'm sorry." Dallas started blinking hard. Was he holding back tears? "I'm just scared, okay?"

"So am I," I said as I paddled toward him. "Right now we have to think smart in order to survive. Now if we relax and lie on our backs, we can float and ride the current to shore. But you have to get rid of all that deadweight."

"Like what?"

"All that jewelry, your shoes, that diamond-plated belt I noticed you wearing," I said, embarrassed this man's accessories cost more than my town house. "I can't guide us in with all that weight."

"Do you know how much that belt buckle cost?"

"Not as much as my life, I can tell you that," I said. "You can keep it and stay here if you want, but I am headed to shore."

"Okay, okay." Dallas stripped off his adornments and somehow looked a little smaller, as if the jewelry had added size and girth to his frame.

I moved behind him. "Now don't struggle. Just try to relax." Dallas loosened his grip on the plane wreckage and allowed himself to lean back in the water. I wrapped my arm around his neck and shoulder blade and began paddling back.

The sun was setting quickly, and I prayed silently that we would make it to the coast before the night air chilled the water. I underestimated the time. What looked like a thirty-minute swim seemed to take hours. My legs and arms tingled, and my toes and fingers felt numb. My eyes were heavy, and I tried to think happy thoughts, like my friends at the clinic and my dad. Just as I felt my body drifting off, we smashed into the sandy beach. It took all my strength to push Dallas off of me. He seemed more exhausted than me.

My legs shook, and my arms felt like they had been holding two-hundred-pound barbells on either side. I just wanted to sleep for a month.

"Help," called a voice so distant and tiny, I thought I was dreaming. I looked at Dallas, who was snoring, with his face half buried in the sand. I looked around but could barely see with the sun closing down for the night. Suddenly, I caught a glimpse of something shiny in the water and wobbled toward it.

I could make out a white shirt buttoned at the wrist and blood soaked. I knew it was the captain. *Do any of these people know how to swim?* I pondered as I dived back in the water. "I'm coming," I yelled. And I meant it, until my legs retaliated. They burned and locked as I tried to tread water. I tried to get my bearings, but my arms hurt too much to stay afloat. I could feel myself sinking. If I died, at least I would know who to haunt. The swim instructors at the Chicago YMCA.

Chapter 9

The fire warmed my dreams first. I felt like I was cooking a salmon dinner. I realized immediately it was a dream, because I never cooked nor ate much fish. Most of my diet consisted of stuff from vending machines, fast food, and the occasional cooked meals from the hospital across the street from the clinic, when my staff forced me to "eat some vegetables." At times, I felt bad for being such a poor example in the eating department, when I advised so many young women about the woes of foods high in cholesterol. But working seventy-five hours a week left little time to learn casserole recipes. But regardless of who made the salmon, I was devouring it. No fork, no knife, just me ripping off the head of a salmon, eyes and all. My eyes opened to a very similar scene in real life.

A fire crackled a few feet away from me as I spotted Dallas, Francis, and the captain all sleeping quietly around the flames. Several fish and an assortment of fruits rested on a flat piece of wood. Had we made it to Palau, anyway? I looked around and saw a figure heading our way. My heart raced, and I wanted to wake the others, but my voice was so weak, I couldn't gather the words.

The dark figure was dragging something with some vines across the beach. I searched for a large stick to fight him off with but came up empty.

"Hello," I yelled loud enough, I hoped, to wake the others. No such luck. "Who's there?"

A stack of fish fell at my feet, and I caught a look of the man. It was the cameraman. But he looked so different. His pant legs were ripped, revealing thick thighs and muscular calves. He had no shirt, so his dark, chiseled chest was on display under the moon's bright light. I felt like I was trapped in some surreal mix of *Lost* meets *Survivor* meets Danielle Steel. Finally, my medical instincts pulled me back to reality when I noticed a huge gash on his shoulder blade.

"You're bleeding," I said to the man, who turned and ignored me as he proceeded to check the firewood.

"Hey." I propped myself up and walked over to him. "I'm a doctor. Can I see?"

The man didn't even look at me. But at least he stood still so I could examine him. It was mainly a flesh wound, much worse to look at than to treat.

"You need to clean this and cover it so it won't get infected." I looked around and saw a few large palm trees in the distance. I trotted over to one and pulled off several leaves, then returned to the man. Luckily, he was brewing water in a misshapen piece of metal, no doubt part of our carriage into this nightmare. I ripped off a sleeve from my shirt and dabbed it in the water and soaked the wound. The man didn't even flinch as the water washed away the old blood, leaving a fresh white patch. I folded the leaves and wrapped the sleeve of my shirt around it.

"You need to change this every day until it scabs over," I said. I wanted to say, "Until you can get to a hospital for stitches," but the reality of the situation dawned on me. Had we reach our destination, someone would have stumbled across us, or Captain America over here would have found somebody.

"Did you save the captain?" I asked as the man walked past me and bent over the fish. He took a sharp rock and started cleaning them. Charming! Stuck on an island with a muscular mute and a pro basketball player who fainted at the sight of water. Then it hit me that this guy hadn't just saved the captain, he'd saved me, too.

I remembered that, I was drowning, my body too weak to float, and a hand so big the fingers spanned my waist grabbed hold of me and pulled me up. I leaned back on his shoulder as we swam to safety. At first I thought it was Dallas or Francis, but they smelled different. This man was free of expensive colognes. His scent was clean and crisp and masculine. When we reached the shore, he carried me to a fire, where Dallas and Francis sat dazed and silent. They refused to look at me or each other. They were quieted by the grim reality of our situation.

The man placed me down, then ran back into the water. He was gone for what seemed like an eternity. For a moment, I feared he had succumbed to exhaustion like me and had broken under the water's strong currents. But, finally, I saw him walking out of the water, with the captain straddling his back. He carried the man, in his arms just as he had me, all the way to our little camp of former bougie Negroes and plopped him on the ground. Then he passed out. I wanted to check on him, but I was so tired myself, I couldn't move. Next thing I knew, I woke up to him bringing back the fish.

"You saved us all," I said. The man was cutting the fish into small pieces, which he skewered on a stick.

"Thank you," I said. But the man never spoke. But he did pass me a stick with several pieces of fish and fruit stuck on it. That was progress.

Chapter 10

You never expect it to get cold on an island. But it does. Sometimes it gets so cold, you could freeze if there wasn't a fire to keep you warm. We found this out our first week there. The day was so deceptive, as we almost burned under the sun's rays. But by nightfall the wind kicked up and hollered at us, angry and spiteful. At first our camp was open as temperatures remained mild at night. But that night, the wind was determined to let us know who reigned on this island.

"We have to do something, or we'll freeze to death," Francis said. We each scrambled in the dark, cold night, looking for bamboo and leaves that would provide a shelter more than a space to lay our heads.

The quiet man was busy breaking bamboo into pieces, which Francis needed to build a shelter. They had a silent rapport. The quiet man never talked, and Francis didn't feel the need to say that much around him. They worked in relative silence as Dallas cussed and moaned while he brought back his portion of the wood. The captain and I gathered leaves and put them in a pile in front of the two men.

We all watched in awe as Francis and the quiet one built a solid structure that allowed the wind to hit us only in one direction. Then we stacked the kindling and wood for the fire and let it ignite. It didn't take long before we were toasty and warm inside our little hut.

"Where did you learn to build a shelter so fast?" I asked.

"Boy Scouts," said Francis. "I know you were expecting me to say while rebuilding houses for Katrina victims or something more magnanimous than that. But the truth is, it was the Boy Scouts."

"Well, I am just glad you knew how to make it, so we didn't freeze," the captain said, and I nodded.

"Thank you," I said and turned to the quiet man, who seemed to ignore my expression of gratitude. I wanted to catch an attitude, but the man had saved us from freezing. He deserved my thanks, not my scorn.

Later that night, as everyone slept, I thought about the first fort I had ever made. Granted it wasn't made of bamboo, just a carton from the TV my dad had just bought. But I used my scissors to make the window holes, and I picked the place to put it, right under the maple tree in our backyard. I felt so safe in that fort. I brought all my dolls inside and read stories to them. I ate lunch there and invited my mom and dad to have tea with me inside. My mother always declined; my father always wriggled his short, stout body under the box and drank the invisible tea with my Barbie and Rainbow Brite doll.

That was one of the happiest moments of my life. But this fort wasn't for fun. It was for survival. I couldn't get up, walk inside the house, and go to sleep in the safety of my room. This was real.

I got up and took a step outside. I walked down to the beach and looked across in either direction. There was nothing but darkness all around me. The only warmth I felt was from the fire burning far behind me.

Suddenly, I felt arms around my shoulders. "Whoa," I yelled and jumped back to see the quiet one, with a tattered sweater in his hands.

"Sorry," I said. "You scared me." He extended his arms again with the sweater, and I turned around to let him place it on me.

"You did a great job on the shelter," I said. "It looks amazing and is real warm inside." I caught myself raising my voice. I quickly corrected myself. There was no evidence that this man was deaf. He just didn't talk.

He nodded. For a second, I thought I could see the corners of his lips curl. Was he going to smile? Before I could focus, the man turned around and walked back to camp.

I knew, regardless of what happened on this island, it was not going to be boring.

After the shock of our experience wore off, the panic moved in like a plague.

"We are gonna die out here," said Dallas. He threw his hands in the air. "This is some bullshit."

"You need to calm down," Francis interjected. He seemed to be surveying the land. "Everyone knows we're missing by now. They are going to track us. Does anyone have a cell phone?"

"You really think you gone get service out here?" said Dallas. He looked perplexed.

"Of course not," said Francis. He rolled his eyes as he patted his pockets. "But all we really need to do is turn it on. A roaming signal can be picked up. We don't have to get a call out so long as they know there is someone here."

Francis pulled a small phone from his back pocket. "Found it."

He checked his phone and fiddled with the switches. "Shit. The back is gone. Anybody else got a phone?" He looked around at the circle. The captain and the quiet one shook their heads no.

"I left mine in my purse," I said. Dallas reached deep in his pockets and pulled out four different cell phones.

"Jesus," the captain blurted out.

"Yeah, I know a lot of people," said Dallas as he dropped the devices in Francis's hands.

"There has got to be some way to get a signal out," said Francis.

"Great professor," Dallas smirked. "While you are trying to figure out a way to get us off the island, lovee and I will be chillin' at breakfast." Dallas tried to grab my hand. I snapped it back.

"You may be a millionaire, but I am not your wife," I said.

"Well, you are definitely more Mary Ann than Ginger."

"You'll never find out," I replied.

"Girl, you never know," said Dallas. He bent over so his pearly smile was inches from my face. "We may have to repopulate the earth."

"Humanity is a goner," said the captain.

"I need to concentrate here," snapped Francis, who

gave one of those stern, confused, or constipated looks he offered during his celebrity interviews.

I said, "Dallas, why don't you and . . ." It dawned on me that I didn't know the captain's name, or the strange, quiet man's for that matter.

"Captain Andrew Phillips," said the captain. He smiled back at me.

"Nice to meet you, Captain Phillips," I said.

"Andrew is fine," replied the captain.

"Great. Why don't you and Andrew catch us some more fish," I said as I smiled at the quiet man, who got up from his sandy seat and walked away from our camp.

"Jacques doesn't talk," Francis said nonchalantly.

"I see," I said. "But there is no need to be rude."

"He is just very direct. Best cameraman I have ever had," replied Francis.

"That's great," I said. "But we need a little more co-operation than camera angles at this point."

"Damn, you got a mouth," Dallas said.

"And I can back it up, too," I said.

"Hey, Dallas," Andrew said. "Come on. Let's go see if we can catch some fish."

"I guess I am going to pick some more firewood and see if there is anyone else on this island," I said, praying for a moment alone to cry and shout in peace.

"Alone?" Francis asked.

"Yes, alone," I said.

"I am not being chauvinistic, but statistically, you would probably be in more danger from rapists than one of us." Francis never looked up. He just spit out his knowledge like a computer. A computer living in the sixties.

"I think if I can pull a two-hundred-thirty-pound man to shore by myself, I can handle a couple of horny natives," I said. "But if they happen to know where the Best Western is on this berg, I believe they may get a little taste."

I watched as Francis twisted his head at me. His cigar-colored skin was a bright red. *That got his attention,* I said to myself as I walked off.

At first I was resolute, even cocky, in my feminist monologue. But as I stepped deeper into the dense forest, the light was slowly filtered out. And my heart rate increased double time. Suddenly, I was conscious of every sound. The crackling of branches beneath my feet, the cawing of birds above my head, and even the rustling of the wind through the leaves seemed amplified. I dared not look back for fear I would see a ghost, or an alien chasing humans for sport. But when I heard an unfamiliar creeping sound by my right shoulder, I had to look.

There, less than one hundred yards away, were the darkest red eyes looking back at me. I stood petrified for a moment. But a voice kept getting louder and louder in my head. *Run, dumb ass!* I listened and darted through the forest. I prayed the eyes would decide I was boring game and turn the other way. I knew I was too scared to look, because if those eyes were still behind me, I would most likely fall from a heart attack.

But I had to look. I peeked back, and there were those eyes off in the distance, jogging at a pace just behind mine. I screamed and tore through the woods like I was on the track team at my old high school. Branches slapped across my face as I jumped over logs and sidestepped rocks. *Don't fall like a white girl. Don't fall like a white girl.* I begged my legs to stay true to a sista and keep running. Because everyone knows, once you fall, you die. It has been proven in almost every horror movie in American cinema. And I was not going to be the fool to test the validity of this theory.

My eyes caught sight of a clearing just a few yards ahead. If I could make it to the beach, maybe the beast would be too scared to follow. The light grew brighter as I could feel my freedom approaching. I wasn't going to die single and alone on an island, chased by demons. I was going to live to see another day. I stepped one more step into my undoing.

I grabbed a branch, which slowed my locomotion just enough to prevent me from falling off a steep cliff that jutted out just a few feet from the forest. I was leaning over to thank my Lord and catch my breath when I remembered those eyes. I turned around to see them slowly coming out of the forest.

Chapter 11

Red eyes staring into your core, it doesn't get scarier than that. I was wrong again. As I stood clinging to a vine near the cliff, a beast surfaced from behind the shadows. It was a wild boar, but much bigger than they looked on television, and more menacing in person, too. It huffed as it saw me. I prayed it would decide I was too small a prey and retreat back into the forest, but it grunted, scratched the ground with its hoof, and charged forward. If my life flashed before my eyes, it was barren and uneventful.

The only things I remembered were the red eyes and scurrying footsteps. I wanted to close my eyes, but I was too petrified to blink. I watched as the animal came within a few feet of me, and before I could let out a scream, a shape glided in front of me, pushing the animal off the cliff. I looked down on the ground to see the silent man halfway over the cliff's edge and losing his balance. I quickly ran to him, pulling at his feet until he was able to brace his hands on the edge and pull himself up.

"Ohmygod! Thank you!" I let out and hugged him. I couldn't believe I was alive, and I was dumbstruck as to how this man was able to save me. But I was more than grateful.

He looked at me, and I caught a glimpse of his deep brown eyes. I wondered what they revealed about the man in front of me. I didn't have long to wonder. After a half attempt at a smile, the man walked off back into the dark, leaving me alone to deal with my many emotions.

"Wait," I yelled after him. "My name is Josie."

I extended my hand, but the man kept walking. "You don't know how happy I am that you came along," I cried. The only connection between us was the crunching of dead leaves beneath our feet. Then a sobering thought entered my mind. What if he hadn't just come along? What if he had been following me all along through the forest, waiting for a chance to rape me? Maybe the boar came along before he could attack me.

Okay, get a grip, Josie, I drummed into my head. *The man saves your life, and you want him doing five to ten for imagined rape charges.*

"Have you been to the other side of the island?" I asked, trying to change the subject and calm my nerves. "Do you know if anyone else is here?"

The man looked back at me. Was he smiling, smirking? Why couldn't this man speak a language or at least carry a pen and pad with him?

I assumed the man was leading me back to the group, but when he walked away from the path I knew and headed farther into the woods, I felt my heart thumping.

"Hey, did we miss our exit?" I said and laughed, but

the man kept walking. "I'm sorry. Did you hear me? I think we missed our—"

The sunlight stopped me, and when we stepped out of the forest, I had to put my hand over my mouth. A hidden lake lay before us, complete with waterfall. We walked to the edge of the water.

"This is incredible," I said. "How long have you known about this? Is the water clean for us to get fresh drinking water? Is there anything to carry—"

Splash! I felt the slightest shove, and I was underwater. I rose to the top. I wanted to let the man have it.

"What the hell is wrong with you!" I screamed, but there was no one in sight. A few air bubbles later, and he bobbed up out of the water. I was furious for a good minute. But as the cool water relaxed my sunbaked muscles, the gravity of the situation seemed to melt away. The man wasn't being malicious. He wasn't tormenting me in the water to remind me how we almost died. He was giving us what we needed: a break from the fear, the anger, and questions, a childhood moment in a very adult situation. I started smiling and took a second to wipe water from my eyes, but he was gone again.

When he reemerged from the water, I didn't know what else to do at that point, so I improvised. I swam up to him slowly and then pounced on his head, sending him back underwater. It wasn't long before he had me by the legs. "What! Stop!" I screamed.

Too late. Slam! Right back under the water. For a brief moment, my fears were gone. This was not a stranger, and we were not stranded on a deserted island. We were just two people enjoying an afternoon swim under the hot sun. It was one of the few moments of peace we would experience.

Chapter 12

My first medical emergency happened shortly after the quiet man and I got back to the others. I noticed Andrew was sort of slapping water on himself in the tide, in an attempt to bathe. I had been thinking of a similar method of cleaning myself. Suddenly, Andrew let out the loudest yelp I had ever heard.

"Oh my God," he cried as he fell into the water. We all ran out to him.

"What's the matter?" I yelled.

"Something bit me," he answered. He was sitting in the water, and I could see red all around him. Dallas and Francis lifted Andrew by his arms as the quiet man grabbed his feet. Once he was out of the water, I could see his foot had been severely cut. I looked around but didn't see any animals.

"Go set him down," I told the men and continued scouring the area for the cause of the cut. I found it. A large, slick metal plate, most likely debris from the plane, jutted out from the sand. It almost cut me as I pulled it free from its lodging. I didn't want anyone else having the same fate. When I got back to Andrew and got a chance to observe the cut, it thankfully didn't look infected. Still, to be sure, we boiled some water over the fire with a steel container we found. After I cleaned the wound, I put mud on it to cool it and wrapped it up with some palm leaves.

"Thank you," Andrew said. I nodded and rubbed his shoulders.

"You're welcome," I said.

"So how long have you been a doctor?" he asked.

"How did you know?"

"You just have a gentle touch that you either were born with or had to practice over and over." He smiled. "So I took a guess."

"Good guess." I smiled. "How does it feel?"

"Not too bad now, thanks to you."

"It was my pleasure," I said.

"So how long do you think before they find us?"

"That is hard to say," I said. "But I guess you would know more about that."

"I tried to send out a distress signal, but I don't know if it got through."

I shook my head. "That is not good."

"What's worse is this wasn't exactly a fully chartered flight," he said.

"I don't understand."

"You know when rich people want something" Andrew tried to adjust his sitting position and winced—"they get fast service, so they pulled me to fly the plane and kind of blew over all the official paperwork. So I am not sure if they knew exactly when we were leaving and our time of arrival."

"That is not good," I said.

"Probably not," he concurred.

"Well, your foot isn't that bad, thankfully," I said.

"Believe it or not, it looked a lot worse. It just needs a little time to heal up properly, and you should be fine."

"Thanks for taking such good care of me." He smiled. "I guess it is good to know if something does go wrong, there is a doctor around, just in case."

"I am here," I said. "But let's hold off on scheduling the bungee-jumping lesson." We both laughed, and I walked away, exuding a physician's confidence. But I began to worry. We were lucky this time. If there was a real emergency, what would we be able to do? How could we treat someone who lost a limb, an eye, or fell a great distance? They would be dead. And being trapped on an island is one thing. Watching the only people you have left in the world die in front of you is a torture I prayed I didn't have to endure.

You don't realize the skills you have forgotten until you have to use them in an emergency situation. We had to relearn basic skills that science and age had rendered unnecessary. For instance, the simple task of building a shelter was a confusing, tedious ordeal for everyone. But when I was a child, without four-star hotels on my cell phone's speed dial, I could build a makeshift fort out of blankets or bark or sofa pillows within minutes.

We all knew the first night, we needed to build some more sophisticated form of shelter. But the task of building a tent was akin to building a space station. By the time we settled on the type of materials to use (a sloppy mixture of leaves, bark, and mud) and who would go gather what, no one had the energy, patience, or tolerance to sleep under the same roof. But we had to settle in together or risk venturing out on our own in the lonely dark.

Even though my watch had broken during the crash, I could tell it had rained for at least a day. I spent most of my time sleeping. The silent man, Jacques, would walk out in the rain and lightning and come back with fish and fruit for us to eat. Dallas tried in vain to get the games on his cell phone to play, and after several attempts, he settled on using a sock to polish a pair of tennis shoes he found on shore one day, along with his hairbrush. Francis took a large slab of rock from a mound of stones and scribbled notes and maps with his keys. Andrew sometimes conversed with Francis and wrote numbers on the rock. They looked like longitudes and latitude—directions. But after a day of rain, even they succumbed to laziness. We watched the lightning move across the sky like dancers in a ballet. As soon as the rain dried up, our restlessness was apparent.

"I think I know where we are," Francis declared.

"Yeah, lost," Dallas answered.

"To a certain extent," Francis said. "But we are not that far away from Palau. We were only off course for about fifteen minutes, so we can't be more than a few hundred miles away from Palau."

"A few hundred miles?" I asked. That did not sound like we knew where we were at all.

"I know it sounds far, but think of a helicopter," Francis said. "They cover hundreds of miles within hours. I'm sure they'll be able to find us."

"That seems pretty far to me," said Dallas. He sat up and walked over to Francis. "And even if they did fly near this island, how would they ever find us?"

"We were thinking we need to give them something to look for," Francis said.

"A sign," Andrew added.

"Like an SOS sign?" Dallas questioned as he rubbed the sweat off his neck with hand.

"Yeah, a little message that no one can miss," Francis said.

"Like what?" I asked.

"We figured if we have a few signs set across the island and stake camps there for a few days, a helicopter or plane could spot us from any direction they came from," replied Francis.

"You want us to split up and walk through a dangerous jungle just to post a few help signs?" asked Dallas, who was already hating the idea. And this time I agreed. I didn't want the group broken up. It sounded dangerous. What if one of us got hurt?

"If we separate, we cover more ground," Francis said.

"We can always regroup later if we get no response," Andrew said.

"Hmm. Why can't we go as a group and set up each camp?" I asked.

"What if a rescue squad comes and we are on the other side of the island?" Francis said.

"You don't think they would take the time to search for us?" asked Dallas.

"They may assume we already died," replied Francis.

"Wow," I said. I didn't think we would even explore the possibility that we could die on this island.

"We can go in groups," said Andrew. "We will be safe."

"Jacques showed me that there are three great places to put the messages," Francis said.

"Wait a minute," I interrupted. "Jacques showed you where to put the signs? Are you saying he talked to you?"

"Oh, no," Francis protested. "Jacques doesn't talk. But we have a way of communicating." I wanted to explore this line of questioning further, but Jacques came back with more food rations, and I decided if I had questions about our mystery man, I would ask him myself.

Jacques dropped his food in a corner of the tent we had designated for rations and came over to the group.

"Jacques, we're going to go ahead with our plan and set up three help signs throughout the island," said Francis. He talked as if they had been planning this for days. I was so pissed not to be included in plans that could save my life. I was madder that Jacques and I didn't have a special rapport.

"Okay, Jacques is going to climb to the mountain on the west side of the island," said Francis. "Andrew and I will take the other side of the beach, and you and Dallas can set up a fire here at base." Francis was so matter of fact with his plans. On one hand, I was enraged, I was not a part of the planning committee. On the other hand, I was so happy I didn't have to take care of this situation, with a bunch of grown-ass men. I felt a little relieved that under extreme pressure, my brothers were handling business.

Jacques walked over to our growing pile of rations and divided them into three stacks.

"The food and wood that Jacques gathered should last us all while we are away," Francis added. I had to give this brother some props. He was a little pompous, but I felt safe knowing he had a solid plan to get us off this island.

"All right. When do we regroup?" I said.

"We should give it seventy-two hours," Francis said.

"Three days!" I almost yelled. Three days partnered with a spoiled athlete who was once quoted in *Sports Illustrated* as saying, "Since buying my Maybach, I don't know how I could go back to driving a regular person's car," did not sound like an ideal vacation. But then again, this whole trip was definitely not what you see in a brochure. More like a horror movie.

"If someone does not check back within three days, we'll regroup and go look for them," Francis said.

"So when do we do this?" I asked. Jacques threw his rations in his shirt, which he had taken off and shaped into a makeshift backpack. His chiseled physique glistened under the now-scornful sun. He turned and walked off. No wave good-bye, no acknowledgement of our joined struggle. God, he was so mysterious and interesting. I had to make a mental note to stay as far away from him as I could.

"I guess we start now," said Francis. He hunched his shoulders up and headed toward his and Andrew's rations. Soon they were walking toward the other side of the island, leaving me and Dallas alone to either find a way off the island or kill each other.

Chapter 13

Dallas and I spent the first two days being polite and maintaining a proper distance. We did our daily chores for the tent, and by the beginning of the third day, we had enough wood to form the simple message Francis suggested: FLIGHT 346 ALL ALIVE HELP.

After we surveyed our work on the beach, we headed back to the tent to rest and wait for the others' return. We each grabbed a piece of floor on opposite sides of the tent. We sat in silence until Dallas smiled and turned to me.

"Twenty Questions," Dallas said.

"What?"

"Let's play Twenty Questions." Dallas smiled that flirtatious smile that I knew got hundreds of women in trouble.

"Why?"

"You got a surgery scheduled for today I don't know about, Doctor?" He smiled, and I had to laugh.

"Touché," I said. "What are the rules?"

"You have to answer the questions truthfully, with no hesitating, and I will do the same."

"Okay," I said, with more than a hint of trepidation. This could end very badly.

"Aiight." Dallas slapped his hands together and rubbed them. "I'll go first."

"Okay," I agreed.

"Why did you decide to be a doctor?"

"I wanted something I could control."

Dallas raised an eyebrow. "What do you mean?"

"That counts as two questions." I smiled.

"Fine."

"My parents did not have the most stable marriage, and since I was the only child, I was alone to deal with all their fights and arguments. Then they got divorced, and I never felt more alone and vulnerable. As a doctor, I choose what I want to specialize in, where I want to practice. I opened a clinic so I would have control over who I would see."

"So a control freak?"

"That sounds like a third question." I laughed. "And, yeah, I guess you could kind of say that."

"Hmm." Dallas looked away.

"What?"

"It seems like for all that control you wanted, now you are back to none on this island."

"Very true," I said. He was right. I felt so lost on this island. "Okay. Your turn."

"Shoot," Dallas said.

"If you didn't play basketball, what would you do?"

"I'd be a doctor."

"Stop lying."

"Hey, I had a four point zero average in college and got a degree in biology."

"Really?" My mouth fell.

"You sound so shocked."

"Then why do you act so—"

"So what?"

"Juvenile."

"I am twenty-four years old."

"Still," I protested.

"Yeah, well, I know this is a hustle that won't last very long, so I decided to have as much fun as I possibly could for as long as I could."

"Yeah, I guess that makes sense."

"Do you ever think you will get married?"

"Whoa. Where did that come from?"

"It's a legitimate question."

"How do you know I am not already married?"

"No ring." Dallas chuckled. "And you would not be getting on a plane with me if you were married, 'cause you knew what was going to happen."

I sat up. "And what did you *think* was going to happen?" I didn't know why I was smiling.

"You didn't answer my question." Dallas was leaning toward me, cheesing and making me want to both slap him and . . . explore him.

"I want to get married. I really do. But I think for some people, some women, it isn't in the cards."

"And you think you are one of those women?"

"I could be, yes."

Dallas took my hand. "You would never be one of those women. You know why?"

"Why?"

"Because no matter how bad it gets, you have too big a heart for it to go cold."

"Thank you." I smile. "How many women have you slept with?"

"Damn." Dallas buckled over, laughing. "You don't be playing."

"I heard you don't, either."

"Four," Dallas said.

"Bullshit," I protested.

"Hey, I ain't lying."

"We said we would answer these questions truthfully."

"Dana was my high school girlfriend and first," Dallas started. "When I went to college, I fell for Genesee, and we were together through college. Then we broke up when I didn't marry her when I turned pro. I dated a certain R & B singer for a few months and had a one-night stand, my first and only one, with an actress that no one would refuse."

"Who?"

"It's your turn to answer questions," Dallas said.

"Lord, now I am scared."

"You opened the door," Dallas said. "How many?"

"God, I am so embarrassed now." I could feel the heat on my face. My head was throbbing. "Six."

"That is not a large number at all," Dallas said.

"It's larger than yours," I said.

"But you are what? Thirty-seven?" Dallas questioned. I slapped him on is chest.

"Thirty-four, thank you," I screamed. "Do I look thirty-seven?"

"You look beautiful."

"So did you love the women you were with?" I tried to change the subject.

"I guess I did," Dallas said. "But I don't know if I was in love."

"Yeah, I kind of feel the same way."

"I want to be in love one day."

"Me, too," I said. "So what did you think was going to happen with me and you?"

"I am a monogamous guy, Josie," Dallas said. "I flirt a lot, but if I am interested in you, I want more than fun."

"You're twenty-four," I argued. "You say that now, but you have so much living to do."

"I don't have anything to prove to anyone, Josie," Dallas said. "I already am the top in my field, won a championship ring, and have more money than most people make in a lifetime. I can afford to choose what I want out of life."

"And what do you want?"

"Right now"—Dallas inched closer to me—"right now I want a kiss."

"Is that a question?"

"I hope it's a kiss." Dallas closed his eyes and went for it. I should have resisted, but I was curious. So I closed my eyes and let our lips connect. It was sweet, like ice cream on a summer day. It was definitely sexy, just the right amount of lip, combined with a hint of tongue. But it was not *it*. I pulled back.

"Dallas," I said.

"Well, I'm glad you two were able to entertain yourselves while we were gone," Francis said. I looked and saw the rest of our party hovering over us. It must have looked crazy to see me wrapped in Dallas's arms.

I got up and arranged my clothes. I felt like I had a scarlet *S* on my chest, for slut. "We were playing Twenty Questions," I said as if I was answering to my parents when they caught me and my boyfriend making out on the couch when we were supposed to be studying.

"You could be cutting each other with razors,"

Francis said. "As long as you set the fire on our SOS." Francis and Andrew sat down. I looked over at Jacques, who refused to look in my direction. He placed his supplies in the corner and headed back out without saying a word.

Chapter 14

As best we could figure, we had been on the island for seven days. All our attempts to contact the outside world had failed. All cell phones were lost, broken, or dead. The SOS signs we had placed bore no fruit, and we were running out of ideas. But as with human nature, we were finding ways to adapt to our new life.

We expanded our little tent into a large base, which had separate spaces for all of us. We established a men's and a women's restroom area, complete with watering holes for us to take baths.

Our mornings were spent doing chores: gathering wood, changing out water, fishing, and gathering fruits for food. I had the special task of finding herbs and roots for when people had minor cuts and bruises.

Luckily for us, several things from the plane ended up washing to shore. Francis's suitcase, which had stacks of soaked notepads, pens, and pencils; a bundle of Andrew's clothes; and the first aid kit all arrived on the shore.

I was handling our situation pretty well until I was fishing on the beach and literally tripped on my overnight bag. I pulled it from underneath the mound of sand where it had settled. I looked through the contents. Several bathing suits, a shorts set, and several changes of underwear were inside. "Thank you, Jesus," I shouted. Then I discovered my sunglasses. There was also a brush and a few head scarves. Damn, no mirror. Why didn't I pack a compact mirror? Just as well, as I was sure I looked a hot mess by now. I opened the private compartment of the billfold to reveal pictures of my father and mother. Then it hit me. I might never see either one of them again.

My parents were already old, and though my father still worked and owned his own farm, he was still a senior citizen. I was supposed to be the one to care for them, and I was stuck in the middle of nowhere, alone on an island.

Tears ran down my cheeks, and I collapsed on the ground. I pulled my knees up to my chin and allowed myself to cry.

"You okay?" Andrew said as he walked toward me.

"No," I answered honestly.

"What's wrong?" he asked.

"I miss my parents, my friends, my life," I said. "I was complaining about what a lonely life I had, and now I really feel all alone here. No friends to laugh with, no father to beg me to visit him. No mother to complain about my hair or clothes."

"French toast." Andrew sat down next to me. "I miss French toast."

"Huh?" I tried to wipe the tears from my eyes.

"Every morning I was home, Brian would make us French toast, and we would eat it while we watched cartoons in bed." Andrew leaned back and looked into the sky as if he could see his life in the clouds.

"So Brian is your . . ."

"Partner, yep." Andrew said. "He is a flight attendant, and we would usually do flights together so we would be together."

"That's so sweet."

"Yeah, but when I did these private flights, they usually didn't have a flight attendant," Andrew said. "He told me not to go."

"Why did you go?"

"He wants to learn to fly planes, too," Andrew said. "And classes are expensive. I was taking side jobs to help him pay for school. He kept saying, 'We'll get there when we get there.' But I wanted him to be happy."

"You had good intentions," I said.

"Yeah, but now we are separated, and what hurts the most is him thinking I am dead."

"Me, too," I said. "I am an only child. I just don't know if my dad can handle it."

"What about your mom?"

"Oh, she can survive anything." I laughed thinking, *What a true statement.*

"If you got to go home tonight, what would you do differently?" Andrew asked.

"Believe it or not, I would take more vacations," I said, and we both laughed. "I mean, I would take more time for me, and not hide in my work so much."

"It's a common problem."

"What about you?" I asked. "What would you do differently?"

"Honestly, I would ask Brian to quit his job and I would quit mine and we would move to Tuscany and open up a bistro."

"God, that's so . . . gay," I said, and we laughed again.

"It's so white gay, too," Andrew admitted. "But that is what I would do so I could see Brian every day and spend as much time with the most important person in my life."

"Aww."

"Mushy, huh?" Andrew said.

"But that is real," I said. "I admire the fact that you have that much love to give."

"You have love, too, Josie," Andrew said.

"Well, unfortunately, I may not be able to give it to anyone."

"What about you and Dallas?"

"Oh no." I shook my head. "He is a baby."

"Well, he didn't seem like a baby when you guys were kissing."

"Yeah, it was nice but . . ."

"Say no more." Andrew raised his hand in the air. "You are describing a kiss with the number one point guard as 'nice.' That says it all. What a shame. He is mad sexy."

"That he is," I said. "But sexy does not a relationship make."

"You obviously don't hang around a lot of gay guys." Andrew laughed. "Sexy is the basis of a relationship."

"You are stupid."

"Well, if he's not the one, don't worry about him." Andrew smiled. "As fine and funny and intelligent as you are, the love of your life is just waiting to find you."

"I hope you're right."

"I know, stuck on this island, it looks bleak," Andrew said. "But nothing is an accident in this life. There is a reason we are here. And once we figure that out, I am sure we will be able to take what we have learned back home."

"Well, I've learned that I can actually survive without my TiVo, and that is a lesson in itself."

"Gosh, I know," Andrew said. "Just think of all the shows you can catch up on when you get back."

"Yeah," I said.

"So what do you want for dinner?" Andrew said. "We have fish and coconuts, or coconuts and fish."

"Surprise me." Andrew pulled me to my feet, and we walked back to the camp.

"Believe me, you have many more surprises ahead of you." Andrew smiled, and I believed him.

Chapter 15

"We need to make a boat," Francis said over dinner, once again never looking away from the notes he'd etched in the rock near his side of the tent.

"A boat?" Andrew questioned. "But we really don't know where we are or how far away we are from civilization."

"We can't just wait here," Francis protested. "It has been over a week. If they could find us, they would have found us."

"It seems risky," Dallas said.

"So is waiting here to die," Francis said, and it was out there. The word everyone was too afraid to mention but was pulsating in the back of our minds. We could *die* out here.

"We just need to wait it out a little longer," Dallas said, almost pleading. "Someone will find us."

"I can't afford that luxury," Francis said. "None of us can."

"If we did build a boat, what then?" Andrew asked. "Sail out in hopes of running into a cruise ship?"

"No, we take our SOS and make it mobile," said

Francis. He turned toward us and dropped his notepad in the center of our circle. "We have several blankets now, thanks to the salvage we found from the plane. We can use some for a sail and for a roof and to put up the sign."

"Won't a heavy storm soak the blankets?" I asked.

"Yes," Francis conceded. "But we will have leaves and bamboo underneath so we stay dry and the message stays up."

"And how long would it take to build it?" Andrew asked.

"I am thinking maybe three weeks," Francis said. "But at this point all we have is time."

"What about food and water and medical supplies?" I said.

"We store that up as we build," Francis said. "Look, I am not saying it isn't risky, but what other choice do we have?"

He was right. And our silence confirmed his theory. If we ever had any hope of escaping, we needed to do it now, while we were strong and our spirits weren't broken.

"I'm in," I said.

"Me, too," Andrew said.

"I ain't got nothing else to do," Dallas said.

We all looked at Jacques, who was cutting up our meal.

"Jacques?" Francis said. "I know the States haven't been the best for you, but it must be better than living on this island."

Jacques stood up and walked away.

"What is that dude's problem?" Dallas asked.

"He's been through a lot," Francis confessed.

"But he will come with us, right?" I asked.

"I honestly don't know," Francis said. I stood and walked out in hopes of catching Jacques. He was far ahead and already was deep into the forest by the time I could reach him.

My heart thumped a little harder as I entered the dark forest again. Though Jacques had saved me from the wild boar, I was still a little gun shy about entering the forest alone.

"Jacques," I called out to him, both out of concern and a little fear. "Jacques."

I called again and again and didn't get a response. It was unnaturally quiet, and I debated if I should head back. I wanted to help Jacques but didn't want to get mangled by wild animals in the process. I was turning to go back when someone grabbed my arm. I let out a scream until I realized it was Jacques.

"What is wrong with you?" I asked. "You scared me."

Jacques released me and stood looking at me. I hoped to talk some sense into him, but also to get some answers. Since we had ventured off on this journey, Jacques had been an enigma. I had yet to figure him out. I wanted—no, needed—some answers.

"Why don't you want to come back?" I started my probe. "Is it because you think the trip is too dangerous?" He just stared in the other direction.

"Is it because you don't want to face your real life back in America?" I asked. Jacques huffed. "Is it because you don't have a real life back in the States?" I was grasping for anything at this point.

"Believe me, I understand." I said. "I thought until I came here, I was living a meaningful life. Helping people, healing people. But now it seems I have isolated my self from everyone. And I want a second chance to fix that. To appreciate my family and friends and the life I left behind long before this trip.

"I know you may think your life may not be important, but it is," I said. "You can change anything that went bad. You can start over. You have that power, you know."

Jacques began pacing around me.

"What is it?" I said. "I didn't bring any paper, but maybe you can scratch it on a tree or something. I don't know. Jacques, I just want you to know that I am here for you to help you in whatever you are going through. You saved my life, and you just don't know how grateful I am. I want to help you. But you have to let me in. You have to communicate with me so we can figure this out together."

For the first time, Jacques had an expression on his usually blank face. I couldn't make it out for sure, but it looked like exasperation. His hands were on his hips, and he looked as though he was contemplating something heavy. But he kept looking at me, his soft brown eyes locked with mine. He had no shirt on and didn't seem bothered that bugs were nipping at his skin.

I kept swatting and scratching every few seconds.

"What?" I questioned. "What is it?" I walked over to him and put my hand in his in a sign of familiarity. "You can express it to me. Let's go back to camp, and you can write it down."

He leaned into me, his mouth just an inch from my ear. I could feel his cool breath tickling the hairs near my temple.

"Do you ever bloody shut up?" Jacques whispered in a baritone British accent. I stood motionless, trying to decide if I would strangle this man or just slap the life out of him.

Chapter 16

"You can talk?" I cried. I felt foam flying out of my mouth.

"I never said I couldn't talk," replied Jacques. He threw his hands in the air as if to say, *Well, I didn't.* I was busy deciding if my hands were big enough to strangle this man, or if I needed to use a blunt object.

"And you didn't think that information was important enough to share?"

"Talking is easy. It's listening that's the hard part," he said. "Besides, you all seem to do enough talking for everyone."

"Because we're human beings," I screamed. "We are stuck on an island, with only each other to rely on. Of course, we're going to talk."

"And for all that talking, who built the tent, who caught most of the fish, and who supplied the wood?" He was right. While we all planned, it was Jacques who trudged out every morning in silence, coming back with most of what we needed for the day.

"That's no excuse," I combated. "If you can talk, then you can share information."

"What information?" Jacques began gathering wood. "Food, water, shelter. A child knows this without having to pontificate for hours like they do."

"But what about connection?" I said. "Don't you feel you are somehow connected to us, trapped in this mess together?"

"I am here with you all, but I am not connected." Jacques had a small bundle of wood in his hands by now and avoided my eyes as he talked. "I have my own life, like you all do."

"Could you at least look at me when you talk?" I knocked the bundle of wood to the ground.

"You are a bloody firecracker."

"You saved my life." I grabbed his arms. "You keep saving us every day. What if we want to know you? What if I want to know you?"

"Believe me"—Jacques broke from my grip—"you don't want to know me."

"You're not coming with us on the boat, are you?"

"Why?"

"It's our only chance for salvation at this point."

"You think so," Jacques said. "Well, from my vantage point, this is my salvation. An island almost all to myself, plenty of food, and when you all go to sleep, lots of quiet."

"So you think civilization is that bad?"

"I don't think anything." Jacques continued picking up the wood from the ground. "I know. And if you are as smart as I think you are, you'll just drop it, jump on that boat, and head back to your little life and leave me alone."

Jacques sidestepped me and headed back to camp. I crossed my arms, flabbergasted at my discovery. I watched as he disappeared into the foliage. I wanted to chase him and demand answers. I was frightened of a man who could keep such a big secret from the only other humans for miles. Then I thought of Francis and realized it might not have been that much of a secret. I ran back to the camp to confront Francis.

It only took a few minutes to find Francis alone by the shore, writing in his notebook.

"Francis, I need to talk to you," I said as I walked up behind him.

"Drop it, Josie," he said, scribbling away. "It's not worth it."

"So you knew?" I questioned. "You knew he could talk."

"Of course, I did."

"Why didn't you say anything?"

"It wasn't my place," Francis said. "Besides, Jacques rarely talked back in the States. No one knew except family."

"Why keep it a secret?"

"It's not a secret; he just chooses not to speak."

"But why?"

"It's his right, like you liberally use yours to talk." He looked up and smiled at me.

"That is not funny." I tried to hide a smile.

"Yes, it is." He smiled at me, and I saw why millions of television viewers watched him every week. "Sit down. Let me show you something."

I sat down and looked over his shoulder at a sketched drawing of a pretty young girl and a beautiful woman, who had to be her mother.

"They're lovely," I said.

"My wife, Lee, and my daughter, Asia," Francis said.

"Wow, you must miss them terribly," I said, without thinking how horrible that sounded out loud. "Sorry."

"I do miss them," Francis said. "They're the reason I have to get back home. They're the reason I haven't drowned myself in the sea."

"That's definitely a reason to keep fighting, to keep trying," I said, pondering what was pushing me to go home.

"I love my job and miss writing so much, it hurts." Francis's voice trembled as he spoke. "But those two . . . They keep me whole."

"You'll get back to them." I rubbed his shoulder. "We'll all get back."

"My brother doesn't have what I have anymore."

"You're . . ." I stopped for a second. "Wait, you mean Jacques is your brother?"

"Half brother." Francis wiped the tears from his eyes.

"Are you serious?" I shook my head. "Were you guys spies in another life?"

"No, we are just very private about our private life."

"Go on." I urged him forward.

"All I can say is every privilege I was afforded he was not given, yet he managed to excel despite all the discouragement from our drunk father, the disadvantage of being a black in the poorest white town in England, and having chronic seizures."

"Oh my God," I said.

"Yeah, the boy has been through a lot, but like I said, he triumphed, built his own photography business from the ground up, started a family. He sought me out of the blue one day, and we became best friends. I remember him saying to me one day that he finally had everything in life he'd ever wanted. Then he lost it all."

"How?"

Francis stood up. "His seizures got progressively worse, sometimes knocking him unconscious. One day he was driving his family home from a school play his son was in . . . I think he had the lead. Anyway, he was so excited. On the way home, he had another seizure. He woke up two days later. He had crashed the car, ran right off a winding road. Killed everyone in the car but himself. He was unconscious before the car crash, so his body didn't tense up. He survived physically but has been the walking dead for three years now. I got him a job filming my reports so I could keep him close. And the doctors gave him some medicine that reduced the amount of seizures, but even then their prognosis was not good."

"So how often does he have these seizures?"

"Every couple of days."

"Wait." I threw my hands in the air. "Are you telling me he's been having seizures since we have been on this island?"

"A few, yes."

"Are you all fucking crazy?" I yelled. "I'm a doctor."

"What can you do that the others haven't been able to do?" Francis said. "And we're not at a hospital. We're nowhere."

"So how come no one has seen them?"

"That is why he goes off alone, so no one is around when he has them."

"And he doesn't want to leave the island, because he feels he has nothing to live for and no more time left?"

Francis stood up. "That's about it."

"And you're just going to let him stay?"

"Josie, I love my brother with all my heart, but I have to get back to my family. They are my soul. I pray Jacques will change his mind, but I have to think of my little girl."

"I understand," I said.

"We are leaving in three weeks," Francis said. "Maybe you can convince him to go by then."

"If he didn't listen to his own brother, why would he listen to me?"

"Because besides me, you are the only person he has talked to in three years."

Chapter 17

At first I wanted to confront Jacques, but then I didn't know what I could say to change his mind that his brother hadn't already expressed. So instead, I chose to ignore the issue until we were forced to deal with it. To my surprise, we actually started getting closer. He still refused to talk in public, but when we were alone, we talked quite a lot. So I made sure he and I had time alone.

When Jacques got up early in the morning to go fishing, I would grab my sweater and head out onto the breezy shore with him. Sometimes we stood in silence. Other times he would grill me.

"So if you had a choice between saving a child and saving your one true love, who would you choose?" he asked as I tried to help him pull in a fish caught on his line.

"Can't I save them both?" I pleaded.

"Nope, just one," Jacques said.

"I guess I would save the child," I said.

"Wow, such a typical answer," he said. "What if no one was around?"

"What do you mean?"

"I mean if no one was there to say, 'How could you not have saved the child?' who would you save?"

"I know he is the love of my life, but I would have to try to give that child a future. I would hope the love we shared would sustain me when he passed."

"Well, I can tell you, my friend, it doesn't." Jacques pulled in the fish and slammed it dead against a rock.

Some days we sat and watched the sunset, and he would say, "Your hair is lovely in the sunlight."

"Thank you," I'd say.

"But you have a lot of dandruff."

"Jacques!"

"You do." Jacques would laugh. "Wouldn't you rather I be honest than lie to you?"

"A girl always appreciates flattery."

"You don't need anyone telling you how beautiful you are," he said. "But someone who really cares about you will tell you the truth about a flaw that can be corrected."

"Your nose is crooked," I said.

"That is not something that can be corrected," he said.

"Yes, it can. It's called rhinoplasty," I rebutted.

"Well, out here you are stuck with my nose." He put his head on my thigh and looked up into the sky. And I got a weird sensation all over my body. Truth was, his nose was crooked, but in a sexy, perfect way. Like he had been fighting for his woman's honor and got it knocked farther to one side. It didn't matter that his abusive father broke it when he was two and it never quite healed correctly.

A week into building our escape boat, we had

managed to gather all the necessary equipment for the job. Piles of bamboo and chopped wood stood on one side. Miles and miles of vine lay coiled under a tree. We stored fish in a pond, where the water was cool and kept the meat fresh.

Jacques did his share of the work, though only Francis and I knew he wasn't planning on going with us. It was bittersweet to work with this man, who I found mysterious and interesting, but knew I would never see again. Whether we were rescued or died at sea, we would probably never cross paths again. I tried to remain neutral about the situation, but each time we talked, I forgot about the time, and the day whizzed to a close. At first, I was waking up early to accompany him. Soon he was tapping my shoulder when he got up.

"Wake up, ladybug." He smiled. "Another day is here."

Our afternoon routine was the same. After a morning of chores and a light lunch, we hit the lake for a swim. Sometimes the whole group would go, but usually it was just me and Jacques. Each time we reached the cliff that overlooked the mountain, he would take my hand.

"You ready?" he would say, and before I could nod my head, he was lunging forward, pulling me with him. I would always scream on the way down, though I was a pretty good swimmer. We would swim for hours, until my bones shook and my limbs were exhausted. Then we would lie on a rock and tan. It always amused me, because we were both a deep chocolate hue, but it felt so good to bronze under the sun's soothing rays.

"Can I ask you a question?" Jacques asked me one day as we baked.

"Of course."

"Why did you kiss Dallas?" He leaned over to look at my face.

"I guess 'cause when everyone talks about how great it is to drive a Ferrari and someone gives you the keys to a Ferrari, you test-drive it."

"Wow, such a male analogy."

"It's the truth." I felt a little uncomfortable now and suddenly was very aware that I was wearing a skimpy bathing suit.

"So how was it?"

"What?"

"The kiss, silly." Jacques's eyes were fixed on mine. I couldn't look away if I tried.

"Have you ever kissed a girl and known instantly she would be your best friend?"

"Yep." Jacques smiled.

"That was what it was like."

"Interesting." Jacques was blushing and I was smiling, and it became obvious we weren't just hanging out anymore. "So do you think I would be your best friend if we kissed?"

"I certainly hope not." I smiled. "But there is only one way to find out."

I turned my head toward him, and he did the same. He cupped my chin in his hands just like I imagined a man would hold me when he kissed me. And then I felt it. What you were supposed to feel when you kissed. Like you just stepped into an abyss you should never have walked near, but falling down never felt so good. This was not a best friend kiss; this was a *Modern Bride* magazine kiss. I wanted to get up and run away. But for the first time, I couldn't move. I was stuck. Then Jacques pulled me close to him, and we looked at the sky until the sun retreated and the moon took center stage for the nightly light show.

Chapter 18

We decided not to tell anybody about us. Actually, we really didn't discuss it at all. It just was. We went from casual conversations to making out, to daylong excursions away from the pack. The second we reached the woods, our hands would clasp together and we would be us. Sometimes we were silent for hours, drinking in the day and each other. We would lie on a rock or in the grass and just be together. It was so weird and exciting not to have to explain myself, or excuse my job or career for Jacques, because it really didn't matter here. He could keep his secrets because here we were all born again.

The domestic squabbles that ruined other relationships never came into existence. We were stripped of our arrogance and titles and pride, and were just a man and a woman who enjoyed being around each other.

But as we soon discovered, even on a deserted island, misery loves company.

"Yo, man, you spending all your time lounging with

your honey, you missing them chores," Dallas said as we came back from one of our day trips.

"Dallas, you know we did all our work before we even left," I said.

"I am talking to this man," Dallas said.

"Well, he doesn't talk. You know that," I said.

"Well, some part of him must be speaking to you for you to follow him around like a little bitch." I wished I had had the opportunity to really knock this man out the way I imagined. But I had barely dropped my fishing pole and balled my fist before Jacques pounced on him. At first I was so angry, I wanted to kick his head in while Jacques walloped him with his fists. But soon it became apparent there was not much of a fight. Dallas was on the ground, scarcely avoiding huge hands pounding his face. After a minute, it resembled more of a father beating his overgrown, loudmouthed son.

"That's enough," I said to Jacques, but he wouldn't stop. He kept swinging, and blood was spewing everywhere.

"Hey, Jacques, that's enough," I said again. I tried to pull him off Dallas, but then he did the unthinkable. He pushed me off of him. I fell back and landed on my butt on the sand. I stared at the impossibility of this moment. I had been pushed by the man who was supposed to be protecting me from harm. Then I started questioning the motives of this fight. Was it about my honor or just an excuse for Jacques to release his rage? Either way, I was tired of the whole event and brought it to an end like only a sister could do. I got up and grabbed the biggest log I could and ran back and whopped Jacques as hard as I could. He fell off Dallas and to the ground. He was stunned and trying to regain consciousness.

"What the hell!" Jacques screamed.

"What the hell is wrong with you?" I cried.

"I was fucking defending you," shouted Jacques.

"You weren't defending me," I said.

Dallas tried to sit up. "Yo, that nigga can talk?"

"He called you a bitch!" screamed Jacques.

"You pushed me," I replied.

"Yo, you can talk, nigga?" Dallas looked more stunned by Jacques's speaking ability than his fighting skills.

Jacques tried to grab my shoulders, but I pulled back. He said, "That was an accident. I was—"

"Man you weren't even here," I said. "You would have killed him."

"I . . . ," Jacques began. Then he gave me a look that scared me, a look of agreement. He could have killed Dallas. What if he'd lost it like that with his wife? What if he lost it with me? Suddenly, it became clear that I didn't know this man. We were playing house. We lived together because we had to but we were strangers. All the things that build trust between people so they feel comfortable living together we don't have.

Jacques had a look of pure embarrassment and hurt. He looked up at me. "I gotta go."

"Where is that nigga going? This is an island." Dallas questioned.

"Shut the hell up!" I yelled.

Nightfall came, and Jacques had been gone all afternoon. He didn't show up for dinner, and I started worrying. My mind was distracted when Dallas came to me, complaining of headaches. Part of the paradox of being a doctor was you might have to help people you may not necessarily like. But I had to treat Dallas, or else I would be stooping to his level. I used the first aid kit, which I reserved for real emergencies, to clean a large wound on his nose and forehead.

"Your boyfriend really beat my ass," he said.

"You're lucky I didn't get to you." I thumped his head. "Why did you have to call me a bitch?"

"I was just pissed, man." Dallas looked like a little high school student who had lost his eighth-grade girl-friend to the captain of the football team. "I thought we was vibing, and then you start going off with Charlie Chaplin and shit."

"I think you are so cool, Dallas," I started.

"Lord, please, I have been beaten enough." He laughed. "No speeches."

"I am just saying you are great and will have liter-ally a million women who would kill for you."

"But you wouldn't?"

"Not when you call women bitches."

"I just wanted to hurt you."

"Mission accomplished."

"You got class, Josie," Dallas said. "And I really like you, is all. I don't know what your little friend has, but he is lucky if he has you."

"Thank you." I smiled. "Just for that, you get a little alcohol before I stitch this up."

"Is it going to hurt?"

"Lucky for me, it will hurt a great deal."

An hour and several stitches later, I was on my pallet, trying desperately not to think about Jacques. But he invaded my thoughts. I closed my eyes and tried to imagine him next to me. And then, just like magic, I felt a strong arm wrap around my waist and a body sidle up to me.

"I am so sorry if I scared or hurt you," whispered Jacques.

"You did."

"I know. I am sorry." Jacques buried his scruffy beard in the nape of my neck. "Can I make it up to you?"

"It's cold. Just hold me."

"I can handle that." Jacques slid his other arm under my head and pulled me into him, and I never felt so safe and scared in my life.

Chapter 19

After the altercation with Dallas, we were basically outed by the group.

"So you guys are together now?" Andrew asked as we sat around the fire.

"I guess so," said Jacques. He looked at me for confirmation, and I smiled.

"I knew there was chemistry, but wow," said Francis. He gave a look that didn't look as supportive as I hoped. In fact, the scowl on his face would have made the average person a little apprehensive about revealing our secret.

"You look upset, Francis," said Jacques, and I was relieved someone recognized the tension in the air.

"No, I am really happy for you both, believe me," Francis said as his eyes sort of looked away. This was not a good sign. He was Jacques's brother, and I wanted to make sure he was okay with our relationship.

"Cool," said Jacques, who seemed content to change the subject. "How close are we to finishing the boat?"

"It's more like a glorified raft, but I think it is almost finished," Andrew said. "We just have to sew the tarps and blankets together to finish the sail and the covering for the roof."

Was it me, or was he staring a little more intently when he mentioned sewing?

"We could really use your help working on that project," said Andrew as he rubbed my knee.

"Yeah, right, you want the girl to do the sewing," I said and laughed.

"Naw," Dallas interjected. "You are a surgeon. You sewed my stitches."

"Bullshit," I said. "You want the girl to do the sewing."

"None of us can even hold the damn needle in our hand for more than a few minutes," said Andrew. He burst into laughter. "I don't know how people do that."

"Lawd," I said. "I feel like I am being roped back into slavery."

"I'll help you," Jacques said. Every one turned and smirked at Jacques. "What? I had to sew stuff in the army."

"You all have been inseparable for almost two weeks," Andrew teased. "What's next? Marriage?"

"Hell no, man," Jacques blurted out. "I am never getting married again." All eyes once again fell on me and then on the sand. Jacques noticed the silence. "What? I was just being honest."

I knew we would have to broach this subject later, but right now I didn't want a deep conversation in front of so many nosey people, so I tried to change the subject. "So, Andrew, what about home do you miss most?"

"Easy," Andrew said and smiled. "My man."

"Aww," said Dallas as he grabbed Andrew and hugged him. "You'll be back with your boo soon."

"What about you, Dallas?" Andrew asked.

"Driving down the freeway in my vintage Porsche," said Dallas. He smiled. "No other car in the world handles like that."

"You obviously haven't been in my 2003 Toyota Tercel," Andrew said, and we all fell out.

"Steak," Francis said. "A medium-rare steak."

"What about your daughter?" I said.

"That goes without saying," Francis said. "But for a good steak . . . Asia would be in some trouble."

"Francis," I screamed.

"Liar," Jacques said.

"Hey, I am tired of all this fish," Francis said.

"Oh, Ben & Jerry's Cherry Garcia ice cream," I said.

"Twinkies," said Francis.

"Donuts," said Andrew.

"Sausage, egg, and cheese biscuits from McDonald's," Dallas said as Andrew extended his arms and slapped him five.

"What about cable?" I said and meant it. I had missed all the TV shows and movies that kept me company at night and on my rare free weekend.

"Movie popcorn," said Dallas.

"Popcorn butter," Francis said. "My wife hates it, but the stuff is like crack to me."

"Movies, period," Andrew said.

"I miss my Jimmy Choo stiletto shoes in brown, red, and black," I said.

"How very specific," Jacques said and laughed.

"Hey, I love my heels," I said.

"Me, too," Andrew said. "I'm just kidding."

"Sure," Dallas said. "I miss massages."

"Those with or without happy endings?" I interrogated.

"Raunchy," Andrew giggled.

"Any twelve-hundred-dollar massage is always a happy ending," replied Dallas.

"You are so nasty," I said. I felt my face scrunch up.

"You know I'm kidding," Dallas said and smiled.

"Yeah, right," I said and shook my head.

"I miss the news," Francis said.

"You're a journalist. Of course, you would miss the news," Jacques said. "There are people celebrating the disappearance of a nosy journalist."

Francis smiled. "Ya think? Fuck 'em." It was the first sign of a relaxed Francis I had seen since I met him.

"Do you miss writing?" I asked.

"You know"—Francis laughed to himself—"I miss the ideas and the idea of writing. But I actually am glad I am not writing right now. It is a nice break for what's to come."

"What do you mean?" I asked.

"Well, the second I get back, if I get back, they are going to want me to write my story," replied Francis. "And the truth is, I don't know if I can bear retelling this story."

"Really?" Andrew said.

"My brother is really dramatic," said Jacques, palming his brother's head.

"You guys are brothers?" asked Andrew. His mouth dropped.

"I thought you said there would be no more secrets," Dallas said.

"There aren't. We just forgot," Francis said.

"You forgot you're brothers?" Dallas said.

"No," Jacques said. "We forgot we hadn't mentioned it before."

"They are like the Sopranos with the family secrets," Dallas blurted out but looked directly at me.

"I miss my patients," I interjected, attempting to cool down the flames. There had been so many flared egos; I did not want any more fights.

"I kind of miss flying my passengers around the world," Andrew said, picking up on my subliminal cue.

"Well, no offense, bruh, but I never want to fly with you, again," said Dallas.

"Yeah, I don't even know if I want to fly with myself," replied Andrew.

"Yo, Jacques, you been awful quiet," Dallas said. "What do you miss about home?"

"Home is where you place your feet and say I am not running anymore," Jacques said. "It's the spot in the world where you can relax your shoulders and breathe easy. And if that is the case, I think I have home right here." Jacques rubbed my neck with his fingertips, and I wrapped my arms around his waist. After a long pause, Dallas said, "Yeah, I miss pizza." We all slid into a fit of laughter.

Chapter 20

A torrential rain forced the group to leave the camp and seek shelter in a cave near the mountains.

The rain eventually stopped, but our spirits were as low as ever. Our home, for lack of a better word, was destroyed; we were wet, tired, and hungry. And adding to the growing number of fears and concerns, my period was starting. Normally just a nuisance, my monthly cycle in the middle of the jungle was a hassle almost too big to think about. But I would have to think fast before it was too late. I made a plan to grab materials for a makeshift tampon out of the first aid kit. There was gauze and plenty of cotton balls, which I could sandwich together and sew if necessary. God, the little details I never thought about were blazing across my mind every day on this island.

"We should probably get back to the camp and see about fixing the tent," Francis said.

"Oh, and the boat, too," Andrew blurted out.

"Shit," Francis said. "Jesus, I hope it's not damaged."

"Of course, that shit gone be damaged," Dallas

yelled. "We're all damaged. And we are never getting off this fucking island."

"Yes, we are," Andrew said. "We just have to stay strong and keep working together until—"

"Fuck that," Dallas said as he slashed the air with his giant arm. If it were a sword, surely, someone would have been cut in half. "We have been trying for two weeks to survive this bullshit, and everything we do backfires on us."

"What do you propose we do? Just sit here and wait to die?" Andrew countered.

"I don't know what ya'll niggas is gone do, but I am a tired man," said Dallas. He moved around our semicircle and walked off.

"Where are you going?" Francis called out to him. "We need your help."

Dallas shouted, "Help your damn selves. I'm out." We all watched Dallas walk away. We wanted to stop him but didn't know what to say. How did you cheer up a man who'd lost everything this world could offer and had been stuck on an island with relative strangers for weeks. It seemed everything we'd built here to give us some semblance of home, some ounce of our dignity, had vanished like sand under a heavy wave.

Jacques, Francis, Andrew, and I walked in silence back to the beach, in a hopeless prayer that the boat would have at least been spared. But as with everything else recently, luck did not seem to be on our side.

It was actually worse than we'd imagined. A tree had fallen and severed a portion of the boat, leaving jagged bamboo rods splintered all across the sand. Our sail was ripped in several places. All the fruit we'd stacked had been thrown ashore. It was an absolute mess.

I didn't know if it was frustration or the impending period, but I couldn't check my emotions. I felt the tears rising at the corners of my eyes. I put my face in my hand, but even that couldn't control the emotions spilling out.

Jacques came over to me and put his hands on my shoulders. "It's whacked, isn't it?"

"Huh?" I said as I turned to him, hoping he would have some plan of salvation in his eyes. He only offered big, soft brown eyes, which under normal circumstances would have done wonders for my mood. But at present, the puppy dog eyes did little more than remind me that even though we were getting close, Jacques was it. I might be on this island for the rest of my life, and he could be the only man I would be with until I died. Don't get me wrong. Jacques was amazing. He was sweet, considerate, a keeper. But was I supposed to live out the rest of my life with him and three other guys? Was this really it? The idea made me cringe.

"I need to take a walk," I said. Jacques released me, no questions asked. That was another thing I liked about him. He didn't need to solve my problem in order to be a man. He left me to my emotions. I wiped my face and walked along the beach, half praying to be struck by lightning so I wouldn't have to endure making a life away from the world. But another part of me was pleading for God to send a rescue helicopter or boat or balloon, anything to get us home. I didn't know how long I'd walked, but I knew it had been a while when I found Dallas on the other side of the beach. He was sitting on a rock, staring out into the water. At first, I was going to give him his space, but then I figured by now we were all feeling the same thing.

"Is this seat taken?" I called.

"Man, for a doctor, you don't listen to directions very well," he said.

"Sure I do," I said. "I just ignored your wishes like every other doctor." I thought I saw a smile creep over his pursed lips.

"So this is how it all ends, huh?"

"What do you mean?" I said, knowing full well what he meant.

"Us on this island." Dallas pitched a rock toward the water, and I watched as it skidded across the top.

"It's not over until it's over."

"That really doesn't answer my question."

"Because right now you know I don't have the answer."

"I want children," he said.

"Is that a proposition? 'Cause I can barely get through my period out here." Finally, a smile hit his face.

"I'm serious."

"So am I," I said. "Look, it would be crazy for me not to see how bad this situation is, but life can change in an instant."

"Clearly." Dallas tossed another rock.

"Well, there you go," I said. "In an instant, we went from luxury vacation to *Castaway*."

"Yeah." Dallas nodded.

"But as long as we're alive, we have to keep fighting to get home. There are people who are waiting for us."

"I really hope you're right."

"I am." I gave my best smile, though inside I felt like shit.

"So do you?"

"Do I what?"

"Do you want to have children?"

I looked at the sea, finally resting. Waves were cresting just below the horizon. "I do."

Chapter 21

Despite all the emotional and physical damage we'd sustained during the storm, eventually, we rebuilt the tent and fixed the boat. We counted twenty-one days on the island, without a single sign of life or hope of being rescued. We were all in accordance that it was time to go, all except Jacques. He didn't say anything, but after my conversation with Francis, I was worried he might actually stay on the island. I avoided the topic for weeks, but as the time to leave drew near, my breathing room became limited. We had to talk about it.

My chance came when he invited me to an impromptu picnic. We didn't have a basket, just a piece of tarp he tied into a saddlebag. He was the only man who looked sexy with a big purse. We held hands in silence and walked through the woods, taking in the soft breeze that kissed our skin. He guided me to a place I had never been before. The trees circled a patch of grass and sand that seemed untouched by anyone. The trees provided just enough shade to keep us cool. But parts of the ground were exposed, so we could bake under the sun's rays. The intimacy we were beginning to develop made our bond stronger. I never had to explain anything to Jacques. He seemed to understand me without words. He just got me, which scared me more than anything. How could a man I barely knew get to the core of me when men I'd dated for years never digged deeper than the surface? And more importantly, if he felt the same about me, would he be willing to leave it all on this island if I left?

We feasted on the main delicacies on the island, fish and crab, which we cooked over an open fire. We had several exotic fruits to offset the strong fish taste. Coconut milk was the beverage of choice. As we ate, I noticed Jacques was staring at me harder than usual.

"What?" I asked. I smiled as I was sure all the blood in my body had rushed to my face.

"I just never thought I would ever find someone as beautiful as you." He smiled.

"Please." I tried to blow his comment off, but I was almost speechless.

"Not just physically," he said. "You have this heart that could breathe life into a city."

"Thank you." I ran my fingers through my hair.

"What's up?" He rubbed my knee. "You seem a little distant."

"Not distant." I grabbed his hand. "I . . . have a lot on my mind."

"Our most precious asset on this island is our mind," he said in that gorgeous, lilting British accent. "It's what separates us from the animals."

"That and the fact that we've tried to eat all the animals here," I said, attempting to break the mounting somber mood.

"Seriously, babe," he said. "What's wrong?"

"We are almost ready to take the boat out," I said.
"I know."

"Well, your brother mentioned that you may not be going." I felt my muscles tense as I spoke. My heart felt like it was pushing against my skin. He didn't take his eyes off me. He just continued to rub my knee.

"I just don't know if there is a life out there for me." The words cut deep into me. I stood, unable to process his statement.

"Are you kidding?"

"Don't get me wrong," he continued. "I have very strong feelings for you, and if we had more time here, I would love to explore them. But in the real world . . . I just don't know if I can handle it."

"Handle what?" I pulled back.

"This," Jacques said. "Us, life, the real world. I tried to do that before, and it had horrible ramifications. I don't know if I am willing to try that again."

"It's not like playing the lottery. Oh, you lose once and then forget it," I said. My voice was elevated, and I knew I was going to bust a fuse any second. "This thing is real."

"Of course, it's real." He stood up. "I mean, for Christ sake, I—" He stopped himself and turned around. "I care for you, but I think we are having fun, passing time in this place together. Let's not ruin it."

"So we're just having fun," I said. "And you're going to stay on this fucking island all by yourself and let your life pass you by."

"My life has already passed me by," he yelled. "I lost everything."

I got up and brushed the sand and pebbles off my skin. "Correction. Now you've lost everything." I walked away, praying I didn't cry in his face. Once again I was the idiot. Once again I had put my heart out on the ledge only to have a man kick it over the ledge.

"Josie," Jacques called out to me. "Wait."

"Hope you enjoy your island paradise," I managed to say before running off. I bolted through the woods and could hear him following me for a few beats, and then it was just me, as usual. I kept running, tears pouring. I dared not think of Jacques and his soft, masculine smell, like pears, cocoa butter, and musk. I advised myself to forget his thick, soft lips pressing against mine, his soft tongue exploring the inside of my mouth. I thanked the Lord we hadn't slept together, or I would have to run right off a cliff. I had hit a new low. I had managed, despite being alone with four men on a tropical island, to still be the last woman standing.

Chapter 22

The problem with being on a tropical island and having to share everything with everyone was there was no private time, place, or space for yourself. I had so many emotions swirling inside, and I needed a place to let them out. I decided to walk toward the other side of the island. After about an hour, I found what I didn't know I was looking for. There was a mountain of rock behind a mass of trees. There was no one around, but I let out such a bloodcurdling scream, I just knew the others would come running to see what was the matter. I waited . . . nothing. I walked over to the rock. Its smooth, untouched surface was exactly what I was looking for, I thought. Bending over and scouring the ground, I lifted rock after rock until I found the smallest rock I could find.

Then I let it all out:

To whom it may concern:
I don't really know if I am writing to God, myself, or just a rock, but I have to get it out. I am sick of this island. I am sick of these people. I thought I could trust

Jacques, and he's just like the rest. Dallas is an asshole, and I could care less about the other two. I just want a bubble bath. Hell, a shower would do. And what is the deal with the rain here? It's like monsoon season every other day.

I am sure my mother would be proud of me, trapped all alone with four beautiful men, but the truth is, it is lonely. I actually miss women. Not in a lesbian way, but more the communication I once shared with my female friends. What I wouldn't give for a poetry reading right now.

All these guys care about is themselves. Whatever they're dealing with is what they expect you to deal with at the time. Well, guess what? I got my own problems, too. I could run out of tampons any minute. I am sunburned. I think I am developing a rash, because my skin won't stop itching. Be happy this is a rock and not a real journal, 'cause I could go on.

I am worried about my father. I am the only child, and he is very old. I know he is worried sick about me. I fear my mother has no one left to ridicule and may actually be forced to look at her own faults. She would surely die at that point, and I am sure she would blame me on her deathbed.

God, if this is your rock, why are you punishing me? I mean, I know I haven't been attending church much, okay, not at all, but is that any reason to banish me to purgatory? I have read the Bible, and people have done a lot worse. A lot worse! I mean, I was trying to help people at my clinic. I hardly charged anything. I worked well with most people.

And while we are laying everything out on the table, what is the deal with this Jacques guy? He is silent; then he is all talk. He likes me; then he doesn't. Do I need to deal with a noncommitted man on a deserted island, too? Why do all my other friends get to lead normal, healthy lives with real relationships, and I am stuck in some pseudoreality show—like existence. It is not fair. There I said it. It is not fair. It is not FAIR!

Well, now I got a couple of demands of my own. That's right!

1. *Could you please stop sending stupid men to my doorstep?*
2. *I think I deserve to survive this whole island thing.*
3. *I think I deserve to know if I am going to be stuck on this island for the rest of my life.*
4. *If I am going to be stuck here, then you could have at least left an iPod or cassette recorder or something.*
5. *I'm tired of fish! We need a new food to eat pronto, one that we can cook.*
6. *If I do make it back to civilization, I don't want to see anymore movies with guys dressed up as black women. It's demeaning, and you should have told them so.*
7. *Please stop letting people build a Starbucks on every corner in my neighborhood. I love coffee, but not on every block.*
8. *I think, in light of this situation, I deserve to do over the whole vacation thing. This was a bust!!!*
9. *Reality TV . . . Please let it go!*
10. *Finally, please, God, if you see this note, please if I do survive, please don't let anyone take a picture of me until I get a chance to put a comb through my hair.*

When I got done writing, a feeling of relief washed over me. I looked up at my writing, which from afar definitely looked like a crazy woman's ramblings. But for me, it was the most therapeutic thing I had experienced since I'd landed on this death trap.

I walked away, with a smile. I ran back, though, and scribbled one more line.

I'll be back.

"Whoa, slow down, Josie," said Andrew. He grabbed my arm as I tossed more supplies on the already overloaded boat. "What is the rush?"

"I am ready to go," I snapped. "Aren't you?"

"Of course, I am, but I don't want to sink our ship in the process," he said. Andrew was right. We did not need to be lost at sea, to add to our list of unfortunate circumstances.

"Sorry." I put my hand on my waist. "I'm a little frustrated."

"Jacques?" Andrew smiled in that way you knew he had been there. Though I doubt anybody had ever been stuck in the middle of nowhere and fallen for a pseudo-mute Brit, with a dead wife and matching heart.

I managed only what I could. "Yep."

"Josie, the thing about guys like that is, they are exciting and interesting, and in a time of utter distress, they can be a lifesaver. But he has a lot of issues."

"Ya think?" I laughed, more to stop from crying than anything else.

"He will never be of any use to anyone until he decides he wants to live himself."

"I know, I know," I said. "I mean, I know it was the most improbable relationship to start out here, but he just felt so easy."

"Probably 'cause he knew it wouldn't last past this brief moment."

"Ya think so?"

"I am sure there was a connection," Andrew said. "But, honestly, how many times have we felt connected to someone only to find out they didn't feel the same way?" I tried to stop my mind from recalling the list of those I had fallen for who didn't love me back.

"So what do I do?" I asked. I wanted to know. Clearly, I was not in a position to judge the facts for myself. I needed someone to weigh in and say, "Josie, are you fucking crazy? Ditch that negro, and head west."

"You know what you have to do, kiddo. Get on this boat, make it home, and start over," Andrew said. "And the good news is, if you can survive this, you can survive anything." I hugged Andrew. I was hoping his faith in me was correct.

By nightfall we had completed all the packing of the boat. Francis had shaped a map to the best of his ability on one of his dried notebooks. He figured, at worst, in one week at sea, we should reach some form of civilization. I wasn't as convinced but needed to believe in order to sail across an endless ocean without any concrete evidence that we would survive.

Everyone fell asleep early but me. We were all exhausted from the packing. But I was more concerned with the fact that Jacques had yet to come back to camp. We hadn't really spoken the last few days. I had focused most of my energy on our chores. But when he didn't come back in the morning, I became concerned.

Nobody had risen yet, so I decided to look for him

before we began our journey home. It didn't take long to spot him sitting with his feet dipped in our swimming hole.

"So you're not going to say good-bye?" I asked.

"I said good-bye to Francis," Jacques said.

"I meant me," I said.

"Would it make a difference?"

"No," I admitted. "But it would have been a gesture I could live with."

"Well, I am sorry once again to disappoint you."

"You are only disappointing yourself."

"No, I am just not trying anymore."

"Look, I am sorry for your dead wife, but you are still alive."

"You don't talk about her," Jacques snapped. "You don't get to talk about her."

"Maybe you should talk about her, mourn her, cry over her and your child, and then let them go."

"Like it's just that simple." Jacques huffed at me.

"It may not be simple, but it's necessary."

"You don't know," Jacques said. "You have never loved anyone that hard and then lost it all."

"Actually, I am about to." The words spilled out before I could get a chance to stuff them back in my mouth.

"Josie, I—"

"You don't have to say anything," I said. "I just want you to know that despite everything I promised myself about moving on and not falling in love again, I am right back here, again. And I lose again, but this time not to another woman, or a man, or money, or insecurities, or even your wife. I am losing because you are a coward."

"What?"

"You are scared to take a chance, to risk losing someone or them losing you." I moved closer to him. "But you cannot control that. This island is not an escape. It's a prison. And if you let us leave and you remain on this island, you will have lost more than your family. You will have lost yourself once and for all."

"It's not that . . ." Jacques stuttered as he talked. His eyes watered. "It's not that easy. I'm . . ."

"Sick? I know that," I said and grabbed his hand. "But with the right doctors, it can be controlled."

"They're getting real bad now without the medicine."

"Let me help. Come home with us, with me," I pleaded. Jacques turned away, then turned back to me. I thought I had finally broken through. He smiled. And then my worst nightmare came true. Jacques's eyes rolled in the back of his head; he flopped to the ground, busting his head open. He started shaking and choking uncontrollably on the ground. Blood from his head was shooting up like a sprinkler. He was having the worst seizure I had seen in my life. And there was nothing I could do to help him.

Chapter 23

Without any medication or equipment handy, I did all I could to care for Jacques. I stuck a piece of wood in between his teeth, to make sure he didn't choke on his tongue. I moved away all objects that might cause him to injure himself. Then I sat there and watched him flop all over the ground for what seemed like hours but was only a few moments. Eventually, the movement stopped, and Jacques lay still and quiet, drained from his ordeal. I hurried next to him. Stripping off my shirt, I wiped his brow with it and then placed it under his head. He still wasn't talking, so I curled up next to him and held him in my arms.

"Josie," he mumbled, and I shot up.

"Are you okay?"

"No." He shook his head. I tried to be strong, to think of him as a patient, not the man I loved.

"Have you been experiencing more seizures since you've been here?"

He nodded his head.

"More than one a day?"

He nodded again. This was not good.

"You have to get to a hospital as soon as possible," I said in a very cold and clinical way, as if we were down the street from Saint Joseph's Hospital. I quieted my inner hysteria. "Okay. You have to get on that boat."

"No." Jacques tried to raise his hands, but he could barely move.

"I don't think you have a choice," I said. "Stay here. I'm going to get Francis." I darted back toward camp, to find the others already packed and pushing the boat to sea.

"Francis," I yelled as he turned back to face me.

"Yeah?" he said. "I know you need closure with Jacques, but we needed your help out here this morning."

"He had another seizure," I said. "They seem to be getting more frequent and more severe."

"How is he now?" Francis let go of his grip on the boat and gave me his full attention.

"He is not good," I said. "We have to take him with us."

"He said he doesn't want to go."

"He is in no capacity to make decisions anymore," I argued. "He can barely speak."

"How are we going to take a sick man on a glorified raft?" Francis said. "He would be better off waiting here until we send help back."

"This is your brother." I wanted to slap Francis. "He may not make it until help comes."

"Yo, man, what's the hold up?" Dallas yelled from the other side of the boat. "We moving this thing or what?"

"Give me a second," Francis said. He grabbed my arm and gently pulled me to the side. "You know I love my brother. But I have to think of all the other people here. We all may not make it if we take him."

"You mean, you care for yourself."

"I'm going to be honest," Francis said. "If it takes leaving my brother here to have a chance to see my child again, I will do it over and over again."

"So he just dies so you can go back to your old life?"

"It's my daughter, Josie." Francis turned.

"Well, I'm staying here."

"Don't be stupid," Francis said. "You're going to sacrifice your life for a guy who can't give you the one thing you want?"

"I took an oath," I said.

"Not to him," Francis said. "You owe it to all the other people who need your help to leave."

"You know I love him," I said. "But it's more than that. I can't pick and choose when to be a doctor. I am who I am. If there is a chance to save him, I have to stay here and help."

"Then I will send somebody back here as soon as we find the coast guard or somebody."

"Thank you," I said. The weight of my decision was hitting me as I looked at Francis and saw the concern in his eyes.

"I'll be okay," I assured him.

He pulled me into his arms. "I'm going to pray for you both."

We separated, and I helped them push the boat in the water. I waved and walked off.

"Josie, where the hell are you going?" Andrew yelled from the boat. "Hop on."

"I'm staying to take care of Jacques. He needs me," I called.

Andrew jumped off the boat and ran up to me. "Josie, no."

"Someone has to care for him, Andrew."

"But what if something happens to him, Josie?" Andrew said. "I know you love him, but you could be left all alone on this island."

"I have to take the chance."

"Josie." Andrew shook his head, but he must have seen the resolve in my eyes. He just hugged me and ran back to the boat. I looked up and spotted Dallas, who just stared at me. I waved my hand, and he smiled. He waved his hand and winked back at me. I watched the boat as it moved out to sea. The wind kicked the sails out, and the boat glided out toward the horizon. A moment of fear hit me. What if Francis was right? What if Jacques died? I would be alone on this island until help came. And what if Francis, Andrew, and Dallas didn't make it? What if they died at sea? I would be all alone with no hope of rescue.

For a second, I contemplated swimming out to meet the guys and save my black ass. Hell, he couldn't even say I love you. For all I knew, he could die at any moment—or worse, live and be a constant reminder of how gullible I was for love.

Suddenly, I thought of Jacques lying alone on the ground in the middle of the woods. No matter what, saving a life was the right decision. I just hoped I racked up enough good karma to save my own life in the process.

Chapter 24

Dear God/Rock/Rock God

Am I a fool for staying and caring for a man who doesn't want to be saved? Should I have left with the others? I may well have made the choice that ended my life. Or I could be choosing to cling to something so special, it defies the threat of death. Either way, I wish I had some barbecue potato chips to munch on while I contemplate this dilemma.

The others left so quick. It really won't take them long to forget about me and then focus on their larger goals. And, to be honest, I don't blame any one of them. Francis has a wife and child, Andrew a partner, and even Dallas has a star-studded career and an amazing future ahead of himself. What kept me here? I wish I could say it was all about Jacques, but it wasn't. A part of me wanted to stay behind, too. Maybe I was scared to live out my days alone in public. Maybe I liked punishing myself. Either way, I had a chance to save myself, and I didn't take it. What is wrong with me?

With the rest of the group gone, it was up to me to take care of Jacques. I decided to make a strategic plan of action. I helped him walk back to our camp. I made him as comfortable as possible and gave him the little medication we had left in the first aid kit. I jotted down names of herbs I could use to calm his nerves, since I figured the stress was aggravating his attacks.

After he fell asleep, I went fishing. I will admit, I had usually left this duty to Jacques or Andrew, who were superb fishermen. They'd caught and cleaned bundles of fish before the sun set. But since Jacques was still weak, I knew I had to take care of everything.

It wasn't the easiest task baiting the wooden hook. I wasn't scared of worms, but they kept wriggling out of my hands. But I finally managed to secure one, and I cast my line out in the water. Not even a minute later, I felt a tug on my pole, and soon I had to brace my legs in the water as I fought with a small fish for his life. He swam toward me, then jetted in the opposite direction, almost pulling me out to sea. But I held my ground. I fought and pulled in the other direction until I finally got it out of the water. It was a little smaller than the fish my friends had caught. But I was still proud. I repeated my efforts a few more times to make sure I had enough fish to last us.

After gathering some firewood, I headed off to the woods to find herbs for my makeshift medicine bag. I found a patch of mushrooms near a tree and began picking them. I checked their underbellies to make sure they weren't poisonous. I found other herbs throughout the woods. It amazed me how fast time flew under the grueling sun, picking plants. When I arrived back at the camp, Jacques was sitting up and leaning against the back of the tent.

"Are they gone?" he asked. His face looked sunken and hollowed out. It was pale in color. He looked drained of life itself.

"Take it easy. You need to rest some more," I said.

"I think that is all we'll being doing out here."

"You didn't see the tennis courts they built across the way?"

Jacques smiled. "I didn't see them in the brochure."

"Newly built, right next to the swimming pool and day spa." I put my bag of goodies on the ground and sat next to him.

"You will have to give me an official tour when I can get up."

"No problem."

"Why'd you stay?"

"Because you could have died." I proceeded to unpack the herbs and put them in some order. Maybe his words wouldn't upset me so much if I gave myself something constructive to do.

"And what if I did?"

"Do you want to die, Jacques? Is that it?"

"I don't know honestly."

"I don't think you want to die. You're just afraid to live." I put my hand on his head to check his temperature. "If you want suicide, you will have to wait till I make you well. Then you can slit your wrist or jump into a dormant volcano. I don't care. But if you do it, you're going to be effective and stop wasting everyone's time."

"Wow, you're a bitch."

"This bitch just saved your sorry ass."

"I am grateful. I am," Jacques started. "There is just so much you don't know about me."

"Don't you want to be around when I find out?"

"I don't know."

"That seems to be your resident answer for everything."

"Not all of us have answers for everything."

"I don't have the answers to everything, Jacques. But I am willing myself out there to find out."

"You remind me a lot of her, you know," Jacques said.

He grabbed my hand. "I do?" I said. I hated that my body tingled when he touched me.

"Yep, but you're different, too. Feisty, unabashed, in control."

"It's an American thing, I guess."

"It's a Josie thing. I just woke up, and they were gone."

"What?"

"I woke up from the car crash, and they were dead."

"Francis told me you didn't find out until you woke up in the hospital."

"We were in a ravine, and I woke up from my seizure. I turned, and Liz, Elizabeth, was slouching next to me, her head back. You could just see the life was gone. I don't even know if I bothered calling her name. I turned back to look at the kids. . . ." Jacques stopped talking, and he gave me a look of panic and fear I had never seen on another person. It was as if the grim reaper were whispering his due date in his ear.

"I just don't want to endure that with anyone else I love," he finally said.

"Love hurts," I said. "That is why it's so beautiful. It's tragic, too."

"I wouldn't be able to bear it if something happened to you."

"That is why you need to get better, so you can watch over me."

"And I suppose you'll watch over me."

"Of course," I said. "You know when I was much younger, I was at the mall with my father and he had a heart attack. I think I was about five or maybe seven. I can never remember. But I do remember him almost falling over the second-floor balcony. I grabbed his shirt and pulled him back before he went over. He slumped down on the floor and whispered, 'Get help, baby.' I thought I was petrified, but I was actually already running to the security guard at the end of the mall. He called the paramedics, and they took my dad to the hospital. We rode in the ambulance, and he went into cardiac arrest. There was this sister who was in the back. She ripped off his shirt and rubbed some oil on his chest. Before I knew it, she had put these two shiny things on my dad's chest, and he jumped up like a fish. I yelled, 'Stop hurting my daddy.' But after the third time, my dad started coughing and mumbling. She saved his life. I knew I wanted to do what she did. Save lives. And I knew I would never let anyone die under my watch if I could help it."

"You're a brave girl." Jacque leaned his head on me.

"No, I just fight for what I love."

"Josie"—Jacque lifted his head toward me—"I love you."

"I love you, too," I said and cradled him in my arms until we both fell asleep.

Chapter 25

I don't know if it was the herbs or the extra rest that Jacques got, but after a couple of days, he seemed to be much better. So much so that we decided, since it was the two of us, we should relocate closer to the rocks in case another storm hit. We moved only the essentials and left a fire going just in case a boat or helicopter should arrive. But I had pretty much resigned myself to the idea that for now it was just the two of us, that was until I decided to go looking for some different fruits to add to our diet. Jacques warned me not to play Dora the Explorer all over the island, but I was tired of passion fruit and coconut.

After an hour of searching, I hit pay dirt and found a nectarine-like fruit that was firm to the touch and slightly tart to the taste. It would complement our current menu perfectly. I was busy picking them from a low branch, and I guess I didn't see the log in front of me. I fell over hard and landed in a mound of sand. It only took a second before the stinging bites registered in my brain and I looked down. I was covered in red ants, who saw me as the enemy invading their base. They tried to kill me. I screamed and tried to brush them all off, but it seemed like there were just so many.

I must have been making an unbearable noise, because Jacques came barreling through the trees and stopped in his tracks when he saw me.

"What?" he yelled.

"Ants!" His eyes narrowed and he came swatting. He wiped the ants off my back and grabbed my hand and forced me to run.

Before I knew it, we were at our watering hole and jumping head first into the water. The cool water soothed the burning sensation that punished my skin. But the second my skin broke the water, the pain eclipsed my senses. I cried. I admit, I cried. Jacques got out of the water and ran away. I was about to cuss him out, but he soon came back with some fruits and a rock. He smashed the fruits and rubbed the pulp on my arms and back. It felt much better.

"Where did you learn that?" I asked.

"Army."

"Be all that you can be." I smiled and it hurt.

"You have no idea."

I looked at my arm, which was covered in reddish welts. "God, I look awful. Turn away. I am ugly!" I put the back of my hand on my forehead for effect.

"You are beautiful." Jacques kissed my arm. "Dramatic, but beautiful." He kissed my neck, and I giggled like I was fifteen years old.

"You are so beautiful," Jacques murmured. His eyes, deep and brown, glossed over in that way men's eyes do when they get sexual. I knew this was the moment. No candles, no three-hundred-thread-count bedsheets, just us and nature. He placed his arm around the small of my back and lifted me toward him. He pecked at my lips like he was deciding whether they were good enough to eat. He started softly sucking them between his lips. I guess they were good enough to eat.

He began kissing the back of my neck and then worked his way down the middle of my neck. His tongue made a special appearance when he reached my breasts. He stopped and pulled off his shirt. He turned his attention back to me and caressed my skin. He kept kissing me as he unfastened my bra and pulled it off. This was the first time I was really exposed to him. I felt I needed to cover up for some reason. But Jacques held my arms as I tried to put them over my chest.

"Don't hide, baby," he moaned. He reached my nipples and slowly sucked each one as my eyes rolled. It was so sensual, I felt myself trembling inside. For some reason, I was acutely aware that I had nothing else on my mind but him pleasing me. This was a huge surprise for a person who usually made grocery lists during intercourse. I didn't know if he was so good or if being on this island had cleared my mind of unnecessary things. But I felt good physically and mentally.

Jacques drove his tongue south to my belly button, kissing and sucking as he unbuttoned my shorts. He slowly pulled my underwear and shorts from under my butt and off my legs, all the while sucking on my stomach.

I didn't even notice he had taken off his shorts. But when I opened my eyes, there we were, both naked. I felt exposed in the open, but safe because I was with Jacques. I prepared for him. But I was pleasantly surprised. Instead of just going for the goal, Jacques dribbled the ball a bit. He placed his tongue inside me, and I thought I would faint right there. He explored my insides, whispering, "Beautiful," as he proceeded. It was beautiful in a sensual way. But luckily, it was also hot. I could barely contain myself, and then Jacques pulled his tongue back. I looked up and saw it. Perfect. Just like him. When it was inside, I felt the tears falling on my face.

"I love you, Josie," he said as he moved into a steady rhythm. I probably would have given him the deed to my house at this point. He continued the tempo, changing up to every once in a while to keep it spontaneous. But he made sure he looked in my eyes and held my hand until I finally exploded. I shook for minutes as he kept his momentum. Then he placed his arms around my back and took it home.

Jacques closed his eyes and released. He clutched my body tight. Then he looked at me. "I love you," he whispered. I stared into his eyes, felt how they gazed down on me. All my defenses evaporated. The shields I held up against all men slowly lowered, and for the first time, I allowed myself to believe in him, in men, in love.

Chapter 26

That morning I woke up with a new kind of feeling for Jacques. I knew how I felt about him. But it was intensified by our night of passion. I wanted to know everything about him. I could hardly wait to talk with him. And soon I felt his arms reaching around my waist. He started kissing my neck and holding me closer to him.

"Tell me about Europe," I said.

"It's a lovely country." He laughed, and I jabbed him in his stomach.

"No, I mean tell me about growing up in Europe," I continued. "What was it like for you?"

"Not much to tell, but I guess you're not going to really accept that answer, are you?" I shook my head no.

He went on. "I grew up in a small town in lower England with my mum and Francis's and my father. My dad had already had a relationship with Francis's mom, and before Francis was born, my dad was shagging my mom. He was not exactly the nice type and could never really seem to latch on to a job. He did odds and ends, but mostly stayed home, drank, and tried to beat the living hell out of my mother and me.

"Once, when I was seven years old, we were playing football, your soccer, and he kicked a pass to me and I missed it. He didn't say one word to me the rest of the day, and that night, when I was dead asleep in my room, he busted through the door and beat me bloody for missing the toss. 'You gonna be a loser all your life,' he yelled at me. I was seven, for Christ's sake. My mum called the police, and thank goodness they came as quick as they did, or I would probably be dead. Come to think of it, it was shortly after he left that I had my first seizures."

"Wow," I said. I almost felt like an intruder for bringing up such a sensitive subject.

"Yeah," Jacques continued. "It was rough. But once he left, my mother and I got along okay. We never had any money, but we made do, ya know? She was so proud when I got accepted to the university. She died before I got there, though. That's why when I found out from her paperwork that I had a brother in the States, I had to meet him. I saved all my money to go visit him. You should have seen Francis's face when I told him who I was. He was right shocked, I tell ya. But once we started talking and hanging out, we were thick as thieves. I only spent one week with him but felt like he was more my blood than my own father. And when Liz died, he came right over, he and his wife, and they took care of me. They brought me back to the States. They loved me. For that, I will never be able to repay them. I owe Francis so much."

"Sounds like you two both love each other very much," I said.

"Time and distance separate people, but if you

really love someone, you are never rid of them," Jacques said.

"And what about your wife?" I finally asked. "How did you meet her?"

"I used to have a small photography studio, and Liz was one of my students. She used to ask a million questions, like someone else I know, and I would stay late answering her queries. One day it was so late, we decided we might as well get a drink together. We talked about photography, art, and life, and just in that instant, I knew she was the one for me. I never left her side, and she never left mine. We got married within six months. Oliver and Olivia came right quick after that." Jacque paused, and I felt his body quake. Then the tears hit my neck. I turned around to him.

"I am sorry I brought it up."

"No, it's not that," he said. "It's just I miss them so much, I do. But I am also so happy right now. Right here with you."

"I am, too," I said.

"You know, there are moments on the island here when I can hear my babies yelling and playing," Jacques said.

"Really?" I said.

"Yeah," he said. "They always spoke in tandem, like they were identical twins, even though Oliver was a year older. When I first got here and I was off by myself, I could hear them calling for me to play hide-and-seek with them. It was almost like a whisper, like their voices were riding the air currents. I would spend hours looking for them. But, of course, they were nowhere to be found."

"Do you ever feel Liz's presence?"

"Sometimes, like she is watching me," he said. "But it's not as strong as the kids."

"Why do you think that is?"

"Honestly," he said, "I think the kids miss their daddy. But Liz sees I have someone looking over me. So she is letting go." I wanted to ask more. I wanted to know if her letting go meant that he had, too. But I knew that was enough for one day. You can ask a man to expose only so much pain before he has to put it back under lock and key. We were alone together on this island and had nothing but time to explore each other.

The phase "it was like a dream" had never made sense to me. Was it a dream where everything was surreal and people were riding bicycles, or was it so real and yet unobtainable? The truth was, I was focusing on the wrong thing. When people said, "It was like a dream," they knew whatever "it" was would eventually have to end.

But the first couple of weeks Jacques and I shared alone on the island were like a dream. We made love every morning and every night. When we finally would force ourselves to get up, we would eat together, legs connected at the ankles, hands intertwined. We would talk for hours about what we thought was current politics, or about our favorite television shows, or what kind of ice cream we favored. The connection we shared out there alone was unreal.

Jacques could yell something obtrusive and rude, like "Ugh, you smell like wet dog today," and it was okay because it was our little secret. But then he got sick again. He tried to hide it by saying he was getting fresh water. But I could tell from his trembling hands that something was wrong. The next morning I woke up to him staring in my face.

"You may have to make a boat and leave me here," he started.

"Not this again."

"That's not it," he protested. "You know how I feel."

"Then I don't want to talk about this again," I said. "If someone comes, we both go. Or we both leave together—but not apart."

"They're getting worse," he said. I turned to him and could see genuine fear in his eyes.

"The herbs aren't helping anymore?"

"Very little," Jacques said. "I think the seizures are just too strong now."

"Then we have to leave together."

"I don't think I would make it."

"Of course, you would."

"I'm serious," Jacques said. "I can feel my energy leaving me right now."

I turned around so I could face him. "We will make it."

"I'm sorry."

"For what?" I held his head in my hands.

"For putting you through all of this."

"This has been the happiest moment I have ever had."

"Then you need to get out more." Jacques knocked his head against mine. Not hard, but just enough for me to go, "Ow," so he could kiss the spot he bumped.

"Corny," I said.

"That's my specialty. Corny jokes."

I smiled and kissed him again. "You have a few more specialties than that."

"Hmm," Jacques moaned. "Let's count them off, shall we?"

I pushed him back. "I thought your energy was zapped."

"Yeah, for talking." He grinned. "Not for other stuff." I giggled, as we had had sex all afternoon. It was the last time we would be intimate on the island.

For some reason, my hair was really bothering me that day. Without a stylist and proper equipment, it was blossoming into a gigantic nappy bush. I tried to use one of Francis's combs we found from the crash, but the teeth were too narrow and could not cut through the cotton field that was now my hair.

"We may need your knife to cut all my hair off," I joked to Jacques, who still lay on the pallet. "I am thinking of going bald, like Natalie Portman did for that one movie. What was it called?"

I turned to Jacques. His head was turned away. "Don't tell me you're still asleep."

I moved over to him and gently kicked his leg, which felt a little cold. I kneeled down and touched his face. It was blue. His eyes were open. I shrieked. I check his mouth. He had choked on his tongue and couldn't move. My head was screaming inside, but my hands, trained to deal with emergencies, went to work. I pulled his tongue out of his throat and opened his airway. Still no breathing. God, how long had he been like this? Was it too late? I began CPR on him, pounding my fists on his chest, then filling his lungs with air. I did this several times in the kind of silence you never hope to hear. I could hear the thumping of my hands on his flesh, the whoosh of air from my mouth into his mouth. But then I heard a sound I had not heard in a long time. A thunderous whirling of wind and steel. What was that? I tried to recall as I worked on Jacques. Finally, he started coughing and gulping for air, and the silence was broken between us. But I still heard that sound I couldn't quite place yet. I looked around.

"Are you okay?" I asked. Jacques nodded. "Okay. Be still. I will be right back." I walked out of the shadow of rock and tree and looked to the sky. I saw a sight that only seeing Jesus himself could have topped. Flying a few miles out was a helicopter. Its trajectory was unmistakable. It was heading toward the island. I ran to the shore. By the time I got there, the helicopter was preparing to land at the edge where the sand and water met. Before it reached the ground, a man jumped out, head tucked low, but I knew him immediately. It was Francis.

He ran over to me and lifted me in his arms. We held each other for a long time. Then he looked down at me and said, "You all right?"

I nodded. "Yeah, I'm okay."

"Jacques?" He looked like he was trying to brace himself for whatever answer I gave him.

"He's alive," I said. "But he needs medical attention immediately."

"I brought them." He pointed back to the helicopter as two people unloaded a stretcher and equipment. They came jogging up to us.

"Where is he?" a man asked. He wore a paramedic's uniform and dark shades.

"He's not too far. I can show you," I said. I was turning to show them when Francis grabbed me again and hugged me.

"I prayed you two would be alive. I prayed every night I made the right decision," he said.

"You did, and we are."

"Everything will be fine now," Francis said. "I promise." It was at that moment that a single phrase entered my mind: famous last words.

Chapter 27

"He's all right now, ma'am," said the paramedic with the shades, assuring me as we flew high above the island, heading to what was my "real" home. I watched him inject medication to stabilize Jacques. He moaned slightly but then was quiet the rest of the trip. They told me he would be taken directly to the hospital as soon as we landed to do more accurate tests.

"Wow, you did a great job taking care of him," the other paramedic said. "And those herbs you gave him really slowed down his seizures. How did you know to do that?"

"I read a lot," I said. "And I'm a doctor."

"Well, he is extra lucky," the paramedic with the shades said. "To have such a beautiful woman, who is also a doctor, taking care of him." He winked. *Welcome back to reality, girl. Where men flirt over comatose bodies.*

I nodded and turned my attention back to Francis. The whirring of the chopper was so loud, I inched closer to Francis to hear him.

"So what happened?" I asked.

"Turns out we were about four days away from Palau.

But there are all these uncharted islands along the way. That's why it was hard for the authorities to find us. We kept getting happy seeing all these islands, but I kept telling Andrew and Dallas we had to keep pushing until we saw some air traffic. They were furious until the fourth day, when we saw a plane buzzing ahead, heading toward this huge land mass. 'That is where we're headed,' I told them. Once we hit ground, it didn't take long for people to call the police and paramedics and get us checked out."

"And Dallas and Andrew are both okay?" I asked.

"Yeah, they're fine."

"Good," I said.

"As soon as I called my wife to tell her I was okay, I headed back to find you two."

"Wait. You haven't seen your wife and kids?"

"I had to find you before—"

"He's okay." I gripped Francis's hand.

"I know," he said. "I just feel so bad for leaving you all back there. But I had to find a way to get back." Tears gathered around the corners of his eyes.

"I understand. You have a family," I said. "I would have done the same thing."

"Well, I had my company get us a chopper and a medical team to come look for you. The police wanted me to wait and give all these statements. I didn't have time for all that."

"How long did it take you to find us?"

"I tried to chart a map," he said. "So it really only took about a day to find you."

"Well, I am glad you did," I said. "And I know Jacques is glad too."

Francis seemed relieved, like a pulling on his chest

had stopped. He released a smile, and I was glad he could relax a little.

"Your parents are on the island, waiting for you," Francis blurted out.

"What?" Immediately I welled up.

"Yeah, my company rented a jet to bring all our families to Palau to greet us."

"Wow," I said. "Thank you. Thank you so much."

"So I need to warn you about something," Francis said.

"What?"

"This has become a big media circus," Francis said. "The press is everywhere, and they have been digging dirt on all of us."

"Well, I don't have any dirt."

"You may not, but everyone has a past, which can be misconstrued and warped to fit any agenda."

"What are you trying to say?"

"I am just saying be careful, Josie," Francis said. "These guys will do anything for a story."

"And what about you?" I asked. "Are you going to do a story?"

"Actually, I quit," Francis said.

"What?" I said. "You can't quit. You're the most competent and the cutest black reporter we have on television."

Francis laughed. "Yeah, well, on that island, I realized how much I was gone on assignments all over the world. So I am just going to spend time with my wife and kid."

"That is amazing!" I said. "So what are you going to do?"

"Teach my daughter French and Spanish, take her to school. Learn to braid her hair, read my wife's screenplays, which I always say I never have time to edit. Make love to my wife, and not just have quickie sex before I go off on a monthlong assignment. Live basically."

"Sounds amazing," I said, with a smile.

"We'll see how long my wife can stand me messing up her schedule," Francis said.

"She'll love it." The chopper made a sharp turn, and I looked out the window and saw the island, with tall buildings and millions of lights illuminating the sky. It had been so long since I'd seen artificial lights. It hurt my eyes.

"We'll be landing at the hospital in just a few minutes," the captain yelled back to us.

I maneuvered over to Jacques to see how he was doing. His eyes were closed, but he kept shifting in the bed. I gripped his hand, and he gripped back. I rested my head on his chest, careful not to crush him. I rubbed his stomach and adjusted the blanket that was wrapped around his midsection. I knew we weren't completely okay yet, but getting Jacques to the hospital was critical for a full recovery. I knew once we got there, I could make sure he got a handle on his seizures and help get him well.

Jacque moaned as he tried to open his eyes.

"Hey, baby," I whispered to him as I wiped my wet face. "We're going home."

"Lizzie," Jacques said. I jumped back. My heart felt like it had incinerated inside my chest. I lost my grip on his hand and stumbled back to my seat.

"What's wrong?" Francis said. "Is he okay?"

"He's fine," I said. I looked out the window in silence, cursing the day I'd decided to go on this blasted vacation in the first place.

Chapter 28

We landed on top of Easterbay Memorial Hospital, the island's main hospital. They lifted Jacques and carried him to the elevator. A small group of doctors and nurses were waiting for him. I wanted to follow, but my heart didn't have the energy to pursue him one more step.

Francis grabbed my hand and escorted me to the side steps.

"Let's take the stairs," he yelled above the background noise. We got into the small stairwell and walked a few flights of steps.

"The press has been hiding everywhere, trying to get this story," said Francis.

"Why?" I asked.

"Are you kidding?" He laughed. "A major NBA player, a TV journalist, and a beautiful doctor all trapped on an exotic island. They are going crazy."

"I guess my actual experience was a little different," I said. We both laughed as Francis peeked down the corridor.

"Okay, let's find a room, and we can call and find out where our families are."

"You didn't mention Jacques in your description," I said.

"I am trying my best to keep him out of the limelight," he said. "If the press starts digging in his past . . . that would not be good."

"Why?" I questioned. I felt like I was missing something.

"Trust me." We crept down the sterile white halls until he discovered an empty room. "In here." We moved into the room, and Francis checked the area like we were spies hiding from the police. He pulled out his cell phone.

"I'm going to find out the best place for us to meet," said Francis. He turned his back and left me to look out the window. Wow. I was almost home. The nightmare was almost over. Yet all I could think of was Jacques. How can you feel so strongly for someone when they do not feel the same way? I just couldn't get rid of the mental picture of him calling his dead wife.

"Wonderful," Francis said and got off the phone.

"There is a car that will take us to the Ritz, where everyone is staying," Francis informed me. I continued to stare out the window, wondering if finding and losing really was better than never having experiencing it at all. It felt like a draw at the moment.

"Josie," said Francis. He rubbed my back. "What's wrong?"

"Just trying to get used to being back," I said. "So you said everyone is at the hotel. Awesome!"

"Are you sure?"

"Yeah, of course," I said, putting on my best fake smile. "I can't wait to hug my dad."

We took the steps down to the main floor and had the car service meet us in the back of the hospital. The ride to the hotel was quick and gut-wrenching. I began fumbling with my clothes. My hair was everywhere. I didn't even want to look at a mirror; I was sure Pamela would distort all she saw. We drove into a parking garage and halted next to a discreet-looking door. The driver opened the car door, and we exited. Francis opened the door, which revealed a private elevator. We rode it to the top floor.

"So here is the deal," Francis said. "Our families are all in the penthouse suite. I figure we can rest with them, but eventually, we will have to face the press."

"What do you mean face the press?" I said. "I just want to go home and leave this all behind us."

"Either you give them the story, Josie, or they're going to make it up," Francis said. "And, believe me, you don't want that."

"I don't want to deal with this," I said.

"I know you don't," Francis assured me. "Neither do I, but I know the media. If you give them a few quotes, you will be yesterday's news and won't have to worry. But if you don't say something, they will keep hunting for dirt until they find something out."

"Ugh." I wanted to scream. No. I wanted to file a class-action suit against all the people who had made me feel bad for not going on vacation and had forced me to embark on this nightmare in the first place. I had been content going to work and watching my TiVo at night. I had my microwave dinners, and, sure, it got a little lonely. But hell, I didn't have to worry about crashing planes; monsoons; good-looking, emotionally detached Englishmen who called their dead wives' names. Nothing.

"When the time comes, I'll coach you through it," Francis said.

"Okay," I said.

"But I definitely wouldn't mention Jacques," Francis said.

"What do you mean?" I said. "I wouldn't tell anybody about us. I would be too . . . embarrassed."

"I mean I wouldn't mention that he was even on the plane with us."

"What? How could I not mention that?"

"No one knows he was on the island with us," Francis said.

"How?" I looked at Francis, who looked away. "Why?"

"One of the reasons Jacques didn't want to come back to the States is because he has a bit of a past."

My knee-jerk black woman's reaction forced hands on hips. "What the hell are you talking about?"

"It's complicated." Francis led me to the main penthouse doors. I stopped in my tracks.

"Break it down for me."

"Later," Francis said. "Our families are waiting for us here."

"Are you crazy?" I asked. "I was alone on an island with this man. Was I in danger?"

"No," Francis snapped. "Of course not."

"Then what?" I said. But before I could pry the answers I wanted from Francis, he opened the door and all I heard was a group of people yelling, "Surprise!" The noise was earth-shattering. With all those voices, my head immediately started throbbing.

I spotted a pretty woman holding an adorable girl across her hips. She came up to Francis. He started crying. She followed suit. They hugged, and I began tearing up.

"I missed you, baby," Francis said as he kissed his wife. He grabbed his little girl and set her on his arm. "You, too, baby."

"Josie." I heard a familiar voice. I turned to see Peter Green standing in front of me. He was holding Pamela's hand.

"Daddy," I whispered. "Mom."

I ran to them and fell into their arms.

"We didn't think we would ever see you again," my father said. His hands were quivering as he caressed my back. I held on to them as if they would evaporate if I let go.

"Oh my Lord, girl," cried Pamela as she started arranging my hair. "You're a mess."

"There was no hair and make-up trailer on the island, Mom."

"I am just so happy you are alive," said Pamela, still trying to pat down my hair. "We'll fix it later."

"Leave your daughter alone, Pam," Peter said. "Ain't the girl been through enough?"

"Don't you start yelling at me in here, Negro," Pamela snapped back. "That is why I left your sorry ass alone in the first place."

"Guys, I hate to be selfish," I said, "but I think this moment is about me."

"Sorry, baby," my mother said. "But you are all right, right? Those boys didn't do anything to you, did they?" She held the word *do* just long enough to make me sick to my stomach. It was as if I had been in some concentration camp, being raped and beaten daily.

"No," I said. "They were all perfect gentlemen."

"I just don't think I could be trapped on an island with three men and not be scared," said Pamela.

"And why did they leave you?" asked my father.

"Wait. There were four guys," I said. "And no one left me. I had to take care of Jacques."

"Who?" my father asked.

"Is that that cute basketball player?" Pamela asked. "I know you are a little long in the tooth now, but he is cute and I read he makes twenty-two million a year. Can you believe that? Now *he* would be husband material."

"Pamela!" said my father.

"I'm just saying," said Pamela. She hunched her shoulders and rubbed my back again. "I just want you to be happy."

"Oh my God," cried a trio of voices, interrupting Pamela's lecture. I turned around, and there were Gayle, Marcela, and Ruby, jumping in place.

"Hey," I said.

They gathered around me in a circle and pounced on me. They lifted me in their arms and almost squeezed the life out of me. I laughed.

"Girl," Marcela screamed, "I am so glad you're alive. I thought I was gone have to search for another job. And you're the only one who let's me do nothing."

"Thanks, girl," I said. "I'm glad you still have your job security."

"Don't pay her no mind, Josie," said Ruby, my surrogate mother, as she inspected me. "You look good, a little scruffy, but still beautiful as ever. You look a little darker, too. Nice sun-kissed skin tone. I love it."

"We told you to take a vacation, honey," said Gayle, smiling. "Not a sabbatical."

"It wasn't my intention, believe me," I said.

Ruby hugged me again. I could hear her sniffling. "Don't ever listen to us again," she said.

"Oh, I won't," I assured her. We all sat down, laughing and reminiscing for hours. The hotel brought in food and drinks, and it almost became a party. I was so grateful to be back. I was discussing some details of the crash with my father when I noticed Francis's wife standing in front of me.

"Hey," I said and excused myself to my father. "I'm Josie Green."

"I know," she said as she hugged me. "It is a pleasure to meet you."

"Thank you," I said. "You, too."

"I know you are busy getting reacquainted with everyone, but when you get a chance, I think we need to talk." She moved in closer to me and whispered, "It's about Jacques."

"What about him?" I asked. "Is he okay?"

"He's fine," she said. "Not here. Meet me in the lobby in fifteen minutes."

She hugged me again and walked off, leaving my mind to invent every scenario possible. My family grabbed me again, but my attention was now officially diverted.

"It's like a reunion in here," Jason yelled, and I ran to him.

"Oh my God," I screamed.

"If you wanted me to come visit, you didn't have to get lost at sea," Jason said. "You could have just bought my ticket. Geez."

"I missed you!" I cried. We hugged for a long time.

"Please, Josie," Jason said. "I can't cry. I am supposed to be butch."

"It will be our little secret then," I said and hugged him again. "Go mingle with the family."

I sent Jason away and kept glancing between the grandfather clock standing in the corner and Francis's wife. I kept my conversations going but could not recall one thing they'd said at that point. All I knew was that the next fifteen minutes crept along. I was aware of every second passing, as if I were watching individual granules of sand pass through an hourglass. When the time did finally elapse, I excused myself and darted to the bathroom. I splashed water on my face and tried in vain to fix my hair. Wow. Mirrors were horrible inventions. I looked like I'd been electrocuted. *Fuck it,* I said to myself and slipped through the people to reach the door. The second I got outside, I felt a hand grab me.

"Let's go to the stairwell," Francis's wife said. She grabbed my hand and took me to the stairwell.

"Wow. This feels really secretive," I said. She lost her smile and opened the doorway to the stairs.

"It has to be," she said. "Francis would kill me if he knew I was talking to you. But I think you deserve to know the truth."

"The truth about what?" I was getting scared.

"Jacques has a past that some people don't need to know about," she said. "But I can tell after hearing what you did that you really know him and deserve a few more facts."

"Like what?"

She pulled a cigarette out of her back pocket. "I only pull one out in emergencies."

"Is this an emergency?"

"It's a nasty habit. Do you smoke?"

"No." I was getting annoyed by the stalling.

"Sorry," she said. "But if I gotta talk, I need something to take off the edge."

"Does this have something to do with his dead wife?"

"That's the thing," she said, letting out a long white stream of smoke as she talked. "Elizabeth is not dead."

Chapter 29

"Excuse me?" I said. The force of her words hit me like a car going eighty miles per hour against my brain. "Are you serious?"

"Yep," the woman said.

"Mrs. Wright, please tell me you are mistaken." I prayed that she would slap me on the arm and say, "Just joking." No such luck.

"I'm sorry. I am so rude. My name is Lee, by the way." Francis's wife was even prettier up close. Her bright brown eyes seemed to shimmer even in the staircase's dull light. She was small but well proportioned. Her nails were perfectly manicured as she held the half-smoked cigarette in her hands. Her other arm lay across her torso and supported her smoking hand. You could see the muscles in her arm as it flexed against her breast.

"Lee, Jacques told me . . . Francis told me she was dead."

"She is in a hospital in D.C.," Lee said. "She is officially termed a vegetable."

"But she is alive?"

"Yep."

"Why would they lie?" I was furious. I felt like I was in some warped game in which I kept losing points by the second. *Bling.* She loses her dignity. *Bling.* Josie loses her morals. *Bling.* Josie loses her integrity.

"Well, the doctors did pronounce her dead," Lee said.

"Then why?" I asked.

"Elizabeth has very religious parents, who didn't want to lose their daughter if there was the slightest chance she could live."

"Was there?"

"She hasn't come out of it in three years."

"Geez, and what about his kids?"

Lee took another drag from her cigarette. "They did die in the crash."

"So I take it Jacques wanted to take her off life support."

"Josie, they were in an accident because Jacques decided he wanted to stop taking his medication. He had a seizure that caused the death of his children and turned his wife into a vegetable. Elizabeth's parents have never forgiven him for that."

"I can imagine," I said. "That would be a hard thing to forgive, but it was an accident."

"Well, he wanted to end the life support, and when they refused, he tried to take them to court. They said if he tried to stop them, they would press negligence charges for not taking his medication."

"Wow."

"It gets worse." Lee exhaled hard. "So they left Jacques with all these mounting medical bills and didn't pitch in a dime but wanted to keep her physically alive. But Jacques could see her suffering. One night he tried to pull the plugs. Security caught him and saved her. But her parents called the cops and told them everything."

"So what are you saying? He's wanted?"

"Yes," Lee said. "And that is why you can't say he was on that island with you. If Elizabeth's parents get wind of the story, they will have him arrested."

"Oh my God," I said. It was a little hard to digest all this information. My stomach felt like it was chomping on my insides. "So how has he survived all these years?"

"Francis got him a job as a freelance cameraman. They set him up with a fake identity to cash checks and live a modest life, but no one knows he's even in the States except me and Francis and now you."

"How did Francis manage to keep Dallas and Andrew quiet?"

"Andrew is under investigation for taking unprescribed drugs on the job."

"You're kidding?"

"Just weed," Lee explained. "He smokes on his off days, but the press got wind and is trying to say he is responsible for the crash because he was smoking at a party the night before."

"Are you serious?"

"Girl, it's deep." Lee rolled her eyes. "So he agreed not to mention anything about Jacques if Francis would help keep the media off his back."

"And Dallas?" I asked.

"That gets more complicated." Lee sat me down. "He said he would only talk to you about it."

"What?"

"I am just telling you," Lee said. "Of course, he

won't take a bribe, because he makes a freakin' billion dollars a minute."

"So how did he even know I was alive? I just got back."

"He said he would only negotiate if he talked to you," Lee said. "That was why we rushed to find you all even before Francis came home."

"I don't know what to say." I sat there unable to process everything. I was in love with a man who was still in love with a ghost. Meanwhile, I was asked to keep secrets, lie, hide all for a man who two weeks ago could not admit his love for me.

"Francis is going through a lot to keep this all secret," I said.

"That's his brother," Lee confided. "Plus, he is culpable for a lot of lies, too. This would not look good if it came out."

"I guess so."

"Francis wouldn't ask you, but I am. Will you please talk to Dallas?"

"I don't know," I said. "Dallas is a little crazy."

"I will go with you," Lee said. "I just want to protect my family. I am sure you can understand that."

Indeed I could. I wasn't even married to Jacques, and I had done everything I could to keep him alive on that island. No matter what transpired between us, I didn't want him to go to jail.

"Okay. I will go see him if you go with me."

"Of course, I will," Lee said. She leaned over and hugged me. "Thank you so much."

"No problem," I said.

"Oh, I almost forgot." Lee reached into her purse, which was dangling over her shoulder. She pulled out a small leather-bound book. "I don't know if you journal, but it always helps me process my thoughts. And I know you have been through so much. It may be useful."

"Beats writing on rocks." I smiled to myself.

"Huh?" Lee questioned.

"Nothing."

"So can I ask you a question?" Lee said.

"Of course," I said.

"What was it like being the only woman on that island?" she said. "I would be afraid of being raped or worse."

I laughed to ease the obvious tension and concern in her voice. "I was afraid of that, too, and many other things. But each day we were on the island, there was sort of this kind of family thing that developed. I mean, of course, I developed feelings for Jacques, and even kissed Dallas, but overall we were like kin. We yelled at each other like kin. We cried together like kin; we ate like kin. By the time Francis and the others left, it really felt the family was being torn apart."

"Wow," Lee said. "I have to just say, you're like my hero."

"Get out of here," I said.

"I am serious," she continued. "I know I don't know you, but I have met a lot of people in my time, and that situation would have broken the best people down. You have somehow remained strong and above it all."

"I was crying a lot out there, too, believe me."

"It's okay to cry," she said. "But you did something way more important. You survived."

"I guess I did," I said. And when I took a moment to think about that, I felt proud, too.

"Francis said you really are a good person, and I believe him now," Lee said. "Jacques would be lucky to have you." I sat there wanting to say, "He sure as hell would be."

Lee and I set a time to sneak away from the crowds the next day, when we would get back to the States, to see Dallas. Francis had arranged a small press junket on the island and a quick follow-up back in New York. We would answer a few questions and be done with the whole thing. I would hopefully be back to my old life by the end of the week. Dallas had agreed not to say anything to anyone before he talked to me. I was so shocked he even wanted to see me after the Jacques situation. I couldn't even think about what he would say to me. But I was glad I had Lee as backup just in case.

I said good night to all my family and friends and was escorted by security to my hotel room. It was so weird. Once inside, I became instantly aware that I had not taken a shower in literally almost a month. God, I must have smelled something foul. I immediately went to the shower. My entire body felt like it had an extra lining of dirt on it. And I was right. After being in the hot, soothing shower for only a few moments, I saw the line of black grime ooze off my feet and spiral down the drain. I let the water pummel my skin as I reached for the loofah sponge next to the faucet and scrubbed down every inch of my body. I thought I would rip the skin off, but only more black dirt fell away.

I was so happy to be clean. It made no difference that the inside of the tub was almost as dark as me now. Then I saw the holy grail of bathroom supplies—shampoo. I jumped in the air and almost tripped and crashed onto the floor. I opened the cap and released a ridiculous amount of the substance in my hand and lathered up. I massaged my head so vigorously, I knew hair would start falling out in clumps. I sighed as the water rinsed the flakes, dirt, and sand out of my hair. I repeated this process at least eight times before I was sure my hair was clean. I washed my body a few more times, till I saw only clear water in the bottom of the tub. I grabbed one of the übersoft towels and dried off. It was akin to heaven.

Once out of the shower, I meandered over to the king-size bed. I thought I would cry. It had a beautiful brown linen cover over white blankets. I didn't deserve it. But I was so happy to get it. I pulled the covers back and just stared at the bed. It was a far cry from rags and bamboo, which had served as our island beds. I eased my way under the covers, and it felt so uncomfortable—for a second. I was so used to hard surfaces. But as my back adjusted to the firm but soothing mattress, it took only a few minutes for me to fall asleep.

I slept undisturbed for a good four hours before I woke up in a sweat. I looked up, waiting to see if a storm was approaching, but heard nothing more than the soft hum of the air conditioner. My room was perfectly still, cool, and quiet. There were no bugs to swat, no snakes to avoid, no fish to catch. I was in the paradise I had planned to enjoy, and I was freaking out.

The display on the cable box read 3:35 a.m. I slid in my bed and reached over to pick up the phone. I dialed zero and got a pleasant-sounding operator.

"Good evening, Ms. Green. How may I assist you this evening?" said the operator. I loved how they already knew my name and cared enough to say it even in the middle of the night.

"Yes, can you give me the number to the local hospital? It's called Easter . . ."

"Easterbay," the woman said. "I'll connect you right now. Did you want the floor where Mr. Wright is being treated?"

"How did you know?"

"We know everything here, Ms. Green." I could feel her grin through the phone. "One moment. Let me connect you."

There was a quiet clicking sound and then a dial tone. Within three rings, someone picked up.

"Easterbay Memorial IC Unit. This is Tammie. How may I assist?" The woman spoke so fast, all I could hear was every other word.

"Yes, this is Dr. Green." I tried my best not to sound like I was making a professional inquiry. "I am checking on the status of Jacques Wright."

"Yes, Dr. Green," the nurse said. "Mr. Wright was waiting all night for your call. He told us to connect you if you were to call. But I am afraid he is asleep right now. Do you want me to wake him?"

I didn't know if I was more amazed at the fact that Jacques was waiting for my call or at the service of the nurses there. My nurses were never that nice.

"No need to wake him," I insisted. "Can you tell me how he's doing?"

"Of course, you know I am not supposed to," the nurse confided. "But as much as that man talks about you and calls out your name, you have to be pretty damn important in his life."

"I guess so," I said.

"He is on a new regimen of medication and is

doing fine right now. The doctors are doing several tests, but I believe he is going to be going back to the States to see a few specialists."

"Oh? When is that?"

"Why don't you stop by tomorrow and ask him yourself?" I could feel the smile on the woman's face.

"Um, that's okay. I just wanted to make sure he was okay."

"Do you want to leave him a message?" the woman said. "I am sure he would appreciate that."

Nosey. "No, that's okay. I will just check back tomorrow."

"All right, Dr. Green." The woman once again must have been cheesing on the other end. "You have a blessed evening, or morning."

"Thank you," I said and hung up. I moved back into my comfortable position in the bed. Thank God Jacques was all right. I knew I wasn't ready to see him, but I was glad he was doing well. I had made a pact with myself not to see him until I knew for sure what I wanted to say to him. At the moment I had nothing more to say than "You are putting me through hell."

I raided the nightstand for a pen and grabbed my little journal.

Dear Rock/Journal/GOD,

I made it back to civilization, but fear whatever Jacques and I had will remain on that island. He called out his wife's name. His wife's name. After I cared for him. Held him all night, made sure he was stable. He called her name. I can't win. But at this moment, there is nothing more I want to do than run to him right now. With each passing day, I feel I am going more and more insane. I love a man who cannot love me back, and I want him more. I want to make this such a romantic tragedy, but in reality, I am just like every other woman—in love with a man who is just not that into her. What a shame. All that education, all those years of dating, and I am just as dumb as everybody else. If I didn't already promise Francis and Lee I would stay here, I would be gone. I am such a fool.

Chapter 30

That night in my dream, I was back on the island, but none of the guys were with me. The wind was kicking up, and the rain poured down on the ground. I could barely see anything. Nothing looked familiar to me. I tried to feel for a tree or a rock, but I could feel myself losing my balance. A hand suddenly grabbed mine and led me to a cave.

"Thank you," I said as I looked at the mop of long black hair that covered my rescuer's head. I looked down and saw her wet cotton dress dripping.

"Do I know you?" I asked. But the woman said nothing. "I was just saying thank you so much for pulling me out of the storm."

Still nothing. I inched closer to the figure and felt cold as ice. I looked down at her hands. At first I thought she was just light-skinned, but her color was more ash than flesh-toned.

Suddenly, I got the sense that I knew this woman. Her face was still covered up. But her essence felt too familiar to ignore. "Have we met?" I asked. The woman shook her head.

"Do you live on this island?" I said. The woman shook her head no again.

"Who are you?" I asked. Nothing. Something told me to leave it alone, but I had to know. I walked up to her. My head was inches away from where I presumed her face would be. Before I could move her hair to one side, the woman jumped on me.

"Leave him be," she said. The woman had a distinctly English accent, and I recognized who I was battling. Elizabeth.

"He is my husband," she said. Her hair moved to one side, and I saw her face. I was expecting a ghoulish figure, with fangs for teeth and black eyes with no pupils. Instead, I got something more frightening. This woman was real. She was beautiful and angry.

"You can't find your own man?" she yelled.

"I didn't know he was married," I cried as I struggled to break free of her grip. But we were stuck.

"You always know," she said. "Their mind is there, but their heart is somewhere else. He called for me."

"I know."

"He called for me," she said. "You just remember, he called for me!"

Suddenly I woke up. My body was drenched in sweat. I was literally too scared to move. I peered around my hotel room from behind my blanket. I was crying. I had never been more scared in my life. I forced myself to get up and turn on all the lights. I checked every inch of the room. I knew I wouldn't find anything, but I was too terrified not to at least check. I ran to the bathroom, to relieve my bowels. The sweat on my body met the air-conditioned room and made me shiver. Of course, then I became convinced that Elizabeth was still in the room with me.

"I didn't know," I kept whispering. "I didn't know." But I did know that if a woman was trying so hard to keep her husband that she was reaching me in my dream, she could have him.

A knock at the door woke me up. I blinked my eyes open. The sun was high in the sky, so I knew it was mid-morning. There was another soft knock at the door.

"One moment," I said and grabbed the terry-cloth robe from off my bed and headed over to the door. I opened it to find a small man dressed in a dark suit, holding several bags of clothing.

"Compliments of Mrs. Wright," he said as he handed them over to me. I reached in my pockets, then realized I had no money. In fact, all my identification had been lost at sea. "Sorry. I don't have any money."

"That is no problem, ma'am," the man said, handing over his goods. "Mrs. Wright took care of everything." I took the clothes and nodded my head.

"Thanks." I shut the door and walked back to the bed. I hadn't paid attention to the labels. But when the bags fell on the bed, I placed my hands over my mouth in delight. Dior, Prada, DKNY, Choo, all my favorite clothing and shoe designers were waiting for me to try their wares. There was a small card attached to the Dior bag. I pulled it off and read it.

Let's give 'em something to talk about.

Your friend,

Lee

I turned the card over and saw it was a gift certificate to the spa downstairs—manicure, pedicure, hair, and make-up. Even when I was in the real world, I rarely had time to pamper myself. And freshly manicured nails never served me well when I was inspecting the insides of women's bodies all day. But today, before I had to go before the world and tell my story, at least I could relieve Pamela's concern that I would look like a river rat. I basked in another sinfully long shower, then put on a pair of casual jeans and a cute top from Prada, of course. I slipped on the Jimmy Choo sandals and headed downstairs for my makeover. To my surprise, Lee was downstairs waiting for me.

"Good morning, sleepyhead," she said. "How did you sleep last night?"

"Oh my God," I screamed. "I never wanted to leave."

"Yeah, the beds here are nice," Lee said. "So I know we are here for other reasons, but I thought you should at least look your best if you are going in front of a camera. And I know how cameras can be."

"Francis mentioned you write screenplays. Are you in the film industry?"

"Not now," Lee said. "I used to write documentary films in graduate school. That's where I met Francis."

"How cool," I said. "I always thought film was fascinating."

"I did, too," Lee laughed. "But Francis and I got married, and while his career skyrocketed at *60 Minutes,* mine floundered. And once we had Asia, I kind of took a backseat and did freelance work so I could take care of our child."

"Lee, that is awesome," I said.

"It's boring," she said. "Not like being a doctor."

"Are you kidding?" I said. "I would kill to be a mother and get into my family and teach my children stuff and make costumes for school plays. I would be ecstatic."

"Yeah, that part is fun." Lee laughed. "But let's not forget when your child doesn't want to obey, or is sick and has runny diarrhea or, god forbid, a seizure."

"Your child has seizures, too?"

"Yeah, I think it runs in the Wright family," Lee said.

"Wow. Maybe there is a way to trace exactly what it is then." I was talking to myself at this point, trying to put the pieces of the puzzle together.

"Not today, girl," Lee said. "Today is just about you. It's going to be rough this afternoon, and I want you looking your best and feeling as comfortable as possible."

"Oh, don't worry," I laughed. "This won't be a hard adjustment." We walked into the salon, and a swarm of beautiful women who spoke no English surrounded us. They were from all over—Asia, Africa, and Europe—and were equally as stunning in their own right. But they knew how to handle their business. They plopped me down in a chair and went to work.

First, they gave me a facial and an exfoliating peach scrub. Then they went to work removing blackheads, bumps, and pimples from my face and neck. I felt like I was in a Bugs Bunny cartoon where Bugs goes over to someone and all you see are a million hands moving in every direction. I was moved to the hair department, where a small woman pushed my head back under a sink and doused it with a steady stream of water. She massaged my head and washed it repeatedly. Then she lifted my head up and took me to her station. She was African and gorgeous, with long, silky hair that fell past her shoulders. She said nothing and just smiled and nodded at me. She pressed my hair and straightened it. A month of new growth had made it inch down my neck. She put some product in my hair and added a few highlights and some much-needed volume.

When she handed me the mirror, my mouth dropped. I hadn't looked that good since college. I wanted to cry, but I knew they were taking me to make-up next.

"Are you okay over there, girl?" Lee shouted. I couldn't see her face, only women working on her toes.

"Yeah," I yelled back. It had been so long since I'd had a real girlfriend to do stuff like this with. I appreciated talking grown-woman talk with Lee. I mean, I had Pamela and the ladies at work, but they were either too old to relate or too young to experience what I was going through yet. Lee was right in the trenches with me. Only, she was happily married to her dream man and was not in the least bit threatened by my presence or involvement in his life. I respected her even more for that.

After I was done, a lady with a gold smock directed me to the dressing room, where my outfits were waiting for me. I picked a flowing pink dress, with matching Jimmy Choos and a retro white cashmere wrap for accent. I looked in the mirror and was amazed at what I saw. I was not a stand-in for an episode of *Survivor*. I was a woman again, and it felt fantastic.

"Girl," Lee screamed. "Come out so I can talk about you." I slowly opened the door and crept out. Lee fanned her face.

"You look stunning," Lee said. "Like Halle Berry, Gabrielle Union stunning."

"You think so?" I was so nervous that my body, which hadn't seen a gym in a month, would not do the outfit justice.

"I am telling you, I would be speechless if I didn't have such a big mouth."

"Well, I guess that is a compliment."

"It is," Lee said. "They are not going to know what to do with you."

"Thank you," I said. "You look amazing, too." And she did. Lee had on a long beige skirt, with a fitted black top with no sleeves. A half-sleeve jacket covered her bare shoulders. Choos blessed her feet, too.

"I do my part," Lee laughed. We touched each other and giggled, and I remembered again how much I missed this kind of companionship with another woman. No judgments, no competition. Just two women who respected each other and enjoyed each other's company.

"Thank you, Lee," I said.

"For what?"

I placed my hands on her shoulders. "For being a real friend. I know we just met, but I feel like we just click, you know, and I really need a true friend right now."

Lee smiled. "To be honest, so do I. And I felt the click the instant I met you. No hating. Just you were my girl." We hugged and I felt safe.

"You know where we need to go before we do the press conference?" said Lee.

"Where?" I was up for any challenge now. My ego was boosted a millionfold.

"We should go to the hospital and say hey to Jacques."

"Are you crazy?" I shouted. "I can't go there, like this."

"Why?"

"Because it will look like I did it for him," I said. "Which I didn't." It was almost true. I had gone to the salon because I needed some long-overdue pampering. But I knew I would be on television, and the likelihood of Jacques watching was very high. No harm in giving him a little peek at what he missed.

"It will just be for a second." Lee tried to coax me. "I'm sure he would want to see you."

"Hell, naw," I countered. "I mean, aren't we supposed to be hiding this dude from the press? If I go over there, don't you think they will catch wind of something? Besides, I am not ready to see him yet."

"Why?"

"What is it with the questions?" I laughed, more out of nervousness than anything else. "I told you, it's just not the right time."

"Oh, just for a second," Lee pushed. "I will be there. He really wants to see you, and I know you want to see him."

"What do you know?"

"Don't worry about all that," Lee said. "Let me go get our rental car, and I will meet you out front." Before I could respond, Lee was trotting off, her heels clicking on the marble floor. I wanted to stop her but had a feeling, when her mind was made up, that was a done deal. I stood alone, looking in the mirror, resisting the urge to primp.

I am not fixing myself for that man, I said to myself as I slowly walked toward the lobby. I took deep breaths and tried to focus my thoughts as Lee brought the car up the driveway. The automatic locks clicked, and I jumped inside.

"Someone seems to be getting a little excited," Lee smirked.

"I am not excited," I said. "Just concerned that his new medication is working."

"How did you know he had new meds?"

"Just shut up and drive already."

The island was so small, we literally turned three corners and were nearing the hospital. I was so freaked out, I had to sit on my hands to keep them from shaking. I tried to strike up casual conversation to fend off my urge to jump out of the car.

"So how old is Asia again?" I asked.

"She is three, an angel who speaks fluent English and German. And Francis is determined to add French and Spanish," Lee said.

"Are you kidding?"

"Nope." Lee shook her head. "We think she's a genius. Sometimes, between me and you, she scares me a little."

"Wow. That is amazing," I said.

"And a lot of work." Lee sighed. "Francis is trying to push her as far as she can go, but I am like, 'Who do you think is sitting down with her all day teaching her this stuff?'"

"I never thought about it like that."

"You'll be married with kids real soon, and you'll have to deal with all this shit."

"I don't think so," I said.

"What are you talking about?" Lee huffed as she turned into the hospital driveway. "You are smart, beautiful, and a doctor, honey."

"All great attributes if I was a man," I protested. "But as a woman, men don't care about all that."

"You don't think so?"

"Are you crazy?" I said. "Hell naw, they don't think about that. I would stand a better chance getting married if I were a stripper."

"I think there are men out there who would appreciate all that you offer."

"I hope you ain't talking about this Negro we about to go see now." Lee tried to hold her laughter.

"Josie." Lee tried to contain herself. "Jacques is a good man, and he does love you. He told me."

"Wait," I said. "When did he tell you that?"

"Francis and I saw him last night, when you all went to bed."

"So was he okay?"

"Going to go see him right now, honey. Calm down," Lee giggled.

"If only you knew, honey," I said. "He is still in love with his wife."

"He loves his wife, but I don't think he is in love with her." Lee parked the car and turned off the ignition.

"When we were in the helicopter, he called out her name."

"He what?" Lee motioned for us to get out of the car. My stomach started churning again.

"Yes, babe," I said. "I was holding his hand, after saving his life, and he called out her name."

"He was delusional," Lee said.

"He was delusional for her."

"I think you are taking that too seriously," Lee said.

"Well, how would you feel if Francis called my name while he was making love with you?"

"I would have to cut him and you." Lee swiped her finger across her neck. "But seriously, yes, I would be upset. But he was sick. It doesn't mean anything. He loves you."

"Oh, and let's not forget he's still married to the woman," I added. "A little fact he forgot to mention."

"He probably didn't think it would matter stuck on an island," Lee said as I followed her inside the lobby. "Look." Lee grabbed me. "I know it's complicated. I am not negating that. But that man in there loves you. And you can front all you want, but nothing is going to change that."

"Let's just go in," I said. "I will say hi, and then we are out."

"Whatever you say, pumpkin," Lee said. I gave Lee a look that said, "Bitch, whateva," and walked to the elevators. She was right about one thing. No matter what our situation was, I had to at least see how the man was doing. I just wished that that was all I was doing.

Chapter 31

In my mind, I imagined Jacques would be sleeping in his bed. I would caress his head and then sneak out. Of course, my fantasies had a nasty habit of crumbling to pieces.

"Well, it's about time," Jacques said. He was coming back from the restroom, holding onto his IV, but his movement was steady. Even in that horrible hospital gown, he looked amazing.

"Hey," I said and waved. He stopped, as if he had to adjust his eyes.

"Jesus," Jacques said. "You are radiant." I smiled, and Lee came up to him and gave him a hug.

"How you feeling?" Lee said.

"Those seizures kicked my ass pretty good, but I am surviving," he said and flexed his muscles, and Lee laughed.

"I'm sure you are," Lee said as she glanced at her watch. "Well, I have to check on my baby and my big baby. I'll leave you two alone for a minute." I watched as Lee almost ran out of the room. I wanted to strangle her for putting me in this predicament. But it was me who got in the car and me who was standing in front of Jacques right now. So it was me who had to own up to this moment.

"You gonna sit or just stand there, looking beautiful?" said Jacques.

"I guess I'll look just as stunning sitting down." I laughed. He chuckled but wouldn't take his eyes off of me.

"What?" I said.

"I just thought I was never going to see you again."

"You did?"

"Of course, I did." He sat on the edge of his bed. "I just remember collapsing on the island and then waking up here without you. I was so scared. I didn't know what happened."

"I was okay." I fought the urge to jump over and hug him.

"Yeah, well, I wanted to know that."

"So you don't remember anything else about what happened? Like our ride here in the helicopter?"

"No, sorry," Jacques said. "Should I?"

"Well, you called out a name."

"Whose?"

"Elizabeth."

"I did?" Jacques said. "Well, you know I was sick."

"I know that, but I didn't know she was still alive." Jacques pulled back and sat back on his bed.

"So you found out about that?"

"How could you not tell me about that?"

"Her family does not even let me see her," Jacques said. "It is like she doesn't exist."

"But she does exist," I said. "And you have a marriage license to prove it."

"Yes, I do," Jacques said. "But you know she is brain-dead, and I petitioned to stop her life support, but her parents refused."

"Yes, I heard all that . . . from other people," I said. "Not from the person who should have told me."

"I am sorry, love," Jacques said. "I didn't think we were going to get this . . . close."

"You didn't!" My anger was rushing to the surface of my brain. "Well, you certainly didn't act that way."

"Look, I lost everything, okay," Jacques said. "Her existence is a constant reminder of my sin and punishment. It's like I am banished to a hell by myself."

"But you wouldn't have been," I said. "I was open to you."

"I know that now," Jacques said. "And I want to be with you."

"You are married, Jacques," I said. "No matter if she is alive or dead, you are married and imprisoned with her ghost. And until you let go of your guilt, you will be by yourself."

I got up and walked toward the door.

"Hey, where are you going?"

"I can't compete, babe," I said. "So I am out."

"Josie." Jacques followed me to the door. "Don't go. Let's talk this out."

"Answer me this," I said. "Could you get a divorce right now?"

Jacques mouth opened. But his head sank down.

"I thought not," I said and turned. "Take care of yourself, Jacques."

I ran to the elevator. I heard him calling my name, but I couldn't stand to look back. I just wanted to reach the elevator so I could cry one last cry and finally put this man out of my life. The doors swung open. I jumped in and waited in silence until the doors closed shut. I balled all nine flights to the lobby.

"Josie, what's wrong?" Lee called after me as she rose when I ran past. I couldn't stop to acknowledge her. I just wanted to forget everything about Jacques, this trip, this life. I jumped in a cab and asked the driver to take me back to the hotel. I sat staring out the window, contemplating how it had got to this point. I tried to push all the thoughts of Jacques out of my skull, but collages of him kissing me, holding my hand, making love to me flashed across my mind. I winced at every image. I was no better than one of those sad girls in the movies who falls for the unavailable man but then complains that there are no good men. He had never really been available. I had just imagined he was because he had reacted to me. I had been more alone on that island than I was at home. And it was time to get back to the place where I could at least be alone in peace.

When I arrived at the hotel, I walked through the lobby, and Francis called out to me.

"Josie," he yelled as he stepped toward me. I darted in the opposite direction.

"Hey," he said as he caught up with me. "Are you okay? Lee said you ran out. She is worried sick."

"I gotta go, Francis," I said.

"We have a press conference in fifteen minutes," Francis said.

"You'll have to do it without me."

"Are you kidding? You're the person they want to see most," he said.

"Please." I sighed.

"I am serious." Francis smiled. "My office has been inundated with hundreds of e-mails wanting to know who the pretty doctor is that got stuck on the island with the three men."

"And that's another thing," I said. "All this lying."

"It's the only way Jacques won't go to jail."

"I don't know if I really care at this point," I admitted. And I was serious. My level of caring was waning dramatically every day.

"Well, I could go to jail for harboring a fugitive and lying to authorities," Francis said. "Do you know what I had to go through to keep Jacques's admission a secret at that hospital?"

"How did you manage that?"

"Let's just say a certain hospital will be getting a full segment on *60 Minutes* in the fall."

"Jesus, Francis," I said. "This is so much to deal with at one time." He gave me that pleading, puppy dog look he tried in interviews with celebrities accused of molestation and drug-running charges. It always got results on TV.

"Jesus, Francis," I whined. "Okay. For you. And only you."

"Cool," Francis said. "Let's do this."

"Wait." I pulled Francis to the side. "Why all this trouble? I mean, I know he is your brother, but why risk everything?"

"Let me tell you a little story about me and Jacques." He walked me over to a small couch, and we sat down. "When I first found out about Jacques being my brother, I was excited and cautious. I mean, you can love your family, but it doesn't always mean they will love you the same way. But we became instant good friends. Of course, we were both married and living on separate continents, so our bonding time was sparse, to say the least. But after the accident, everything changed. My little brother needed me in a way I hadn't dealt with before. I felt this need to protect him. And when his in-laws started acting crazy, I shielded him in the States.

"That was around the time I got the job at *60 Minutes*. And as a news journalist, you don't just hop onto the anchor desk. So I had to pay my dues. They sent me to Afghanistan, Iraq, Israel, all the most war-torn places you could imagine. Lee was horrified and crying almost every night. And one day Jacques said he was going to go on my next tour with me, as a cameraman. I told him it was too dangerous, but he insisted. We flew to Africa next during a civil war in Rwanda. I am telling you the things we had to do to survive while on assignment would defy anyone's grasp of journalistic integrity. And Jacques, he saved my life so many times, I can't even count. He has gone to battle for me as many times physically as I have for him financially and emotionally. We are brothers, Josie, bound not only by our blood, but by the blood and sweat of others. And no matter how much you deny it, you are bonded to him just like I am." Francis sat back after his story, physically drained from the telling. I patted his knee.

"Let's get this over with," I said as he smiled.

Francis and I discussed our game plan as we walked inside. Little did I know what I would be in for as I entered those press-room doors.

Chapter 32

"Dr. Green, it's Virginia Staten from the *Daily News*," said a thin woman with stringy hair. It was the twentieth or fiftieth question of the night. The members of the press ranged from polite professionals to scandal-seeking socialites, to boring slobs. My only solace was that Francis and Andrew, who had flown back from New York just to support me, were at the table, next to me. Andrew held my hand under the table. I think it was more to support him than it was to support me.

"Rumor has it that you were having a romantic affair with one or more of the young men on the island. Can you confirm that?" said the woman with stringy hair. The woman didn't look up from her notebook. She was ready to write down the dirt.

"Sorry, but there were no extracurricular activities going on on the island, unless you count the occasional game of Spades, which we played with a soggy deck of cards," I said. The crowd laughed at my joke, and I made sure to flip my hair, as if to brush off the question.

A portly man with small, rectangular glasses raised his hand. "Captain Phillips, is it true you smoked marijuana the day of your flight?"

"My lawyers said not to address that question," Andrew said as he pressed his hand in mine.

"I have toxicology reports obtained from Village Presbyterian Hospital that say you tested positive for marijuana," the portly reporter said.

Francis interrupted. "James, that doesn't sound like a question. It sounds like you made up your mind."

"I'm just stating the facts," the reporter continued.

"It has been my experience as a physician that marijuana can stay in the system for almost thirty days, and there is no conclusive way to determine when it entered the system," I said. Sometimes I loved being a doctor.

Francis pushed forward. "Next question."

A lanky white man raised his hand. "Jeremy Higgins, *Los Angeles Times*."

"Jeremy, they finally gave you a story with an expense account," Francis joked, and the room burst into much-needed laughter.

"We have been getting reports that when you went back to get Dr. Green, you picked another person up from that island," said Jeremy.

I dared not look at Francis, who grabbed the microphone from the cradle.

"Boy, I have heard plenty of rumors since coming back," Francis said. "I have heard I was mad the network gave a certain female anchor the lead spot on my show, and that I ran away to write a book. I have heard Dr. Green was abducted by an alien. I have even heard that Captain Phillips and Dallas Sterling were having a

heated affair and were flying to an exotic island to continue their relationship out of sight of prying eyes.
Well, I don't know what you write at the *Times*, but at
my job we make sure we get the facts. And the facts are
the only people on the island were myself, Mr. Sterling,
Mr. Phillips, and Dr. Green."

It was amazing how easily fact and fiction could be
blurred. I sat there wondering if Francis felt uncomfortable lying in front of so many people. But I was
sure many a secret had to be concealed in journalism.

"I do have a fact you can print, though," Francis
said. "I am hereby resigning from *60 Minutes*." There
was a millisecond of silence, followed by a frenzy of
questions, raised hands, and yelling. Bulbs popped
and flashed as Francis smiled and put his hands in
the air to calm everyone down. That was it. Andrew's
and my fifteen minutes of fame were over. The next
big story happened right in front of us.

After Francis made his big announcement, and the
reporters got their fill of dirt, it didn't take long for
the press conference to break up and for us to be excused. I hugged Andrew and Francis and ran back to
my hotel. My parents and friends were already back in
the States, and I couldn't wait to get back to them. I
stuffed most of my stuff in a Jimmy Choo bag, stole a
terry-cloth robe 'cause they were just that soft, and was
headed to the door. Francis had been able to get me
a ticket and a temporary passport. Pamela had given
me some spending cash, so I was good until I got back
home and could replace everything properly.

I thought of calling Jacques, but I just couldn't do
it. I had spent all the emotions I could on that man
and had to go.

What I didn't count on was the abject fear I faced

boarding a plane again. I was sitting in my seat, with a blanket over my legs to hide the trembling. But two Jack and Coke drinks later, I rested all the way to New York. I was so happy to be back in the States.

Once there I took a cab to the W Hotel, where Lee had told me Dallas would be waiting for me. Because of scheduling conflicts, Lee and Francis had to catch a later flight. And even though I was a little scared talking to Dallas alone, I knew in order to close this chapter, it had to be done.

I stepped to the front desk. "Hi, I am trying to find Dallas Sterling."

The clerk didn't raise his head. "There is no Mr. Sterling registered here."

I was familiar with this game. "Could you please tell him that Dr. Josie Green is here to see him?" The man lifted his head and looked at me. He nodded and dashed to the far end of the desk. He came back with a small brown package.

"For you," he said as he offered it to me, and I took it. I opened up the package and found a small black cell phone. I turned it on. There was a note inside the packaging, with a number. I dialed the number.

Dallas answered the phone. "Hey, baby girl, I am in the penthouse."

"Why couldn't the clerk have just said that?"

"Where is the mystery in all of that?" he said. I hung up the phone and got in the elevator. I went over my game plan as the elevator beeped past each floor. I was ready to say what I had to say when the doors opened. I was never impressed by material things, but I had to admit this penthouse took my breath way. The floor-to-ceiling windows made it seem like I was walking on the sky. The minimalist furniture added to the cavernous space in the room. There was a master bed that looked bigger than many studio apartments.

"Josie," Dallas called as he walked toward me, wearing his usual ensemble of jogging pants and jersey. We embraced quickly, and I pulled away.

"I am so glad you made it," he said.

"How could I resist your very big request?"

"I mean, I am glad you made it out alive from that island," Dallas said. "When you decided to stay, I . . . I just wasn't sure you'd make it."

"I guess I am a lot stronger than you think," I smirked.

"You saved my life, remember?" Dallas laughed. "I know how strong you are."

I flipped the subject back to the matter at hand. "So, Dallas, why did you want to see me?"

"So before I talk to the press, I just want to get it straight from you that you are actually covering up for that cat." Dallas offered me a seat as he talked, and I took it.

"It's complicated."

"That's why I asked you here, Josie," he said. "To explain it to me."

"Jacques and I had a connection," I began. "And no matter what, he helped us a lot on that island, and he would go to jail if people knew his identity."

"Had a connection?"

"I thought you wanted to talk about me?"

"This is all relevant," he said.

"Yes," I continued. "We had a connection, but now we are done, and I did what I did so we could all have a clean break."

"There was nothing clean about our ordeal, Josie," Dallas said. "It was messy and scary and crazy."

"And over now," I said. "All you have to do is not say anything about Jacques. Francis already provided the press with a big news story, so we just walk away."

"Will you be able to walk away from everything, everyone?"

"I have to try for my own sake," I said. "Look, what happened on that island was traumatizing and a lot to take in at once. It will take a while to forget. But I am determined to get back to my old life. And you should, too."

"What if I can't forget?"

I rose to my feet. "Well, then there is nothing else I can say that will make you change your mind."

"What's in it for me to keep that dude's secret?"

"Believe it or not, you will be saving a good man from a bad circumstance," I said. "I know there are things that made you mad about him or me or both of us. But the truth is, he doesn't deserve to go to jail because I liked him."

Dallas stared at me in silence for a moment. His big brown eyes seemed to be asking more questions even though his mouth didn't move.

"All right," Dallas finally said. "I am canceling my press conference here. I am not going to speak either way. I will issue a press statement saying I am ready to move on, like you said, and get on with my life. Get on with winning championship rings."

"Considering your team's record, that would probably be a good thing." I laughed, but Dallas was stone quiet, looking into my eyes.

"What?" I said.

"I just made a mistake. That's all," he said.

"What does that mean?" I asked.

"All this time I was saying to myself that you were missing out for not choosing me," Dallas said. "You were missing out for not picking the obvious winner in this scenario. I'm a ballplayer with money, looks, and I even went to school. How could you not think you were being shortchanged by picking that British dude? This is the only thought that kept me going all this time. But in reality, I'm the one who's missing out. I'm missing out on a woman so loyal, she is willing to sacrifice everything for a man, even when it's obviously not going to work. I am missing out on a woman so strong, she saved two men on that island, while being able to let us both go. I am missing out on the only woman that made me question the true value of everything I had."

"Dallas," I said. "Regardless of everything, you are a good man. And as you grow, I am sure you will develop into an even better one."

"But despite everything I will gain or have, I won't have you." Dallas said it in the form of a question, and I couldn't help but be flattered. Here was a man who was putting it out on the line. He was brave enough to say what he felt. I just wished our differences were not so vast. I had already been hurt so many times.

I moved over to him and hugged him. Then I walked toward the door. "Dallas, you will make the best decision that is right for you, and that is all I can hope for. I gotta go now."

"So soon?" he asked.

"I have to get back to Chicago," I said. "And back to my life." I closed the door behind me and did exactly what I said.

*** * ***

I found an afternoon flight from New York to Chicago that had available seats. Thankfully, that flight was uneventful as well.

I made my way to ground transportation and jumped in the first cab. I was so happy to be back in Chicago. I knew exactly how many minutes it would take to get back to my house. Sure enough, thirty-seven minutes passed, and I was in front of my town house. I paid the cabbie and jumped out. I walked over to my door and heard a horn behind me. I turned around and saw a tinted limousine parked in front of my house. I was clueless. I half expected the CIA to take me away for questioning at this point.

A man got out of the limo, and I was once again shocked. "Josie," he called.

"Dallas?"

"Yeah," he said. He gave a crazy wave and grin as I stood looking back at this man in shock.

"I know it's crazy of me to come to your crib like this and all." Dallas forced a laugh. "But I just needed a few minutes of your time."

"Dallas." I shook my head and started laughing myself. "It has been a crazy, crazy month. And I am just exhausted, babe."

"Two minutes is all I ask."

I stood wondering what the hell I had to lose at this point. I mean, I was home now. I was safe. One conversation would not kill me.

"All right. Come on up." I shrugged my shoulders.

After spending five minutes convincing my doorman I was still alive, he let us inside, and I ran and collapsed on my couch. I rubbed the soft pillows and stretched out.

"Thank you, Jesus," I screamed.

"That how you usually treat your couch?" Dallas asked as he cautiously moved into the living room.

"I am just so fucking happy all my shit is still here."

"Well, I am happy for you, boo," he said.

"So you have two minutes before I sleep right on this couch."

"Okay. I wanted to talk to you because I had a question for you."

"Shoot," I said.

"Okay, all I want to know is if you really loved that English dude."

"God, no," I shrieked. "Please. I beg of you. We can talk about anything else as long as we don't talk about that. Please. Please. Please!"

Dallas laughed. "All right. Damn," he said. "Then my next question is, why not me?"

"You're here to kill me, aren't you?" I rose from my couch.

"What?" Dallas frowned. "Of course not."

"Yes, you are," I countered. "You're here to just snuff the last bit of life I have in these old bones."

"Damn, you are dramatic," Dallas laughed. "All I am saying is that I really dug you and not just for sex, even though your body is official and your face is bananas."

"Thanks, I think," I said. I noticed that Dallas was nervous. He was fumbling with his fingers and twitching his knees from side to side. It would have been cute if I hadn't already been drained of all my life force by Jacques.

"I know you got people sweating you everywhere. I just wanted to come here and ask for a chance."

"You flew here from New York to ask me that?"

"Yeah." He looked like a teenager asking the head cheerleader for a date to the prom.

"Okay, Dallas," I pleaded. "I really cannot process this right now."

"I think I love you."

I let out a sound only dogs could hear. I wanted to throw something. Hell, I wanted to throw Dallas. I wished I were strong enough. But instead, I moved over to him.

"You are not in love with me, Dallas," I said. "You are challenged by the fact that I rejected you when no other woman apparently has, and you can't get over that."

"No, that's not it. And I knew you were going to say that."

"Well, I am glad we are on the same page." I turned around. "Good night. Turn the lights out before you leave."

"Josie, come on," Dallas said. "Do you think I would travel all this way because you rejected me?"

"Yes, I do," I said. "I believe you all want what you want when and how you want it. And the second, the second you are required to do anything other than lay your pretty dicks in our pussies, you freak out. Well, life is about more than laying pipe and looking hot. Relationships take work."

"Hey, I have had long-term relationships," Dallas said. "You're the one that hasn't been involved since the seventies."

"And I suppose it's my fault."

"You are smart and beautiful, girl," Dallas said, "but

when it comes to men, you're just like all the rest of them. You blame guys for not being emotionally available, but you turn the guys that are ready away. You cling to these fantasies of a nigga sweeping you off your feet, so you don't see the nigga coming to your house every day, begging for your attention."

"Bullshit," I said. "I have made myself available."

"How?" Dallas said. "You probably dump dudes for the stupidest reasons but blame them for not coming back for more punishment. You are just as bullshit as all those guys out there. No, you're worse, 'cause you don't realize." Dallas got up from the chair he was sitting in. "This was a mistake. I'm sorry."

"Dallas," I said. "I am sorry. I just don't see it."

"Aiight." Dallas walked to the door and opened it, but turned around. "Just remember who was at your door, trying to get at you in the middle of the night, Josie. Not your fantasy, but a real dude. Me."

He closed the door, and I fell back on the couch, praying the apocalypse came tonight.

Chapter 33

The next day I woke up with a hangover. A love hangover. I just didn't feel like moving. My first instinct was to try to bounce back into work, but I couldn't, so I had to do the one thing I dreaded doing. I had to call Pamela.

"You made it," Pamela yelled through the phone. "We were praying you would be all right."

"Yeah, Mom, I made it."

"Thank the Lord." Pamela sighed through the phone.

"So I have a question for you," I said.

"Of course, honey. Let me take this roast out of the oven first." Pamela put the phone down on what I assumed was the kitchen table and hummed her way to the stove. I heard it creak open, then slam shut. "Hot, hot," Pamela sang as I heard noise on the receiver again.

"Okay, baby," Pamela said. "Is everything okay?"

"Yeah," I said. "I just have a sort of weird question."

"I expect those from you," Pamela said in a stern, serious voice.

"All right. How do you know the difference between having bad luck at love and sabotaging love?"

"Are you sitting down?" Pamela asked, which could only mean one thing. "Let me tell you a story. When I was twenty-one, I was in college. This was a year before I met your father. There was this young chocolate drop named Thomas who was in my English class with me. He was tall, dark, a basketball player, and for some reason, he took a liking to me."

Pamela loved to say "for some reason," when everyone in the family had been told the stories of how beautiful she was back in the day. She was regal now. But she was a fox back then.

She went on. "He started courting me every day, asking to carry my books, escorting me to class. I thought he was wonderful. But at the time I had quite a few gentlemen callers calling, and I wasn't paying him no mind. He eventually asked me to go steady. I will never forget what I did. I laughed in his face. In his face, Josie. I was convinced I could do better and told him so. He was crushed, and I didn't see him for a month after that. Well, one of my many gentlemen callers who I was also ignoring spread a horrible rumor that I had given up my virginity to him, and all the callers stopped calling. The only person who ever talked to me again that semester was Thomas. Only he was engaged now and just being the caring person he was. I had to sit at his wedding and watch this great man marry another woman, one smart enough to see what she had before her. I vowed never again. Two months later I met your father, and I was determined not to throw away another good catch."

"But you divorced Dad."

"That's because he was a damn hot mess," Pamela

screamed. "But I was married to him for fifteen blissful years."

"You were married eighteen years," I corrected her.

"And I enjoyed fifteen of them."

"And the lesson in this is?" I blew in the phone, even more frustrated than before.

"Love is what you make it," she said. "I was looking for the perfect thing. No such thing. When I got that, I found happiness."

"Okay. I have to pretend to do something else now, Mom. Bye," I said.

"Listen to what I'm saying to you, child," she said.

"I heard you," I said and hung up.

I got off the phone and took a long shower. I figured if I couldn't find love, I could at least love a new wardrobe. I got dressed in my own clothes and pulled out the Amex card I kept in a shoe box for emergencies. I walked out of my house, determined to shop my cares away, until I noticed the same damn limousine from last night parked in front of my driveway. The window came down, and there was Dallas, waving again.

"Please tell me you didn't stay here all night?" I said.

"I went to a hotel, but I had my driver keep watch to make sure you didn't leave." Dallas gave me his million-dollar smile again.

"You made your driver stay up all night to watch me?" I asked.

"Hey, I gave him the next few nights off," Dallas said. "This is a new driver."

"So not the point." I rolled my eyes.

"I know," he said.

"Okay," I said. "I don't know what to say at this point."

"Just say you would love to have some breakfast."

"Are you serious?" I asked.

"Dead serious," he said. "Come have some waffles and sausage. Put some meat on your bones."

"So now you're calling me skinny?"

"You know you fine, girl," Dallas said. "I am just trying to help you out."

"Thanks," I said. "Okay. If I have breakfast, will you go back home?"

"Yeah," Dallas laughed.

"And by home, I mean your home state, not your hotel."

"Oh, no doubt."

I smiled and got in the limousine. "I hope you got your credit card, 'cause I want to go to an all-you-can-eat joint."

"Your wish is my command."

Chapter 34

"So what do you want to be when your grow up?" Dallas asked me over our scrambled eggs.

"I don't understand."

"What do you want to be when you grow up?" he asked again.

"I think this is it." I laughed.

"No, this is just a phase in your life," he said. "There are so many more transitions you're going to have, if you're blessed, before you die."

"Well, why don't you tell me what you want to be when you grow up?" I asked.

"I want to be a dentist." He smiled and flashed his white teeth. There was not another better advertisement. I almost spit up my sausage.

"What?" I laughed without thinking.

"I am serious." He laughed with me. "I am serious. I have always wanted to be a dentist."

"You are a pro athlete making what? Ten figures a year?" I could not stop smiling. "You're telling me you're going to give that up and go to dental school?"

"I can play ten solid years," Dallas explained, "then

go to school while already investing in several dental practices, and when I come out, I will already have a job, 'cause I will own the offices." I had to hand it to him. His plan was solid.

"Why a dentist?" I asked.

"I always look at people's teeth." Dallas put bites of food in the corner of his mouth as he talked. "No matter how great looking or unattractive or scary a person looks, if they have nice teeth, it is somehow always an improvement."

"Wow," I said.

"So what about you?" he prodded. "There must be something you have always wanted to do besides be a doctor."

I giggled at the image my mind conjured up.

"What?" said Dallas.

"It's silly."

"It's not silly if it's your dream," he protested. And I proceeded.

"I always wanted to be a concert pianist."

"Really?" Dallas stopped devouring his toast and looked at me. "Wow. I thought you would say own a business or something."

"Why?"

"I don't know." He scratched his head with his fingers. "Sometimes you can be a little . . . stiff."

"You follow me across the country because I'm stiff?"

"I followed you across the country because you are the most amazing woman I have ever known."

Any anxiety I felt toward his previous comment dissolved once he said that.

"Thank you," I said. "Anyway, I have always wanted to be a pianist."

"Like in the symphony?"

"I figured I would be a solo pianist."

"Did you ever take lessons?" Dallas asked.

I nodded as my mind took me to the beautiful black piano that sat in the corner of Ms. Harper's apartment. It was the biggest thing in the room and took up most of the space in the cramped studio. But it was a gorgeous instrument. STEINWAY was emblazoned in gold across the front, and I always touched it before I sat at the piano.

Ms. Harper was a slight black woman with glasses as big as crystal balls. They made her eyes look like fishbowls. We practiced our scales over and over until I was perfect at them. If my fingers were bent wrong, she would politely maneuver them to the proper position. I loved traveling from our Southside Chicago neighborhood to the Gold Coast, where Ms. Harper lived and worked. She would always have a single cookie for me to munch on after practice. She would regale me with stories about her singing and playing classicial music and jazz with people I'd never heard of at the time: Ella, Duke, Thelonius. I didn't know who those people were, but I knew I wanted to be a pianist just like her when I grew up.

That was until all my extracurricular activities resulted in me getting a B+ in math class. Any grade lower than an A in our household was considered treason. The result was death, or at least being grounded for a month.

"Piano lessons are for A students," my mother said. That was the end of all my other activities. I just continued to excel in school until I could decide what extracurricular activities of my own I wanted to indulge in myself. The funny thing was there was only school and work.

"Hey, are you still with me, Josie?" Dallas's voice brought me back to life.

"Yeah," I said. "I'm here."

"Where did you go?" he asked.

"I just miss playing the piano. That's all," I said.

"That's the good thing about growing up, though, Jos," Dallas said. "You can go back to that piano anytime you want."

"Maybe I will go ahead and take up lessons again." I smiled to myself at the thought of a woman taking up another career, an artistic one to boot, in her thirties.

"I bet you'd be amazing at it," he said.

"You know, you may be right," I said.

"Josie." Dallas slipped his hand over to my side of the table and grabbed my hand. "I bet anything you put your mind to is amazing."

"Thank you, Dallas. I . . ." Before I could react, Dallas had leaned over and kissed my lips. His kiss was different for sure. Not as confident, but sweet and innocent. He didn't explore my upper lip and inside my mouth like Jacques had. He pecked gently, as if asking permission to proceed with further investigations. It felt like a first kiss every time he touched my lips.

"You know I want to be with you, right?" he said.

"I know you do," I began, "but, you see, I had feelings for someone else."

"I don't care about that if you're with me now."

"I . . . It's all so sudden," I said.

"I am willing to go at your pace," Dallas said. "In the end, I just want to be able to see your face for the rest of my life." I looked at this young man, who could have had anyone he wanted in the world, begging me to be at his side. Yet he had chosen me and was willing to wait for me to feel the same way about him.

"Let's go out to dinner tomorrow and take it from there." I smiled back at him.

My new schedule went as follows:

9 a.m.–3 p.m. Work at clinic.

4 p.m.–5 p.m. Call Dallas.

6 p.m.–8 p.m. Have dinner.

8 p.m.–11 p.m. Watch Dallas play on TV. Try to get paperwork done.

11:30 p.m. Either cheer Dallas on if he won a game or try to coax Dallas out of his depression if he lost a game.

For once in my life, I had decided to take Pamela's advice and not let another opportunity slip away. Dallas and I had had our breakfast, which had turned into dinner the following evening, which had turned into nightly phone calls and, finally, a sleepover. That was two months ago. My coworkers were still in shock.

"You landed the most eligible bachelor in the universe," Marcela had said. I guess she was right, Dallas had turned out to be sweet, nurturing, and he was all into me. I never worried about groupies, because he called me on the phone to talk about them.

"These hos is crazy, yo," he would say, and I would

chastise him about calling women hos. Until he would relay what some of the woman had said they want to do to him.

"Oh, they some hos," I would say, and we would fall over laughing.

When he was away, he would send me gifts every week. Anything from a bouquet of lilies to having my car stuffed with teddy bears. Though it took an hour to find the driver's seat, I was still impressed with his efforts. I knew things were heating up when he rented a place in Chicago so he could spend time with me when he had off days. I thought it was a waste of money, since he usually spent the night at my place. But he insisted I have my own personal space, and he didn't want to intrude.

Dallas invited me to a playoff game in New York, which I was very happy about since I hadn't been there since our meeting there. I immediately called Lee up and asked if she wanted to come to the game with me.

"Anything to get away from this smart-ass child," Lee said and laughed. To her credit, Lee was very diplomatic about the Jacques thing. She never mentioned him, and since I didn't either, we maintained a happy friendship, talking about shopping, work, and babies, which I was ready to have if I ever got married.

And then, while changing into some very tight pants in the mirror, I realized that a reality I was trying so hard to ignore was becoming very clear.

It can't be! I yelled to myself in the mirror. *Not now. Not now.* But I knew better. I knew when, suddenly, the same eight glasses of water I normally drank sent me rushing to the bathroom every fifteen minutes. I knew when I stopped having regular bowel movements. And this stomach. Ugh. I wanted to cry, but if other people could live their lives in denial, so could I. I tucked my speculation inside a mental box in my head and decided it was best to wait until I got some sort of positive confirmation.

The stadium was packed, and the Nuggets were down six points. I knew I was going to hear it if he lost, so I made sure he could hear me cheering from my seat, which were conveniently located a few feet behind him. Occasionally, he would turn and smile at me, but mostly he tried to focus on the game. That was good for me, because occasionally, when the games got boring, I would sneak a book in with me to read.

But that was unnecessary that night, because I had Lee there with me.

"Yeah!" Lee cheered on the Knicks.

"You do know they may kick us out of these seats," I said. "This is the Nuggets' side.

"This is New York, sweetie. It's all the Knicks' side." Lee laughed and pushed me.

"Whatever," I said.

"So how are you and Dallas doing?"

"We are doing real good," I said. "He actually is renting a place in Chicago."

"Are you serious?" she gasped. "That is for real."

"Yeah," I said. "Who would have thunk it?"

"Well, you can do a lot worse than to marry an NBA player."

"Nobody said anything about marriage," I said. "See, you are always jumping the gun."

"I am not jumping the gun, but it seems like the next logical step."

"Maybe," I said. "But he is still young, you know. And we are very new."

"He is twenty-five and rich, and knows what he wants."

"Well, I am twenty-seven and am not sure that is where I want to go yet." I winked.

"Twenty-seven." Lee laughed. "Someone made a serious typo on your driver's license."

"Don't think I won't stab you in a public place."

"Not before I stab you," Lee gently poked me in the stomach with her fingers and then drew back her hand. "Girl, um, I say this with love, but you are getting a little thick."

"Oh my God," I screamed. "You noticed that?"

"I did, just because I am an evil bitch and needed something to bring you down with," she said. "But it isn't really noticeable to the untrained eye."

"I don't know what it is," I lied. "I have been hitting the gym and everything. But this little pudge just won't go away."

"You're getting older, honey."

"Must be, 'cause I can't even eat the same things I used to be able to eat anymore."

"Really?" Lee jumped up to cheer as a point guard made a three pointer from the top of the key. "Amazing."

"Yeah, I used to be able to dog out a vegetarian pizza. Now I can't stand cheese, or any dairy, for that matter. I get nauseous."

"That's not good at all," Lee said.

"But I am in love with all fish now. I had like three

whole salmon cakes yesterday, and Dallas called me a fatty."

Lee stopped her cheering for a second. "Wait a minute, girl. Something is not adding up correctly in this scenario."

"What do you mean?" I knew I had let out too many secrets. Lee was too smart not to piece it all together.

"It just sounds like—"

"Sounds like what?"

"Well, you're the doctor, but it sounds like—"

"Nope," I interjected. "Dallas and I always strap up. There is no way."

"Okay, but I am just saying."

"Stop saying it," I said.

"And I really hate to bring this up," Lee said.

"What, girl?"

"And I promised I wouldn't." Lee squirmed in her seat.

"Just spit it out."

"When you were on the island, how many condoms did you have?"

My mouth dropped. She had said the one thing I had been trying to deny to myself this whole time. I couldn't deal with it if it was true. I just couldn't. Suddenly, the lights went dark in the auditorium. A single spotlight hit the center of the court.

"Ladies and gentlemen, we have a special announcement to make," an announcer said over the intercom. "Dallas Sterling of the Denver Nuggets has a question he wants to ask a certain lady in the audience."

Lee pressed her hands over her mouth, and I wanted to ask her what she was screaming for when a flash of light hit me.

"Josie Green, can you please come to center court," the announcer said. I looked like I was about to be run over by a truck. Lee pushed me forward, and I swear, it was only gravity that forced me down the few steps and onto the court. The light was so bright in my eyes, I could only see shadows. A hand grabbed mine and pulled me to the center.

"Josie Green," Dallas said as he kneeled down in front of me, "will you marry me?"

The crowd went silent. I could barely see with the light in my face, but when Dallas opened up a small black box and pushed it in my face, I swear my corneas burst. I was caught on national television with a dilemma on my mind and an offer in my hand. I did what any girl in my predicament would have done.

"Yes," I nodded and began crying. The crowd erupted, and Dallas lifted me in his arms and kissed me in front of about fifty million viewers that night. The rest of the night was a blur. I somehow managed to sit through the rest of the game and put Lee in a cab. She only agreed to leave if I promised to call her the next day.

I took a cab back to Dallas's hotel and sat on the bed and stared at the mountain of a ring on my finger. I didn't know how many carats it was, but I did know it was almost as big as my knuckle and weighed on my finger like a brick.

My cell phone was ringing off the hook, but I didn't have the energy to pick it up. I knew it was either Lee, Pamela, or the ladies at work. I felt weird with the ring on, having only discussed my issue just a few hours before. I needed to be sure of a couple of things before I did anything else. I took the elevator downstairs and ran across the street to the local Duane

Reade. I couldn't afford for the people in the hotel to see what I was purchasing.

I made my buy and scurried back to the hotel room. I went into the bathroom and took the test so many women my age prayed they didn't have to take unless they had a ring on their finger. I had the ring, and I still didn't want to take the damn test.

I paced back and forth, praying that I was misinformed or crazy. I mean, I was a gynecologist. I couldn't have been that stupid as to miss my own diagnosis.

I looked at my watch, and the three minutes were up. I hated even thinking about the idea of having to look at this damn stick, but it had to be done. I picked it up and closed my eyes. Flashes I hadn't seen in months entered my head again.

Shit! I yelled to myself. I opened my eyes. There it was in black and white, stained with my own urine. Pregnant.

The bathroom door opened as I was holding the stick in my hand. "Hey, baby, are you in here . . . ?" called Dallas. He grinned from ear to ear. "What you doing in here?"

"Nothing." I hid the stick behind my back.

"What is that?" He ran up to me and grabbed my arm before I could toss the evidence. "What you hiding from me?" He looked at the stick and then read the words. He was stoic for a moment, and then he wrapped his big arms around me.

"You have made me the happiest man in the world tonight. Do you know that?"

I was a wreck that night, but one thing I knew for sure was we had to make love like we never had before or Dallas would know something was up. So I worked him out. Whatever he wanted, I supplied, and he did so in return.

"I love you, baby," he kept whispering in my ear.

"I love you, too," I whispered back louder. I did love him. And I was going to be damned if a pregnancy was going to ruin that.

That night, when Dallas was asleep, I grabbed my cell phone and went into the bathroom.

"I knew you were going to call," Lee said, sounding a little groggy.

"Did I wake you?"

"It doesn't matter," she said. "I will wake up for details like this."

"I'm pregnant," I said.

"Oh my God, congratulations," Lee said.

"I didn't just graduate from high school, honey. I said I am pregnant, and that causes a bit of a dilemma for me timing wise."

"I know it is shaky," Lee said. "So what are you going to do?"

"I have no idea," I said. "I am usually lecturing my patients about situations like this."

"Well, what do you tell them?" Lee asked.

"To get a DNA test," I said.

"Well, why don't you do that?"

"I cannot go into the other room and ask the man who gave me an engagement ring the size of a compact car to take a paternity test to see if the baby he wants so bad is his." I shook my head. This was a complete *Tyra Banks Show* kind of nightmare.

"Well, there is another option," Lee said.

"Suicide." I laughed.

"You can have the third party take the test."

"Oh, it's official," I said. "You are nuts. Do you

know how long it took me to get that person off my mind?"

"I'm guessing about three months," Lee deadpanned.

"Cute, girl, real cute."

"I think it is the only way not to make this into a media disaster."

"I wouldn't even know where to look for him."

"You do know he is my brother-in-law."

"I am vulnerable, Lee," I whined. "Please have mercy on me."

"I'll have mercy next week. This week you need answers."

She was right. The only way to deal with this was to meet him and get it over with. "Set it up."

"I'll call tomorrow with details," Lee said. "And, Josie, it'll be all right."

"Somehow I can never quite believe that statement," I said and got off the phone, praying Dallas hadn't heard me.

Chapter 35

The next day in the hotel, after eating breakfast and seeing Dallas off, who had to play in New Jersey that evening, I got dressed, and headed to the Brooklyn Zoo. That was where I was supposed to meet Jacques.

I arrived early, hoping to be the first one there, so I could determine whether or not this was a good idea before he got close enough to recognize me. If I felt weird, I could just duck behind the monkey bars and make a dash for freedom. I asked Lee to arrange it so I wouldn't have to talk to him on the phone. I was nervous enough as it was. I didn't need the prospect of an awkward phone conversation.

The zoo had few visitors that morning, and I got a good view of both paths that led to the monkey cage. I had a crumpled-up piece of paper from which I rehearsed the few lines I wanted to say.

Hey, Jacques. How have you been? You look great. (Wait for his response.) It's been a while. I wanted to talk to you about a kind of serious matter. Well, it looks like I am pregnant, and better still, I don't know who my baby's Daddy is. To avoid going on any talk show and finding this infor-

mation out, I was hoping you would be so kind as to take a paternity test so I could figure out whom to wrangle for child support. (Keep it light, funny, and simple.) No, I don't expect you to be in the child's life if you are the father. I am happy now, and I can provide for the baby quite well on my own. Just need to know.

I was mouthing the words to myself when a pair of hands covered my eyes. I swear, my heart stopped. I could smell him on my skin. *Pull it together.* I gently broke away and turned around.

"Josie Green," Jacques said as he softly kissed my cheek. He pulled back to look at me, and that's when I caught a glimpse of him. Jesus, how was it possible for this man to look even better than he had? He was cleaned up, with a European suit that hugged his tall, muscular frame. He had a freshly trimmed five-o'clock shadow and designer glasses. He looked liked an actor portraying himself in a movie—a movie entitled *Josie and Her Many Handsome Mistakes.*

"Hey," I said, stepping back and trying to give myself a bit of breathing room. We hugged, and I forced myself to let go again.

"Wow," Jacques said. "I guess it would be cliché to say it's been a long time, but it really has been."

"I know," I said. "How have you been?" Geez, I was going way off script.

"I'm okay," he said. "I went back to England for a while but found some different work here in the States. Teaching, actually."

"Really?"

"Yeah, I am teaching English to French students." He smiled that smile that always got me.

"That is great," I said. "But how were you able to get a teaching job with an alias?"

"I am able to use my real name now."

"Why?" I was so curious as to why we had done so much lying for this man a few months ago, only for him to just grab a teaching job at a school all out in the open.

"Liz's parents dropped all charges against me after she died."

"Wait." I threw my hands up. "She died? When?"

"Shortly after I left the hospital in Palau," he said nonchalantly. I wanted to crack his skull. How could he have kept such information from me? Then again I had walked out of our drama-filled relationship.

"My God," I said. "So they forgave you for what happened?"

"I think they knew it was time to let her go," he said. "And when she was gone, there was no real reason to carry a grudge against me anymore."

"Well, I am glad you were able to get your identity back."

"I am, too," Jacques said. "But I am even happier to see you."

I was not able to crumble. I just wanted to get a little information and be on my way. But so many questions kept popping up. "So how are the seizures?"

"I went to several doctors here in the States, and no one could see anything in the charts and X-rays, until I met Dr. Garrison. He didn't check for tumors and such. He did some other tests, which showed I had undergone some slight brain damage, probably from all the beatings I took as a kid."

"Oh my God," I said.

"Yeah, it was crazy, but he also told me of an untested medicine that helps to regenerate tissue, and so far it has had a tremendous affect on the seizures.

I haven't had one since I started on my new meds."
Jacques was smiling, and I was trying not to react.

"That is good."

"God, I missed you," Jacques blurted out, as if he
had been cradling the sentence on his tongue all day.

"Thanks," I knew I was blushing but ignored it.
"Yeah, I uh . . ."

"I missed you."

"I . . ."

"I wanted to call you so many times," Jacques said.
"But I will admit, I was a coward."

"Jacques, I have to say something," I said.

"So do I." Jacques grabbed my hands and held
them in his. He was about to start when he noticed
my ring on my hand.

"Jesus," he said. "What is that?"

"What?"

"Is that a ring or a doorknob?" I let out the fakest
laugh known to man. It was all high-pitched and
squeaky. Very unbecoming.

"Yeah, I'm engaged," I said.

"Oh," he said and pulled back a little.

I prodded him forward. "Go ahead. Finish your
thoughts."

"Wow." He gasped for air. "I kind of . . . forgot what
I was going to say."

"No, you didn't."

"Yeah." Jacques was turning pale.

"Just say it."

"Who's the lucky bloke?"

Here was the part where I got caught up. Now I was
pale and speechless. "Dallas."

"What?" Jacques said. "The wanker from the
island?"

"He's not a wanker, whatever that is," I said.

"So you two really were carrying on back then, too?"

"Of course not."

"Well, you're going to marry him," he said. "Something must have happened."

"Yeah, he stuck it out with me," I said. "Something you never seemed to be able to do. Lee didn't tell you this?"

"She refused to talk about you. Said it would interfere with her friendship if she did."

"We started dating shortly after I got back."

"Wow." Jacques turned around. "This wasn't what I expected at all."

"Well, it certainly wasn't what I expected at all, either," I spat back. "And here is another unexpected gem. I'm pregnant. And I think it may be yours."

Chapter 36

Maybe it was because he cried when I told him I was pregnant. Maybe it was because I cried when he kissed me. Either way we ended up in the back hallway of the monkey exhibit, making out for thirty minutes. It felt so good; I almost forgot I had a new life. But that is the thing about an engagement ring. It reminds you rather quickly of your obligations, especially when it is the size of a tennis ball.

"Stop," I moaned.

"Why?" He kept kissing my neck. I finally pushed him away.

"See, this is what we do," I said.

"What? Have passion?" Jacques rubbed the back of his neck.

"Sex and silence are not passion," I said. "That is sad. We are not in a relationship. We never were. I know this because I am in a relationship with someone who engages me, talks to me, and listens to me. He calls me and pays attention to me. He isn't afraid to say I love you. In fact, he isn't afraid to marry me."

"Josie," Jacques started. "I had some complications."

"Oh, there is always some excuse, honey," I said. "Your dead wife, your alive wife, your fake identity, your prison record. Jesus, I am just sick of it."

"Do you think I wanted to fall in love with you or with anyone else?" Jacques said. He sat down on the steps. "I was content living out my life alone. But then I found you. And, believe me, I know I resisted showing you how I really feel about you."

"But here is the thing, Jacques." I attempted to button up my shirt. God, I felt so dirty and stupid. "You had time to show me you love me. I know you say you love me. But you never show me. It's love on your terms."

"What the hell does that mean?"

"I mean, it's love when we're having sex, or are alone on an island, with no accountability. But the second you have to enter the real world, you close off."

"So you run to the NBA player," Jacques shouted.

"That is not fair, and you know it," I said. "This is not about Dallas."

"Well, he has something to do with it since he is your fiancé."

"He was there for me. He loves me."

"Then why did you even agree to meet me?" Jacques's hands were flying everywhere. I was afraid he might hit me. Not on purpose, but owing to his flailing hands.

"Because I am pregnant, and I need to know whose child it is," I said.

"Why?" Jacques continued his line of questioning. "I mean, you have already made up your mind that you are going to be with him, right?"

"Yes, I have."

"Then why come here and meet me?" He slapped his hand on his head. "The bloke doesn't know it's my baby."

"We do not know if it's your baby," I yelled. "That is why I need you to take the test."

"But he is right there. You could have found out the same results just by having him take the test."

"Yes," I said. "But I don't want him to know until I know, okay."

"Why?" Jacques asked.

"Because I am embarrassed," I screamed. I was sure the monkeys in the cage were filing a noise complaint as we spoke.

"You're embarrassed of us?"

"You pushed me away," I said. "You have a wife, and you didn't even tell me."

"But you're here now," Jacques said. "You must be here for a reason."

"I just need to be prepared, is all," I said. "So can you just take the test?"

"What if it is mine?"

"It isn't."

"What if it is?" he said. "Will you tell him then?"

"I don't know," I said and meant it. "It's complicated."

"So it's okay for your situation to be complicated, but I'm just a liar."

"I'm not saying that."

"You might as well have."

"Jacques," I said. "He already thinks it's his. I couldn't tell him I have doubts about it now."

"Wow. I see why we got along so well," Jacques

fumed. "Everything you called me you are yourself—a liar, a coward, and a sneak."

"I am not. I just don't want to hurt him."

"You think sneaking around a zoo, kissing me, won't hurt him?"

"I didn't set out to do that," I tried to explain, but I was getting flustered.

"I didn't mean to do anything I did to you, either, Josie," Jacques said. "I just wanted to love you. I really did."

"So when your wife died, why didn't you come find me?"

Jacque slammed his hand against the door. It made a banging sound. He startled me.

"I wanted to. I did," Jacques said. "But I just thought I was such a fucking mess. I didn't want to make your life any worse off than I already had. I mean, you lied for me, you saved my life, and I couldn't give you the one thing you wanted. The one thing I wanted."

"It's all a mess now, Jacques," I said. "But I just don't know if we can clean it up."

"Of course, we can," he said.

"Just take the test," I said.

"If it's my child, I want to be in its life."

"How is that even possible?"

"Because we will be a family," Jacques said.

I shook my head, then gathered my coat and bag. "Jacques, I already have a family waiting for me at home." Before he could react, I walked away. I had planned to put him out of my life for good, but before I reached the exit, he grabbed me. He started kissing me again. I felt his hot lips on mine. I felt his hand press against the small of my back as he drew me to him. This was wrong. I knew it. But I succumbed, anyway.

I felt like a complete whore. I had been spending more time in hotels with men than even the most active prostitute. I couldn't believe I slept with Jacques. I glanced over and saw him snoring softly into his pillow. I gathered my clothes, which were sprawled on the floor, with purposeful abandon and crept into the bathroom. Not three months ago, I'd been a borderline bitter single woman jilted by love. Now I was the one hurting people. Was it really that easy to jeopardize a relationship? Within minutes what was supposed to have been my good-bye turned into a love triangle, where someone was bound to get hurt.

I fumbled in the bathroom to put back on my clothes. Suddenly, I heard my phone vibrate. I looked in my purse and pulled it out. Shit. It was Dallas. I threw the phone back in my purse and continued to get dressed, feeling more guilty by the second. First, I'd cheated on him; now I was ignoring his phone call. I could have answered the phone, but what would I have said? What if Jacques woke up and called out to me? Suddenly, all the actions I deemed sneaky by men came into focus. Yes, on the surface, self-preservation was the main motive for my actions. But there was also a need to protect the other person from a truth I felt too ashamed to face.

After I was fully dressed, I tried to make it to the door without disturbing Jacques. But he was roused.

"Hey, love." Jacques looked at me, eyes squinting. "Hey, where are you going?"

"Back where I belong, Jacques," I said.

"Are you serious?" He stood up in the bed. "After everything we went through today."

"What did we go through, Jacques?" I asked. "We just had sex."

"You are carrying my child," he said. "And I want to be with you."

"I am already with someone else," I said. "And we don't know if it's your child."

"It's not his," Jacques rose from the bed and fiddled with his pants. "Look, just come back to bed. Let's calmly think of a way out of this situation."

"I already have," I said. "I am going back to the man who has given everything to make sure I am with him. I am going back to the man who would die for me, not for his former wife or his own selfish issues. But for me."

"Things are different," Jacques said. "And you know that."

"How are they different?"

"I am not married," he said. "I am free to choose who to love."

"You had a choice back then," I yelled.

"I had a wife," Jacques said.

"It didn't stop you from having sex with me on the island. It didn't stop you from holding me and making me believe we had a chance together."

"That's not fair," he said. "You know I love you."

"Loving me and being with me are two different things," I said. "I have a man who will do both."

"I am ready." Jacques ran to me. "I am here now. I know I made mistakes. But can't we start over?"

I looked at Jacques. His eyes were fixed on mine. "I already started over, Jacques. I can't go back now.

Maybe our time was only on that island. Maybe it could only survive in a vacuum."

"You are being dramatic," he said.

"I am being real," I said. "I don't want to see you again."

"Josie." His eyes began to water. "Please don't say that. I can't hear you say that."

"It's done, Jacques," I said and walked out. Jacques didn't follow me. I walked slowly to the elevator, then through the lobby, and got into a cab. Once inside I dialed Dallas's number.

"Hey, baby girl," Dallas said. "How is your day?"

"Fine," I said, trying to appear upbeat on the phone. "How was yours?"

"Practice was brutal, as always," he said. "And I have a commercial I have to memorize lines for, but other than that, it's all good. Can't wait to see you."

"Can't wait to see you, too," I said. "See you tonight."

"Bye, babe," he said, and we disconnected. When I arrived at our hotel, I almost sprinted up the stairs to the suite. I peeled off my clothes and jumped in the shower. I worked every inch of my body with the loofah sponge, trying to rid myself of any scent reminiscent of Jacques. I scrubbed so hard, I felt my skin ache, but I kept going, every once and a while letting the water wash away the soap, dirt, and shame that covered my body.

When I felt semiclean, I got out of the shower and gathered all my clothes and put them in a plastic bag. I walked over to the desk in front of the bed and picked up the phone.

"W Hotel," a voice announced. "How may I assist you, Mr. Sterling?"

"Oh, it's not." I stumbled for the right words. "I have some trash that needs to be picked up immediately."

"Right away, ma'am," the voice said. "Is there anything else we can get for you?"

I stood, with the phone cradled between my ear and shoulder. As fancy as this hotel was, with its laundry service and gourmet strawberries delivered twenty-four hours a day, I was sure they didn't sell clear consciences in the gift shop.

"No, I think that will be all I need for today," I said and hung up the phone.

Dear Diary/Journal/ROCK/GOD,

Am I just that stupid, or am I just looking to punish myself? I cannot believe I slept with Jacques after everything I did to get him out of my life. I just don't understand my problem. Of course, it was good. It's always good. In fact, he is by far the best lover I have ever had. And the most tender. But is that the point? I have made a commitment to a man I love, and I am not going to keep getting jerked around.

When I got back to the hotel, I could hardly look at Dallas. I could tell by his eyes he was concerned. But I just felt so dirty. When Dallas left this morning, I had to get out of the hotel. I got dressed and walked the entire length of Central Park. I tried to clear my mind and focus on nothing, but that damn Jacques just kept creeping back in my mind. I cannot mess this thing up with Dallas. He is good for me. He loves me and obviously has consistently tried to be there for me. I would be playing myself for even thinking about Jacques. But every time I think of those lips or the way he says I love you, I am a goner. My mother says I will never be happy. Maybe she is right. Maybe I will nitpick and overana-

lyze my way out of every relationship I ever have. Maybe I will die alone, not because men didn't love me, but because I didn't have what it takes to fully love them back. Dallas is waiting for me to give it all to him, and I am holding back. Meanwhile, Jacques rations off his love like it is food on a deserted . . . bad analogy.

My point is, I can't keep playing games and expecting them to keep holding on. I am dedicated to Dallas, and that is who I need to be with.

I stopped writing and looked back at the last several journal entries. I thought this damn thing was supposed to be therapeutic. All I ended up doing was rehashing the same questions and emotions in my mind. And it all boiled down to a love of the heart or a love that endures.

Chapter 37

Clearly, my friends and family had been preparing for a wedding for a long time. When I mentioned I wanted to speed up the ceremony, they were right there with a strategic plan, including color swatches and contact names.

"How long have you had these bridal books?" I asked my mom, who was unpacking stacks of material from a little black suitcase. I had decided to have a little girls' weekend in Chicago, where we could all plan this wedding and have a couple of drinks in the meantime. Ruby, Gladys, and Marcela were just a few miles away, but I had to pick Lee and Pamela up from the airport. By the time I got home, Marcela already had the vodka and cranberry drinks mixed and the music blasting. I expected Pamela, a reformed sinner some two years ago and now a devoted Christian, to cause a stink about John Legend playing in the background. Instead, when she heard the music, she yelled, "Whoa, that is my song," and started gyrating her hips clockwise, leaving the entire room on the floor, laughing.

"Since when did you start listening to John Legend?" I asked.

"There is a lot you don't know about me, young lady," Pamela replied and continued dancing. She took a drink from Marcela, who giggled when Pamela gulped down the majority of it before the second verse of the song came on.

"I am just so happy my baby is finally getting married," Pamela shouted. "I have been praying for this for so long."

"All right, Mom," I said. I patted her on her shoulders, hoping to guide her to a seat on the couch.

"Ya'll just don't understand," Pamela said. "She had flocks of men always coming to our doorstep, trying to woo her. But she thought she was too good for everyone."

"I did not," I protested.

"Yes, you did," Pamela countered. "Your father put that madness in your head, and you been stuck-up ever since. But, finally, it took an NBA player to win you over."

"It's not because he's an NBA star," I said. "It's because he's sweet and caring, and a big, cuddly bear."

"And rich," Lee mumbled. I threw a pillow at her.

"And fine," Marcela said and tipped her glass.

"And young," Gladys said. "I am just putting it out there. Ya'll are both in your prime. So I can imagine. . . ."

"All right, and so ends the raunchy bachelorette section of this party," I said.

"Damn," Dallas said as he busted through the door. He brought along a couple of basketball players behind him. "I missed all the nasty talk."

"There was no nasty talk," I said. Dallas came over to me and kissed me hard. He touched my belly, and I immediately pulled back.

"We haven't gone there yet with the group," I tried to whisper as softly as possible.

"Oh, my bad," he said and bent down and kissed me again. "You are so beautiful." His smile was infectious. "Can we use the flat screen in the bedroom to go over these practice DVDs?"

"Please. No feet on my comforter," I said.

"That was one time. Damn," Dallas said.

"And an eighty-dollar cleaning bill," I said.

"You know I got you, Shawdy," said Dallas. It was amazing I was a grown woman being called Shorty and reminding my future husband to keep his humongous feet off my comforter. But I loved it. It felt real and safe, and the consistency he provided was reassuring. I only thought of my other life every so often.

"So it was a pleasure as always, ladies," Dallas said. "Come on, fellas." One of Dallas's friends could not take his eyes off Lee. He stared so hard, he bumped right into the bedroom wall. Everyone fell over laughing. Lee lifted her left hand and said, "Sorry, baby. You're about ten years too late."

"Or you were ten years too early," Marcela said and smacked her lips. "Goddamn, he was fine."

"The fine ones are always the most trouble," I added.

"Mmm," said Marcela. She sucked on her tongue, grossing me out in the process. "Well, I would like to find out how much trouble I could get in with that one."

"You are so nasty, girl," Ruby, who was silently sipping drinks until now, interjected. "You need to calm your hot ass down."

"She's just young and experiencing life," Pamela said. That surprised me. Pam was always too worried about me experiencing life, namely, getting knocked up and embarrassing the family, to let me get away with anything. Little did she know.

"All I have to say is, do whatever it is you want to do in life. Just make sure you are happy," said Lee. She stepped over to me. "Now Josie here is happy. She has the perfect man, the perfect job, and the perfect life. But most importantly, she is happy, right?"

Lee looked at me; I could see her smirk a mile away. If I could have kicked her in her shin, I would have. But I had to face her shit-eating grin and bear her secret chiding of my relationship. But, most importantly, I had to give the right answer.

"I am happier than I have ever been in my whole life," I said.

"Then that is all that really matters," Lee said. "Then let's make a toast." Everyone scrambled for a glass. I rolled my eyes at Lee, who seemed to be enjoying herself too much.

"You're cute," I whispered. She smiled and continued.

"To Josie and Dallas," Lee said. "Her one and only true love. May they be happy and have lots of babies together." She stressed the word *together*, and I thought I would faint. Of course, no one caught it, and everyone cheered and clicked their glasses and drank way more than they should have, but I was mortified.

"You are a real shady bitch," I whispered to Lee.

"Hey, If you're happy, I'm happy."

"I am telling you for the thousandth time, I am happy," I said.

"Funny. Guess I don't know why I still don't believe you." Lee walked away.

Chapter 38

"So let me know first if this is going to be a fabulous or a ghetto fabulous wedding," said Anne Hatcher. She was sitting behind her desk. Her black Donna Karan suit was fitted around her slight figure. She kept brushing her hair behind her ear, a trait I found annoying as our meeting progressed. Everyone had said she was the best wedding planner in the business. They'd also said she was the most irritating soul you could ever come across. But she was professional and worked fast, and that's what we needed.

"Excuse me?" I couldn't help but blurt out. I felt Pamela's hand cover mine.

"Look, ladies," Anne said. "I have covered all kinds of celebrity weddings. My client lists have had all kinds of actors, two MVPs, a record label president, and a hotel mogul. And I can deliver whatever you want, but I need to know if it will be ghetto, 'cause then I will need to hire security, and I'll want my money up front."

"We are aware of your work," Pamela interjected.

"And we're looking forward to working with you. And we want tasteful but fabulous. No ghetto necessary."

"Okay then," Anne said. "How soon do you want this wedding?"

"Three weeks," I said, hoping she would say, "Hell no," and we could leave.

"All right," Anne said as she slid back in her chair and looked at her computer. She pecked at the keyboard with her fingers, then sighed and turned back to us. "I charge a flat rate of fifty thousand dollars for rush jobs."

"Are you kidding?" I yelled.

"At this late stage in the game, most places are going to say no to you, unless my name is attached," Anne said. "And, unfortunately, because your soon-to-be husband is a ballplayer, there will be even more apprehension when booking venues."

"Why?" I said.

"Because they think black people tear shit up," said Anne.

"That's ridiculous," I protested.

"Hey, I am just telling you what vendors tell me," said Anne. "So if I am walking you in, I gotta make sure I get my money."

"That's fine," Pamela said.

"You will also be required to put down an additional fifty thousand as a refundable deposit for a half-million-dollar insurance claim," Anne said while scribbling something in her planner. She didn't even look up at us.

"Am I being *punked*?" I said as I looked around for hidden cameras.

"When you marry into the big time, Dr. Green, there are big-time expenses," Anne said.

"Josie," said Pamela as she looked at me. "Dallas said he didn't care about the cost."

"Well, I do," I said. I felt the heat pulsing on my face.

Pamela looked at Anne, who had pulled out a compact and was checking the beautifully subtle yet vibrant highlights in her hair. "Can we have a moment to discuss?"

"No problem," said Anne. She grabbed her purse and cell phone and headed into the other room. My head snapped back to Pamela before the door could fully close.

"No way," I said.

"Josie." Pamela had a pleading tone in her voice.

"It's just insane to pay that amount of money for a wedding," I said.

"Hear me out," Pamela said. "I agree with you. Your average person would be bankrupt paying for something like that. But you and Dallas are not average. You could pay for this whole thing and not blink an eye."

"That is because I would never pay that much for a wedding," I snapped back.

"Well, you tell me what's worth that much."

"A house," I said.

"Your husband's already buying that."

"A college education."

Pamela shook her head. "I am sure you already have enough money stashed away for five of your kids to go to Ivy League schools and not have to worry about a thing." Actually, I had only saved enough for three of my future kids.

"What is your point, Mom?" I said.

"The point is sometimes in life you have to splurge

a little." She grabbed my hands. "And you, my dear, owe it to yourself to splurge a little. Just this once."

"Fifty grand just on a wedding planner?"

"This is a moment you will never forget," Pamela said. "Would you like to remember china and rose petals, or plastic cups and paper towels?"

"Ugh," I screamed.

"Just this once, enjoy yourself and let her take care of everything."

"Okay," I said.

"Great," said Anne as she walked back in with contracts in hand. She obviously knew the persuasive power of my mother. "Let's get this party moving."

"Okay," I said and opened my purse.

"Oh, and we don't take checks," Anne said. "Sorry." I slammed my platinum card on the desk and made a note to add *hit man* to the list of things to go on the bridal registry.

With Anne's leadership, the wedding plans came together quickly. We were able to book a chapel, purchase a dress and tuxedos, and pick and send out invitations in two days. I guess it didn't hurt that Dallas was willing to fork over any amount to get things done. So with the wedding planned, all that was left was to fight over where we were going to live. This had been our only source of stress since our relationship started. Dallas was already traveling the country to play basketball. He didn't want to have to keep traveling to Chicago if he couldn't get traded there. He wanted me to spend time with him.

I, of course, had a practice to think about. I had already cut back hours since we started dating because

I wanted to put aside some time for my man. But my patients needed me, and Chicago was my home. We had been skipping past the argument for weeks. But I could tell, with nothing else to discuss, it was going to come to a head. We sat at the dinner table, a rarity for us, the Monday after I sent my mom and friends home.

"Wow, this chicken is amazing," I said and thumbed my approval at Dallas, who had decided he wanted to cook. A consummate Southern boy, he was not only a way better cook than I was, he actually kept the house cleaner and more organized, too.

"Thank you, babe," he said. "When we are chilling in our new home in Denver, I'll cook for you every night."

"You bought a new house?"

"I was thinking about getting a new one so we could have a fresh start."

"You weren't going to consult with me?" I asked. The thing about being with a millionaire is their impulse buys are way more extravagant than an average person's. But could I get mad because he bought what was tantamount to a nice pair of shoes for my budget?

"Yeah, I was," he said. But I knew he was lying. When he set his mind on something, he just got it. "I would want you to come check it out."

"We haven't even finished the relocation issue."

"Baby, I have talked to my people about being traded to Chicago, and they suck right now. But it would not work. They have no one to offer my team."

"And I told you I have a clinic to run."

Dallas stood up and came behind me. He started massaging my neck and shoulders.

"Okay, I have an idea," he said.

"Oh Lawd," I moaned.

"That is not fair," he whined. "I have had some good ideas."

"Like frozen chicken wings on a stick?"

"That would have been a great franchise."

"Until all your customers contracted salmonella poisoning."

"I told you they were supposed to cook it first," Dallas huffed.

"Go on, baby," I said. I didn't want him getting distracted and going on a rant. He kissed my head and continued.

"Anyway, how about you still keep your clinic here but ask another doctor to handle the practice here and you open one in Denver? That way more people are served, and you can make sure they get the quality care they deserve."

Damn. His plan made sense. Shit. It was actually good. "Well, it's kind of expensive to start another practice, Dallas.

"Boo, I got you," he said.

"I don't want to just depend on your money."

"It's our money, babe," he corrected me. And I had to admit, thinking I had twenty-seven million in the bank instead of seven thousand dollars sure made me feel a lot better.

"Well, look at you." I smiled. "You thought of everything."

"I told you I got you." He smiled.

"So it's only until you get traded to a better team, to a better location, preferably Chicago?"

"Yes, yes." He moved around and grabbed me. "So you cool with it?"

I sighed. My last bit of resistance was gone. "Yes."

"Whew," Dallas yelled and threw his fist in the air like he'd won a championship ring.

"Me, you, and baby are gone be so happy in Denver," he said. "They have a whole bunch of cultural stuff, like museums and galleries."

"I'm sure."

"Hey, I was thinking about baby names." Wow. This guy was on a roll. Since he'd won one argument, I guess he decided to try to take advantage of the situation.

"Amber if it's a girl and Adrian if it's a boy."

"Your parents' names," I said.

"Yeah, I always liked them."

"They are kind of old school."

"Hey, girl, I am kind of old school. Hell, you are old school."

"Watch yourself, little boy."

"I am just saying there is nothing wrong with traditional names."

"I guess not."

"What do you want to name them? Stick or Morpheus or something?"

"Cute."

"That is me, girl. Always cute." He kissed my cheek as I pretended to move away.

"I was thinking Oscar or Philip if it's a boy, and Cheyenne or Spirit if it's a girl."

"Spirit." Dallas laughed.

"What is wrong with Spirit?" I asked.

"I don't want to invite no ghosts or shit in my house."

"It's a name of a child."

"It's the name of a demon. And I am not bringing no old spirits into my life."

"Okay, okay," I said. "No Spirit."

"Cool."

"How about Beelzebub?" I teased, and he chased me around the dinner table. "I am joking. I'm joking."

"I cannot wait to spend the rest of my life with you, girl."

"Me, too." I smiled and hugged him tight. That night we made love and fell asleep on the floor. I dreamed a spirit was chasing me. Little did I know how prophetic that dream would become.

Chapter 39

If the wedding was the main event, the rehearsal dinner was definitely a dry run. I was more than a little nervous. Not only was I afraid my growing stomach was starting to show (Lee assured me it wasn't), but I also had to meet Dallas's family whom he described as "music video ghetto fabulous." The good news at least was we were having the wedding in Chicago. Dallas might have won the relocation battle, but I had won the wedding location war. We were having it in Chicago, and that was nonnegotiable.

I was looking forward to seeing my dad again. He was so happy I was getting married, he volunteered to pay for the wedding. I declined the offer but said he could make a donation to the clinic instead. I also invited Andrew, whom I haven't seen in months, and his partner. Thankfully, Andrew had been cleared of any charges. Lee had told me he quit his job. There were so many people I wanted to meet and get reacquainted with.

Dallas and I arrived late and hurried into the dining area of the Astoria Palace, where we also planned to have the reception. The dining area was downstairs, in a beautiful space with a marble floor and a gold-trimmed ceiling; the upstairs was more conservative, with deep red runners and velvet drapes.

We walked into the lobby and were greeted by Francis and Lee.

"Josie," Francis said and hugged me hard. "It's so good to see you."

"You, too, Francis," I said. "What have you been up to all these months?"

"Well, I am actually thinking about writing a novel about our little adventure," he said. I rolled my eyes.

"You can relive that all you want. I really am not trying to experience that again. Not even in paperback," I said.

"I thought I wouldn't, either, until my publisher showed me the advance check." We all chuckled, and I thought, *Great. Now everyone is going to get rich off my misery.*

"Hey, Dallas," said Lee. She hugged him and then pointed down the hall. "I think your parents are looking for you."

"Cool," said Dallas as he rubbed his hands together. "Let me see how Mom and Pops are doing." He walked away, and I immediately sidled up to Lee.

"What do they look like?" I asked.

Lee moved close to my ear and whispered, "I won't spoil it for you. But I will say, I can't wait to see what they gave you for a wedding present." Lee snapped back into bougie princess mode. "All right, girl. We're going to raid the shrimp table, so don't be long before you get to that toast, sweetheart. We are old folks here."

"We'll hurry along just for you," I said.

"Josie," Dallas called, and I turned around to see him towering over what had to be what was left of MC Hammer's entourage before he went broke. Mrs. Sterling had on a gold, shimmering dress with matching bonnet. Her blond-streaked hair cascaded all the way down her back, which turned out to be a good thing since her dress stopped mid-thigh. Luckily, her knee-high boots covered up most of her legs. Mr. Sterling was equally stunning in his ruby red velvet suit with matching fedora. His pimp cane was politely tucked under his arm, and his red gators shined so much, the ceiling lights reflected in them.

"Damn," said Mr. Sterling. He immediately grabbed me in his big dry hands. His palms were so ashy, they pulled at the fabric on my cotton sweater. "Dis girl right here is fine."

"Thank you," I smiled.

"Give me some sugar," he said. He had me in a hand vice, and I felt my breath leaving me.

"Let that girl go," Mrs. Sterling said. She pried his hands off me. I looked up at Dallas, who was covering his mouth. But I could see tears falling from his eyes.

"Let me look at you," Mrs. Sterling said matter-of-factly. She put her hands on my shoulders and looked me up and down. "You got a little white girl figure," she said, so loud people down the hall looked our way. "You need some food if you expect to have one of him come out of you." She pointed to Dallas, and I was mortified. She clicked her tongue against her soft palete. "Yeah, when this baby come, I'm gone have to at least spend a few months getting you fit to feed it."

"Yeah, baby like his milk," said Mr. Sterling, displaying his armory of gold and platinum teeth.

"Daddy," Dallas yelled. "That is so nasty."

"It's all right," I said and waved my hand in a dismissive fashion. But I was secretly wishing I had magical powers to whisk myself away from this whole conversation.

"Your hair is so short, girl," Mrs. Sterling said. "Why don't I give you the number to my stylist? She lives in Houston, but ya'll got money. You can fly her here."

Why don't I give you the number to a psychiatrist? "Thank you, Mrs. Sterling," I said. I smiled and looked into the crowd for anyone to save me. I found him.

"If you'll excuse," I said, already walking off. "I see an old friend I don't want to let go."

"That's all good, baby," said Mrs. Sterling as she waved her acrylic nails. "We'll be right here."

"I'm sure you will," I mumbled as I ran toward Andrew, who was standing next to a very handsome man. It was obvious they were trying not to hold hands.

"Andrew," I almost screamed. We hugged, and I moved my mouth to his ear. "Save me! In-laws."

"Ugh," Andrew's friend said. "I hated Andrew's for years."

"I cannot believe you went there with a total stranger," said Andrew.

"You know her," Andrew's friend said. "And if you met his mother, you would feel the same way."

"Josie," I said and extended my hand.

"Brian," Andrew's friend said and gave me a big bear hug. "And the gays hug. Mostly 'cause our fathers never showed us affection."

"Okay," I said and laughed.

"That's my little comedian," Andrew said.

"Well, you can do a three-hour show if it will keep

me away from them," I said, looking in the direction I'd come from. "Don't look."

"Who? Solid gold and dolomite?" Brian said.

"Brian," Andrew said and frowned at him.

"He's right. They were in a black exploitation film at some point in their life," I joked. We all laughed. "So I hear you quit the flying business," I said to Andrew.

"Yeah." He sighed. "Even though I was acquitted, the airline didn't like all the negative publicity, so they offered me real early retirement."

"Was it at least a nice offer?" I asked.

"We bought two Ducatis and a Porsche Cayenne last month," said Brian. He lifted his hand high, and we had an impromptu high five.

"Wow. I can't wait to retire," I said.

"Uh, Josie," Andrew smirked. "I don't think you need to work now."

"I pull my own weight," I said and folded my arms over one another. "I am an independent woman."

"Well, you do it, Beyoncé," Brian said. "But if this one here made that much money, I would be lying in the living room, getting fat by the second."

"He ain't playing," Andrew teased. "He is already getting a little thick."

Brian punched Andrew. They were so cute together. "You may have to book a wedding and a funeral tomorrow," quipped Brian.

"I am just so glad you could come," I said.

"Wouldn't miss it," said Andrew. He smiled and hugged me again.

"All right, everyone," Pamela called, then clanked a glass with a sterling teaspoon. "Can everyone take their seats so we can begin?"

Always the hostess, Pamela guided everyone to

their seats and made sure to sit Dallas's parents at the far end of the family table. That's why I loved her. She was more stuck-up than me.

Once everyone was seated, Dallas stood up and pulled me up with his big hand. I looked at him. I just couldn't believe it was happening. I had found him, my knight, so to speak, the man who loved me and cherished me above himself. He was not threatened by my success, my vocabulary, or my choices in life. He might not get everything about me, but he loved me for me. He glanced at me, and his facial expression, the sparkle in his eyes, that lost look as he stared in my eyes said it all. Why did I feel like I wanted to throw up?

"Okay, ya'll," Dallas started. "You know I ain't the best with words, but I have been working on this for a minute." He pulled out a piece of paper from his suit jacket, and a moment of panic flashed over me. Was he going to read poetry? I was going to have to call off this wedding immediately if one sentence rhymed.

Dallas continued. "Aiight, so ya'll know I met this woman right here at an airport on the way to Palau. Of course, you know that didn't work out like that. But what ya'll may not know is this woman saved my life. My big ass butt can't swim, and when our plane hit the water, I thought that was it. But Josie Green saved me. She saved me then and has been saving me ever since."

He started sniffling, and I could hear the crowd sniffling in response. He went on. "We had a weird start. I called her an unforgivable name because I was angry, but she showed me that acting like a boy had ramifications, and I thought I lost her. But when she agreed to come back into my life, I made a vow to always love and protect her above all else.

"Some of ya'll don't know, but she is carrying my shortie. And I know I love her so much, I would love that child even if it weren't mine." He paused to look at me; then he laughed, and the crowd followed suit. I felt sweat forming on my fingers. Suddenly, my hand felt hot in his. I needed to let go. But I couldn't.

Dallas continued. "Josie Green is a doctor, a leader, a friend, a daughter, and so many other things to so many people gathered here tonight. But for me, she will always be my love."

He raised his glass. "To Josie." The crowd chanted, "To Josie!" so loud I felt like I was leading an army.

Everyone clapped and then started staring at me. I guess, I was expected to reciprocate. It had never dawned on me I would have to make a speech.

"Um," I said. "I don't really know how to top that."

"Try," said Mrs. Sterling. She waved her finger at me, and everyone laughed.

"I had this love thing wrong," I said. "I truly believed there was this cosmic force that brought two people together, and those people were destined, locked by time and space, to be with each other forever. That is a fallacy. Love is work. It is a second, sometimes third, job. Dallas has worked overtime to love me. He has been the sweetest person, gentle, caring, and a natural-born provider. His smile could light up this building for a month. He has proven to me over and over again that love does not have to be complicated to be real. It can be tender, quiet, and real. I feel his love whether he is cooking for us or getting on me for not shaving my legs."

The crowd laughed, and I looked up. I thought I

caught a glimpse of a familiar silhouette in the corner. I did a double take but didn't see anyone.

I went on. "Dallas is not a ghost hiding in corners, afraid to take a risk. He knows that just like in his profession, the most important thing to do is show up. Even if mistakes are made, if you don't show up, you never learn. If you don't show up, nothing improves. If you don't show up, you end up being more legend than man. Dallas is here. He's real, and I love him with all my heart." The crowd went wild. Dallas picked me up and kissed me. I looked out into the crowd and didn't see the shadow again.

The funny and aggravating thing about a wedding is, you never know who will show up and why. This was one of the reasons I didn't like weddings. But as the rehearsal dinner progressed and I kept looking at Dallas, my apprehension dissipated. Maybe it truly was because I was on the other side of the broomstick. I was the bride and no longer the ridiculed bridesmaid. And suddenly a pang of fear crept through my body. I prayed I wasn't going through with this wedding just so I wouldn't be an outcast any longer. And just as I was about to hide in a corner to mull over my mental predicament, I felt a hand touch my arm.

"Josie," said a voice. I turned and there was Craig. He was beaming as we locked eyes. I just knew I would have to deal with more drama. Then I noticed his left hand was connected to a petite hand. I looked and saw a gorgeous little chocolate-colored woman, with long, slightly curly hair and bangs that were clipped perfectly. Not many women could rock bangs, and this woman was doing it.

"Hey, Craig," I cried. He pulled me to his chest, and I immediately knew it belonged to her now. "Wow. How are you?" I asked, hoping to get right into the details of his companion, who was smiling hard at me.

"Thank you for inviting me," Craig said. I stopped and tried to remember if I'd put his name on the list and then thought of dear old mom.

"You're very welcome," I said. "Glad you could make it."

"Oh, let me introduce you two," he said. He looked over at the young woman by his side. "This is my wife, Serena."

"Your wife," I gasped and then threw my hands over my mouth to hide the shock. "Wow. That is amazing. Congratulations."

"Yeah, we would have invited you," said Craig, "but we figured after all you'd been through, the last thing you'd want to do is come to our little wedding."

"I would have come," I said and extended my hand to Serena, who took my hand with both her hands and began pumping.

"It is such a pleasure to meet you," she said. Then she released my hand and wrapped her arms around me. "You are my hero for surviving on that island like that. I could never do that."

"You'd be amazed what you can do when you have to," I countered.

"Craig and I were just so stunned at your ordeal," she said. "And then, after all that, you marry an NBA player. You are truly the luckiest woman in the world."

"Well, thank you," I said. "You didn't do so bad yourself with this old man right here."

Craig blushed and then looked at his wife. "Hey,

baby, can you get me and you another glass of wine? I want to talk to Josie for a second."

Serena smiled the smile only women who really knew their men could give. It said, *I got this nigga, so gone ahead and talk.* We watched her perfect little hips shake as she walked toward the buffet table. I looked back at Craig, who was still watching. I smiled.

"You did good, man," I said.

"Thank you," Craig said.

"You're welcome," I said.

"No, I mean thank you for everything," he said. "After you dumped me, I started thinking about what you said about me and our relationship. You were right. I only seemed to chase the unavailable. I only wanted what I couldn't have and pushed everyone else away. But once I started thinking about why I was so afraid of relationships, it just seemed silly. And I thought about all the good, smart, funny women I'd let go because of my stupidity. Especially you, Josie."

Now I was blushing. "Thanks."

"But thanks to you, I was able to open up to Serena and find real happiness," he said. "I wanted to be like you and not settle. But I also wanted to open myself up to the woman I would spend the rest of my life with. And I never thought of a woman as someone I would spend forever with, until we broke up."

"Thanks, I think," I smirked.

"You know what I mean," he continued. "It was a shift in thinking that allowed real love to come. Because you taught me if it isn't real, why go through with it?"

I stood there, stunned. My own personal mantra of never settling was wagging its self-righteous ass in my face.

"I wish you nothing but the best, Josie," Craig said. "And thank you for letting me go to find myself and Serena. I will always love you for that." He kissed my cheek and rubbed my back and was gone. I watched him grab his wife's hand and walk away, and I felt proud, happy, and jealous at the same time. Not because he'd found happiness, but because the mistakes on that island were messing up my own happiness. Or was it because I thought this was a mistake. Either way, I definitely wasn't feeling as sure about love as Craig and Serena. Maybe men and marriage weren't hopeless things. Maybe I was the one who couldn't get it together. Maybe I was the hopeless one. Either way, the one thing I did know was that I definitely couldn't wait for this rehearsal dinner to be over.

Chapter 40

The night of the rehearsal dinner was winding down, and people were finally starting to leave. I had basically worked the entire room, either with Dallas or by myself. But for some reason, something felt weird.

I knew I wasn't going crazy, but I felt a presence. "His" presence to be specific. I guess that was the problem with thinking you were linked to someone: you started imagining connections to people. I chatted with old and new friends, but after an hour of standing, hugging, and shaking hands, I needed a break.

I nudged Dallas. "Babe, I'm going to get some air."

"You okay?" Dallas looked down at me, his big eyes full of concern. "You want me to go with you?"

"No, I'm all right." I patted his hand. "You keep mingling. Keep dropping the names of the china patterns and appliances we'll need in the new house." We laughed, and he made sure to kiss me, something he always did before I left a room. It was a habit, I realized. It was probably the sweetest thing anyone could ever do. I needed air.

I walked out to the terrace and looked out at the

stars, which were on display that night. I breathed it in, and then I smelled it. His scent, soft, unassuming, masculine—him.

"Are you going to hide in the shadows all night?" I asked.

"How did you know?" a voice answered.

"It's my curse to know when you are near me."

"I wouldn't consider it a curse," said Jacques as he appeared from the shadows. He was dressed in a black suit and a black tie. With his sunbaked skin, he could easily slip into the night without being noticed. I had a feeling he'd dressed that way on purpose.

"Glad you could make it."

"Surprisingly, I didn't receive an invitation."

"It's hard to send out invitations to someone without an address."

"I have an address with my name on it now."

"Oh, that's right. You're real now." I was very aware of how terse the words coming out of my mouth were, but I didn't care.

"I just wanted to see you before tomorrow."

"Not coming to the wedding?"

"Probably not the best idea." He laughed. Damn. I hated his laugh. God, I missed his laugh. "So where is the honeymoon?"

"We're not taking one," I said. "They tend not to work out."

He smiled. "Touché."

"Yeah, we are just going to settle into our new house in Denver," I said, making sure I flaunted my ring in his face one more time.

"Wow. Denver. Hear it's country out west. You'll be attending hoedowns and stuff." He moved to the edge of the terrace and leaned on the banister. "I knew you had a little cowgirl in you."

I rubbed my belly. "I think my line dancing days are numbered."

"I would still watch you, belly and all." I looked at him and resisted grinning. I could not give him the satisfaction. I turned my face.

I knew we were going to have to bring up the baby thing, but I was terrified. Up to this point, I had completely succeeded in pretending there was no problem. But after Dallas made his comment, I realized everyone knew there was a possibility it could be Jacques's baby.

"I went and took the test," said Jacques. He seemed to be reading my mind.

"So what . . . so what were the results?" I asked.

"The results really don't matter, Josie," he said. "It only matters how you feel. As you can see, Captain Marvel over there would love the baby no matter whose it was. And I would do the same."

"Can we not go here with this conversation?"

"On this road, there are only two directions, love, here and there." He turned to face me.

"I am going to get married tomorrow and live a life with a man who will love me to the end."

Jacques moved so close to me, I could feel his cool breath on my nose. "He may love you till the end, but you need someone *you* can love till the end."

"Maybe," I said. "But I know when I wake up, that man will be there."

"I'm ready . . ."

"Only 'cause I'm not."

"You keep saying that, but the truth is you're the one who's scared to walk in unfamiliar territory."

"Jacques." I shook my head. "You are familiar territory. You are like all the other boys who are beautiful and play an amazing game but, in the end, don't have the mental capacity to stick it out. Anytime it gets too rough, you bounce. Well, I'm too old to roll like that."

"Answer me this question then," he said. "Why in the hell would I fly to Chicago, be up here at your rehearsal dinner, when your boyfriend could have security throw me in the river at any given moment?"

"You are here like all the rest," I said, "because I have found happiness. If I were to tell you I love you and jump back in your arms, I would once again be yesterday's news."

"Not true."

"You couldn't leave your dead wife, because it was easier to cling to something intangible than something you can hold on to."

"Josie, I can't keep doing this," Jacques said. "I can't keep coming back, begging you to believe me. If you say no tonight, I can't come back."

I looked at Jacques. I could see the pain in his eyes. Of course, he was pained. He was losing. But still this might be the last time I would see him. What if it wasn't bullshit? Could people actually change? Could a bad boy reform, get a minivan, and live in the suburbs? Or was that a domestic urban legend women told themselves to justify continuously dating men that were obviously bad for them?

I stared in his eyes. I knew I was too old and too tired to gamble my happiness again.

"Take care of yourself, Jacques," I said as I rubbed him. "My life is in there."

I walked away knowing I had made the right decision.

Chapter 41

In order to appease his parents, Dallas and I agreed to sleep in different rooms that night. It was only one night, and we knew by day's end tomorrow we would be in each other's arms. I sat in my room in silence. I refused to do anything that might wreck my wedding tomorrow. I resisted the urge to fondle my wedding dress and possibly get marks or dirt on it. I put up my shoes, avoiding the possibility of trying them on and tripping and falling out a window. I wanted everything to be perfect. So I sat motionless in the bed, trying not to do anything. Suddenly, I felt a kick in my belly. I shot up. I could feel my baby moving. And for the first time, I knew the decision I had to make was about more than me. I sat up in the bed and used a few pillows to pad my back.

"Hello? Can you hear me?" I waited for some kind of response, maybe another kick. Nothing. "Okay. I am going to be real with you. I made a huge mistake here. I messed up and got pregnant and don't know who your father is. Worse, I can't really find out without hurting everyone involved. I know how important it is to have a father in your life. Believe me. I do. I don't want you not to have that. But as you'll soon find out here, life is a little complicated." I laughed to myself.

"You know, I judged one of your possible daddies for saying how complicated life was. But really he was right. Sometimes you have to make decisions you never thought you'd ever have to make. Sometimes a solid presence is way more valuable than a sketchy future. You'll see the compromises you have to make. You'll realize the dreams that have to die. But I don't want you thinking this world is all bad. Oh, there is music—you'll love that—and art, and my parents are pretty great. I don't know if you will see your daddy's parents before your retinas are fully developed. But there is God and love. Oh, love is a tricky one. I suggest you don't engage in it if you can. And if you do, wait until you're at least thirty so you will have enough disposable income to distract yourself with cable and shoes. But whatever happens with you and your journey through love, know that your mother will always be there to love you, guide you, and discourage fast girls or boys from tricking you."

A soft knock on the door interrupted my mother/child conversation. I got up and walked to the door. I peeped through the peephole but could only see a jersey.

"Yes?" I called out.

"It's me, baby," Dallas said. I opened the door and let him inside.

"What are you doing?" I asked. "Your mother would throw her wig at you if she found you here."

"Watch it, pussycat." Dallas kissed me. "What you doing up?"

"Just talking to the baby," I said. "It kicked."

"For real?" Dallas bent down and placed his ear on my belly.

"It's my stomach, not some headphones at Tower Records." I laughed.

"I wanna hear, too," he whined.

"Come here." I took him to the bed, and we both lay down. He curled up around me, and I palmed my stomach like a basketball.

"I'm sorry," I said. "Why did you come here?"

"I miss you two." He pulled me closer to him.

"Dallas," I said. "About the baby . . ."

"It's like I said, Josie," Dallas said, rubbing my belly. "No matter what, I will love this child. It is my baby whether it's biological or not."

"And you don't care about what happened in the past?"

"If I let the past bother me, I wouldn't be here," he said. "I can see you for who you are today and hopefully tomorrow. The past is gone."

"I love you," I said.

"And I love you, too," he said. We fell asleep in each other's arms, and I knew I'd made the right decision.

The sun had barely left the horizon when there was a banging on my door.

"Get up, Josie," Pamela yelled. "We have a long day getting you together, and we need every second we can spare."

"Pamela, give me a minute," I said as Dallas giggled in bed. He got up from the bed.

"Well, babe, I am going downstairs to have a heart-choking breakfast of sausage, eggs, ham, omelets, pancakes, and whatever else they can fit on my plate," said Dallas. His arms stretched to the sky and almost touched the ceiling.

"Not fair," I said. "I want breakfast, too."

"Naw, I think they have to sew that dress on you." He giggled again.

"I am so scared. I think I saw plastic surgery jotted down on her day planner for today," I said.

"They better not hurt that face."

"I won't let them." I rubbed my forehead on his chest. "Lord, I will be happy when this is over and we are married already."

"Me, too," Dallas said. "But you know what? In a few hours, you will be Mrs. Dallas Sterling."

"Mrs. Josie Green-Sterling," I corrected. "I'm hyphenating."

"I don't like how that sounds." He frowned.

"We could always go with Sterling-Green and have you change your name." I smiled.

"Yep," he said. "I'm out."

"Good-bye. Eat some breakfast for me."

Dallas swung the door open, and Pamela almost fell inside.

"I am not even going to ask," Pamela moaned. "Get up, baby. We've got to start getting you ready. The ladies are already up and talking."

"Did they eat?"

"Yep, they had some breakfast special," she said as she pulled me from the bed. This was going to be a long day.

Chapter 42

"Josie," Lee said as I stepped out of the dressing room. "I have never seen you look more beautiful." I looked at all my girls and Pamela. They were crying. Even Dallas's mom was trying to wipe tears away with her knuckle. I turned around and almost stunned myself. It couldn't have been more perfect in my wildest fantasy. The top was simple satin that fit me perfectly. My shoulders were slightly exposed, and the dress was fitted and came all the way down to my feet. A long, elegant train of satin cascaded from the back and flowed out of the dressing room.

"You a black Cinderella," Mrs. Sterling shouted. "You even hiding that big baby belly." The room was quiet as I contemplated eighty ways to slap this woman.

"Wait a minute," said Marcela. She stepped up to me. "You pregnant?"

"That's what you get for missing the reception rehearsal dinner, baby," Gayle said.

"Baby, I am a grown woman. I knew you were pregnant way before Dallas announced it," said Mrs. Sterling. She smacked the gum in her mouth and pulled it with her fingernails. "I spotted the load the second I entered the room. And I also knew by the things Dallas said about you on the phone."

I faced Pamela. "Did you know?"

"Mothers always know," said Pamela.

"She's right," Ruby concurred. Gladys nodded.

"So I am the only one who didn't figure out this was a shotgun wedding all along," Marcela said and threw her hands in the air.

"This is not a shotgun wedding," I yelled. "Dallas and I were going to get married, anyway."

"So, Lee, you knew, too?" Marcela questioned.

"Well, she told me, but, yeah, I questioned her about it," replied Lee.

"Damn, I need a drink," Marcela said.

"Right before a wedding is usually not the time to drink," I said.

"Baby, it's your wedding, and you're the one who's pregnant," Marcela said. "I am single and use condoms."

"All right, everybody, we got the bride dressed. It's time to get dressed ourselves," said Pamela, the diplomat. "Go on. I got it from here."

Everyone trailed out of the room, and Pamela commenced rearranging everything she touched.

"Josie," she said. "I want you to know that I am very proud of you."

"Thank you, Mom," I said as I adjusted the trim on my sleeve.

"I don't think you know why I am so proud."

"Why?"

"I am proud of you for never settling for what you want," she said as she rubbed my arm. "I know I gave you that big speech about letting opportunities pass you by, but you held out for what you wanted in life. You held firm in your career choice, your first home, your friends, and even your lovers. And I am so proud to say you are my daughter." The words came as a complete shock, and I was speechless. She gave me a light hug.

"Don't want to smear make-up on the dress," she said and chuckled.

"Mom," I said. "I'm scared."

"You should be," she said. "This is your life. I am scared of these girls who have no fear walking down the aisle. To me, that means all they care about is the show. And they are never prepared for the morning after.

"The morning after," Pamela repeated as she smoothed the wrinkles on my train. "The next day, when you realize that the man you are next to is accountable to you for the rest of your life and you to him. You have to be there for him even when he did something that would make you want to cut his throat. The next morning, that's when you know you made the right decision. 'Cause all the pressure is off. All the people are gone. Then you smell his bad breath or see the corns on his toes. He sees the little lines forming under your eyes. That's the for better or worse part. So you better make sure you choose wisely."

"Thank God for divorce," I joked, trying to break up my growing fear.

"Even after I divorced your father, I was still connected to him." Pamela continued primping. "I will always be connected to that man. I still wake up with a flash of pain when he is sick. I can even tell when he enters a room." My heart felt like it would freeze right there.

"But you said when you saw Daddy, you saw a golden opportunity," I said.

"I did," she said. "For love. I was so busy playing around, I missed true love. But when I felt it with your father, I took it. He is as crazy as a loon, but I never regretted marrying him."

"I love Dallas, Mom. I do," I said. "But I am not sure if it is . . . the type of love that could survive the morning-after epiphany."

"Well, you better find out fast, 'cause you have a wedding in a couple hours, and that morning after is approaching quickly." Mom moved back and inspected her work. "Yep, that is all I can do. You look amazing. I gave you my two cents. The rest is up to you."

"Thanks, Mom," I said. She turned and looked at me. I could see tears begging to be set free.

Pamela pressed down on her dress. "Josie, I have a confession to make. I know I have always been a little hard on you and very demanding. And I know I was kind of hard to live with growing up."

"You?" I smiled. "Never."

"I am serious, girl." Pamela threw her hands, with their perfectly manicured nails, in the air to silence me. "I didn't make life for you that easy. But when you were lost on that island and I thought I would never see my baby girl again, I . . . I love you very much, Josie, and I grow more proud of you every day. My only wish is that we can be closer over time."

"I would love that." I felt my knees shaking as we talked.

"Oh, damn it." She ran up to me and held me so tight, I thought I would pop. It never occurred to me until that moment that Pamela and I rarely hugged. I was always a daddy's girl and was more cordial with

Pamela. She was the military to his circus show. Sitting there feeling Pamela's sobbing under my chin was one of the most unforgettable moments of my life. I held her in my arms until we both ran out of tears.

Immediately after we let go of one another, she ran to the bathroom and got some Shout wet wipes and cleaned our dresses, restoring their sparkling shine.

Just a few minutes before the wedding was to start, I watched Anne flutter around, whispering things into her headset. "Move those flowers to the center! I asked for satin ribbon! Replace them now! That limo has a dent in the back, so get another one!" She was mean but very effective. The ladies and I had transported ourselves from the hotel to the chapel ladies' room. As I looked at my friends, all moving around to make sure my day was perfect, I began to cry. The day I thought was impossible was finally here. I was getting married. And it felt fantastic.

There was a light rap on the door, and Jason entered, looking snazzy in the form-fitting tux he'd got to be a groomsman in the wedding.

"I am not marrying the bride, so I figured it was okay for me to see her," Jason said and shook his head. He came up to me and hugged me tight. "I am very happy for you."

"No jokes," I said. "No digs at my big feet in these shoes, or my make-up making me look like an Asian whore."

"Tempting," he said and smiled. "But the truth is, you look breathtaking."

"Thank you," I said.

"By the way, our old Jeanne is in the chapel, hating that she isn't a bridesmaid and that your wedding is more expensive."

"Figures."

"I think I will say hello to her, just to make sure she knows how amazing you look."

"I love you."

"I love kicking up shit," Jason said. "FYI, I heard she's getting a divorce."

"Already?" I asked. "They just got married less than a year ago."

"Hey, don't kill the messenger," Jason said. "All I know is that she came alone and refuses to talk about him. My gift to you."

"That is so sad."

"Serves her right for being a bitch," he said. "And think how she'll feel when she sees you walking down the aisle with the man of your dreams, while she goes back to eating Lean Cuisines for one."

"Jason," I laughed. "I told you not all single women eat Lean Cuisine dinners and watch Lifetime."

"Oh? Well, that's what I see women doing on Lifetime." We both laughed. "This is your moment, Josie. Enjoy it. I love you." We hugged again long and hard, and I began to get nervous. Even my big-time joker friends were taking this wedding seriously. This was big; this was reality.

"Um, everyone," I said. "Can I get a few moments alone?" Everyone in the room nodded and quietly walked out. I was about to turn around when the door burst open. My heart raced as I wondered who it was.

"You get five minutes," Anne said. "No more. Or we'll be off schedule, and I don't go off schedule."

She was the boss, and I nodded in agreement. She closed the doors, and I walked over to the tiny window in the restroom. I looked out and saw the horde of people who were arriving for the event. They were dressed in their finest, laughing and smiling, awaiting the moment when Dallas and I would say, "I do."

But I was more anxious than all of them. I couldn't wait for it to be done with so we could get on with the rest of our lives. If we could just roll past the "I dos," I was sure this would be so much easier for me. *Just get it together, girl,* I said to myself. I looked back out the window. I couldn't have asked for a more romantic backdrop. The tiny church was on a hill, behind cascading trees and a winding road leading up to the main entrance. The sun was at its peak and blessed us with light and warmth to match our dispositions. Even the birds seemed to be chirping in unison at the moment of my wedding. Everything was in place for my perfect day. And yet . . .

Anne burst back in the room and walked over to me. "Are we ready yet?" What she really wanted to say was, "We're ready. Let's move it!"

"Yes," I said. "I guess."

"What do you mean you guess?" Anne said. "Look, my deposit is already in the bank, so it doesn't make a difference to me if this place blows up. I am still buying my summer home when we are all done. But I will say this: I have been doing weddings a long time, and I have never seen a man as eager to get married as the one you got across the hall. So whatever your dealing with, honey, put it in a journal, and move on. That one's a keeper."

"I know he is a great man," I said.

"And I have heard nothing but good things about

you," Anne added. "But people talk, so let me say this. In the end, after all the romance and infatuation and hot sex, it's the one who stays that you marry. Passion can fill a romance novel, but it doesn't make a marriage."

I nodded my head. She was right. "Thank you."

"My accountant thanks you," she quipped. "Now let's get you married."

Chapter 43

The organ played softly as I watched Lee walk down the aisle. She looked amazing in her natural-colored jacket and skirt suit. She turned back and winked at me. Then the doors closed behind her. I felt an itch rise up the back of my dress, and that itch made me want to rip off my dress. I started squirming.

"You okay, baby?" my father asked.

"I'm fine," I said.

"Just a few more minutes and you can get to your man." He grinned at me. "He is quite a handsome fellow."

"Thanks," I said.

"Did you know he scored thirty-seven points against L.A. last week?"

"Dad," I snapped. "This is my wedding, not *Sports-Talk*."

"Sorry," he said. "You just seemed a little nervous. I was trying to take off the edge."

"Vodka takes off the edge," I said. "Not point averages."

"Well, we certainly can't drink with you pregnant," he said while adjusting his watch.

"Jesus, does everybody have to keep bringing that up?"

"The pastor made some kind of announcement earlier saying you two were burning in hell." My father looked at me, and we both busted out.

"Stop! I am supposed to look regal as I come down the aisle, not red from laughing."

"Hey, whatever gets you in the mood," my father said.

"I just need to breathe, and I will be okay," I said as the doors crept open, and Anne slid her tall, wispy frame through to our side.

"Okay, happy bride," she said, then showed me all two thousand of her teeth. "I need the happy, happy bride to get ready. I am about to open the doors."

"Okay," I said.

"You don't look happy," said Anne.

"You don't look toothless yet," I said.

"All righty. We're ready," said Anne. She smiled and slowly pulled back the French doors.

"This is it," I said.

"It's a marriage, not a death sentence," my father said as he squeezed my hand. "Lighten up."

The room stood to attention as the organ blared the single woman's most requested song, "Here Comes the Bride." I stepped slowly, watching the smiling faces of almost everyone I had known my entire life. They were cheering me on like I'd just won the Super Bowl. I could see Dallas crying at the podium. I dabbed my eyes, but there were no tears. Was I all cried out? As I stepped closer, I saw Lee, Ruby, Marcela, and Gladys all looking at me, welling up. I checked my eyes again. Still nothing. When we reached the end of the pews, my father let go of his grip and extended his hand. But before I could step forward, I felt arms lifting me up in the air. I was in shock, because I could see both of Dallas's hands in front of him.

"Sorry. Just need a second," I heard Jacques say. I turned my head to discover it was him carrying me to the back door. He slammed and locked the door just as a force began pounding on it.

"Open the fucking door," Dallas yelled. I stood in silence until Jacques pulled me into a tiny room and locked the door behind us.

"She'll be right back," Jacques shouted. He turned back to me. "I realize now why you cannot trust me. I never once was able to express genuine feelings. I seemed to be coasting along. Well, let me tell you I am done coasting. I bought a little house, in Florida. It is awful small, but I bought it because it reminded me of our time together. There are lots of storms, but when the sun shines down, you would swear it's the most beautiful place on earth. But it's not the island that was the most beautiful place. It was your heart."

Jacques's mouth began trembling, and his voice went up three octaves. "Josie Green, if you could see it in your heart to let me back in your heart again, I would never take it for granted again. I can't lose you, Josie. Even when Elizabeth died, I knew I could let her go. I can't let you go."

"Jacques," I said. "This is my wedding day."

He was balling now. "I know, I know, and I know you've had your share of men who only miss things when they're gone. But I am telling you, I can't promise you a lot of money, but I know wherever you go is the only place I want to be for the rest of my life."

The pounding on the other door stopped, and then the pounding began on the door in front of us.

"You have a choice here, Josie, of who you want to be with," he said. "But I don't."

I stood there listening to him speaking as the door in front of us began to crack. Finally, the wood gave way, and Dallas was inside. He didn't speak. He just came up to Jacques and commenced beating him down. I screamed, but he just kept on beating him. Jacques however, provided no resistance. He took each blow in silence until I finally grabbed Dallas's arm.

"Dallas," I said. "Stop." He got in a few more blows, but finally ceased. I walked out of the small room and saw a crowd trying to peek through the doors.

"A little privacy," I yelled as people slowly scattered. Dallas came out of the room.

"Did you kill him?" I asked.

"Would you really want me to?" he said. It was obvious he was crying, too. My heart hurt.

"Dallas, I . . ." The words wouldn't surface, but we both knew. "I have to . . . I'm sorry."

"Whatever you say won't compare to what you did to me this day," he said. "And the reason I know you still love him is because *you* will get over what you did to me." There were no words of apology to explain ruining someone's life. "Just leave out the back, and if that child is mine, I never, ever want to see it."

He walked out the door. I felt like the lowest person on earth. I walked back into the little room, where Jacques was trying to nurse his wounds. I pulled the handkerchief I'd stuffed in my sleeve for wiping mascara off my watery eyes and dabbed at his blood.

"We better get out of here before the mob puts us on a stake," I said.

"So where are we going?" he asked.

"Same place I always go with you. To the hospital," I said as I grabbed his hand.

We stayed in the hospital overnight so they could stitch all Jacques's wounds. I lay in the bed with him and fell asleep in his arms. The next morning, I woke up to Jacques's bloody face in my hair and his strong arms around me. *I can live with that,* I said to myself and fell back asleep.

Chapter 44

Dear Josie/Journal/ROCK/GOD,

This is my final entry. I don't think I need to write in you anymore, and I am almost out of pages, anyway. I know I have done a lot of ranting, and so I thought it only fair to end my story with some good news. Let me tell you about my real wedding.

There was no humongous church with arched ceilings. There was no wedding planner or train of bridesmaids. There was just me and the man that I love. There is a hill in Tallahassee, near the house Jacques built, that whispers of generations gone by and real love sustained. There is a tattered swing that quietly rests, waiting for a strong breeze or an energetic child to give it purpose.

It's a willow tree with sad, strong limbs that cling to bright green leaves. Under this tree, which sits next to our little house, is where we decided to wipe our slates clean and start over. Before our ceremony, Jacques bought a shovel and dug a hole. Not one to bury a body, mind you, but big enough to lay some bones to rest. We dropped the past there and piled dirt back over it. If you dug it up, you wouldn't find anything real. But to us, it was just that important to let the past die in peace.

We thought of inviting friends, family, and neighbors. But we just moved here and knew no neighbors. And our family and friends probably would be a little put off that we'd decided to have another wedding so soon after our national embarrassment. (We made sure to save the YouTube of me and Dallas's almost wedding so our child can see all we went through to be together.)

At the only church near our house, there is a rotund Presbyterian pastor who presides over our neighborhood. We asked if he would be kind enough to marry us. He was overjoyed. In fact, even though we wanted no guests, he insisted his wife, Mrs. Brown, be a witness at the ceremony.

I held my obviously round belly as Jacques and I faced the pastor and our house behind him. The wind kicked up and rustled the leaves lost from the trees and tossled the grass below us.

Jacques's face was healing nicely, and his smile was looking more and more his own every day. He held my hand as the pastor said a few words and then let us do most of the talking.

Jacques turned to me and said: "My Josie, I knew I wanted you the moment I laid eyes on you, and it hurts me beyond measure that it took so long to be by your side. But I am here. And I am never leaving. You helped me to see life again, and I am a better man every second I stand next to you. I will protect you through any trial we could ever face, and we have already surmounted too many trials to count. When I see your smile, I know life is worth living, and I thank God I get to see it every day."

Of course, I was crying when he said those words. But he seemed to be crying more than me. I lifted my head and said: "I only have one heart, but it has always been yours since the day you touched me. *There are people that come into your life for a reason, but I know you are the thing that gives these bones a life. I love you yesterday, today, and tomorrow. I will follow you wherever you go and lead you when necessary. I am your equal, your servant, and your wife until our future generations stop making up words for the end."*

The preacher made his usual announcement and gave us permission to kiss. I looked back at the ground where we had buried the past and the house down the way, where we hoped to start our future. And I knew it would be all right for forever more.

The End

Epilogue

Sean was two years old and had taken well to playing with Terry, Lee and Francis's one-year-old girl. We sat quietly in the backyard of our home in Tallahassee, sipping tall drinks and swatting at mosquitoes. Asia was reading a French version of a Harry Potter novel. Our dog, Homer, was chasing a rabbit unfortunate enough to have slipped through our fence.

"Will someone please save the poor rabbit," Lee pleaded.

"That's what he gets for trespassing," Francis teased her.

"Homer wouldn't kill a fly," I assured Lee.

"But he plays so rough," Lee argued. "I just don't want to see him crush the poor thing."

"So, Josie, I hear your parents are finally coming here for a visit," Francis said.

"Yeah, I think they finally forgave me for embarrassing them," I said.

"They still don't like me," Jacques said.

"I don't like you," I said and pinched his arm. He grabbed me in his arms and started kissing me.

"I beg to differ," Jacques said.

"Can you two calm it down just a little in front of the babies?" Francis said.

"You jealous bloke," said Jacques, chiding his brother. "The spark went out of your marriage."

"Please, we can take whatever you guys dish out," Lee said.

I pointed to the beach just beyond our fence. "Last one in the water has to clean up the dishes," I yelled. Everyone eased back in their chair for a moment, then sprinted for the gate. Jacques and Francis jumped over it, while Lee and I grabbed our babies and fought to get through the gate. Asia gave us all a look of disgust but soon followed us to the shore. Of course, Jacques, the sprinter, reached the beach first. He threw his hands in the air à la Rocky Balboa and started dancing around. We ran to the ocean. The rabbit no doubt had found his escape route, because Homer attempted to chase it on the beach a few yards before finally giving up and heading back to us.

Lee politely sidestepped Jacques and took off her top and jogging pants to reveal her swimsuit. She ran in the water. "Thanks for doing the dishes, man."

"What are you talking about?" exclaimed Jacques.

"The bet was last one in the water, boo boo," said Lee. Now it was her turn for the dance. Jacques ran after her and grabbed her by the waist and threw her in the water. Before I could turn around, Francis had me and was walking me into the cold water. I screamed until he dropped me under the waves. We swam in the water until we noticed our children were asleep on the beach. We finally crawled out of the depths and dried off. I grabbed my son and Lee grabbed her daughters, and we headed inside.

I knew the house was ours the moment Jacques first showed it to me. It was a small tudor, with a bay window in the kitchen and a backyard leading to the ocean. Light loved our house and danced inside every corner. The upstairs was small, but more than enough for me, Jacques, and Sean.

It took a month for Jacques to paint the glowing stars that would illuminate Sean's room when we turned off his light.

I put Terry and Asia to bed and then laid Sean down. Before I let him go, he looked up at me, with eyes just like his father's, and said, "Love you, Mommy." I hugged and kissed him till I feared he would drown in saliva and finally put him back in his bed. I headed back downstairs and took a second to look at my life. Yes, I sometimes missed that big ol' engagement ring. But it was gone; so was the million-dollar home and the dream man. I had a beautiful small house steps away from the beach; a healthy, crazy little boy; and Jacques.

I tried several times to apologize to Dallas, but he wouldn't return any of my calls, and I heard he got married three months later to a supermodel. That day in the hospital, Jacques had showed me the paternity results. The baby was his. Even if it wasn't, we would have worked around it. But it just felt right. I moved my practice to Tallahassee, where I discovered there were many sistas here who needed my help, too.

I knew I would miss Gladys, Marcela, and Ruby, but they supported what I had to do to be happy.

Mrs. Sterling smashed every window in my Mercedes before she went back to West Cadalacky, or wherever she was from. Mr. Sterling sent me an e-mail saying he understood and thought his son would soon get better. He included a picture of him in a Speedo "just in case." I deleted the e-mail.

Elizabeth appeared to me again, but she was much more civil this time. Her hair was combed as she sat up in her hospital bed. I walked over to her, but this time I was not afraid at all.

"Hello, Elizabeth," I said. She smiled at me and put her hands out. At first, I was apprehensive, but then I took them.

"I have to go now," she said.

"I know," I answered. "I will take good care of him."

"I know you will," she said, and then she disappeared. I woke up not cold and sweaty, but calm and relieved.

After I explained that Jacques hadn't really kidnapped me, my father calmed down and actually grew kind of fond of him, especially when Sean was born. Pamela, ever the diplomat, sent apology letters to everyone in attendance at the wedding. She returned all the gifts and stayed with Dallas a few days until he felt able to be on his own. Pamela gets the saint award for enduring Dallas's parents calling me a degenerate every day she was there. She chastised me every day too, until one day she sent a postcard.

On the front was a picture of the Florida Keys. On the back she wrote:

Josie,

I saw this card in the gift store and thought of you. Wow. You are a special child. The only one I know who would leave a million dollars for a British pauper. But that is what I love about you, baby. You make your choices and live by them. You are my constant worry and my hero.

Love always,

Mom

I kept her postcard on my refrigerator just in case I needed to remind myself of just what a wonderful life I had. I rarely needed reminding. Jacques and I had the type of love only pain, suffering, and reconciliation could form. There was sorrow in the corners of our laughter, and humor in our pain. I had finally realized when it came to love, no one was hopeless. And I found a love that could withstand anything. But, no, we didn't take anymore exotic vacations. No sense taking any chances.